THE CELESTIAL PALADIN

By Gil Hough

Paperback Edition

Cover Art and Design by Popa Tudor 2020

Second Cover Art by Ash Arceneaux 2015
Original Cover Art by Ginny Manning, 2011

ISBN-13: 978-1507635308

Acknowledgments

Writing has been a lifelong dream, and it has only been made possible due to the support of a lot of people, notably my amazing wife Kelly and our wonderful children Jonah, Steven, and Autumn. I want to give a special thank you to my editors Eddie Lunsford, my wife Kelly and daughter Autumn.

My parents, of course, should never be left out of acknowledgements of any of my accomplishments.

Contents

CHAPTER 1
ENDINGS

"Move along, move along," Rodregas said. He prodded the prisoner up the roughly hewn stone steps of the tower, none too gently, with the butt end of the lit torch in his hand. "We don't have all night."

The rough handling of the prisoner was a brash act for a man of over sixty years and average build, since the young man could have broken him in half. He was powerfully built, and towered head and shoulders over Rodregas.

The man was clearly Celestial Born, descended from the gods with features that resembled a hero from a bard's tale. With his square jaw and short black curls of his hair and fine dark eyes. In contrast, Rodregas sported a bulging paunch, scrawny legs and loose teeth which gave him fits when he chewed on anything harder than a half-baked wheat cake.

Rodregas' confidence in the prisoner's lack of retaliation came from the expression of dazed uncertainty on the man's face, a look he recognized on other prisoners whose world came crashing down around them without warning. Their previous life changed forever in the blink of an eye.

It was hard to feel sorry for the muscular man. He was the kind of fellow Rodregas had lost out to all his life. Still, somewhere in the recesses of Rodregas's soul, a glimmer of compassion flashed forth. It was hard not to feel pity for the man, if only because of what awaited the prisoner. Unfortunately, Rodregas knew there was no hope for the man.

On the other hand, knowing the there was a glimmer of hope for the female prisoner mounting the stairs behind him thrust Rodregas deeper into a foul mood. Her long auburn hair fell in waves about her shoulders, and her pointed ears. Her startling green eyes were almost too large for her angular face. Her skin was the golden hue of the High Ælf, the most magically powerful of all the Ijosalfar people.

Her auburn hair and slim athletic build marked her as a half-breed, slim like a Ælf, but too curvy and muscular for one of their slim kind. Her ears and features suggested that the other parent had been a Nymph.

A woman such as she drew many an appreciative stare. She was not beautiful in a way that Rodregas was used to, yet the odd combination of her features captivated Rodregas.

She was young, and he had heard that her innate abilities in the magical arts to be immense. The possibility that she would ever achieve such power diminished with each step nearer the tower roof. Unlike the other prisoner, her eyes were alert, and she gazed around her for an opportunity to escape. The gag in her mouth and the iron bands on her arms prevented her from calling on her magic to help her.

"Sergeant," said the other Eternal Guardsmen. "If we don't hurry, we will feel the master's wrath when we get to the top."

Rodregas grunted in agreement, "I will double your ration of food tonight and it will be fresh if you move a little faster," he told the prisoners.

With that hope dangling before them, both prisoners climbed faster up the stairs.

Rodregas thought the other guard would laugh out loud at his comment. As a senior guard familiar with the impending ceremony, the fellow damned well knew that neither prisoner would worry about food within the hour.

Rodregas groaned to himself as the group picked up the

pace on the tower steps. Over the last few years, his right knee acted up whenever he mounted stairs. That was just one of many complaints advanced years bestowed upon him. How ironic that the young prisoners were on their way to die, when old useless men like him, and scumbag fellow guards, continued to live.

He suppressed a shiver of excitement at the notion that this time would be different. This time, he would not just cry out to the gods while innocent people burned.

He filled his lungs with stale air tainted with burning pitch and tried to sink into the mindless guard mentality that kept him functioning for the past decades. Once a man loses all hope of a decent life, it is astonishing what he will do to stay alive. For the last twenty years, following orders and doing his duty, along with his better-than-average training for a guard, had served him well. He had been safe from the bounty on his head and for the most part. His life was more boring than anything else.

They approached the door to the tower roof with the prisoners. Instead of formulating a plan of action. His mind kept going back to the horror of last week's practice when his master the Immortalist sorcerer, Ravenhurr, declared a rehearsal of the ceremony with the senior guards. Rodregas had assumed they would merely walk through the procedure, but this ascension ceremony was unusually important. Ravenhurr was the kind of man who demanded perfection. The Sorcerer demanded it both in himself and from those around him.

That perfection required no less than an exact replication of the ceremony. As usual, he agreed to his master's wishes and did as he was told. He knew the value of following orders; it had kept him alive.

When he placed his hand on the tower door, an involuntary shudder racked Rodregas's body at the idea of following those orders one more time. He looked over again at the half Ælf maiden. To a woman like her, a balding, overweight man like himself would be invisible under normal circumstances. It might tempt some other guards to take what would not be given, but not him. Like his mother used to tell him so long ago, a person did not have to own a beautiful sunset to enjoy it.

The door to the top of Raven Tower was large and deeply carved in intricate designs and runes. As a boy Rodregas had trained in the basics of magic, a secret he was careful not to share, but the magical runes were far beyond his understanding. He led the prisoners through the door and walked out onto the top of the tower. The circular roof was flat and open to the sky. The only covering was the landing for the stairs down.

The cool night air refreshed his spirits somewhat. Before the prisoners could look around, he shoved them to the right side and strode over to Ravenhurr, who was peering into the night sky through a long tube with tiny glass panes at each end.

Ravenhurr loved to boast that the tube brought the stars closer to him. He was never one to hurry about anything, at least not before tonight. At that moment, though, his lean body quivered with excitement.

"Master," Rodregas said, with a respectful bow, "The prisoners are ready."

Ravenhurr looked up. His eyes passed over Rodregas to glance at the prisoners. He nodded without a word and went back to peering through the tube.

Rodregas had never understood how the stars in the night sky could make the world closer or farther away from the Celestial Realm, where the Gods lived. While it was common knowledge that great magics took place during the fall and spring equinoxes when the Infernal and Celestial

Realms could manifest in the natural world during the three days of the Wild Hunt. Rodregas did not know how any of this could affect magic, but Ravenhurr was more than a little concerned about the placement of the stars. The Sorcerer thought it critical to the success of the ceremony tonight.

Ravenhurr was an attractive man, like all the Immortalist Sorcerers. If you can pick your body, why would you ever choose an ugly one? Rodregas looked over again at the man that he had brought up the stairs. With the ability to select your body you would choose someone like that: attractive, talented and a natural athlete.

Rodregas stood to the side, waiting for Ravenhurr's signal. Ravenhurr raised his head up from the tube again and scanned the rooftop, making sure all the parts of the ceremony were in place. Rodregas had always thought it was Ravenhurr's eyes that gave away the fact that what was inside him was not as attractive as his exterior. Ravenhurr's eyes had an intensity about them, a habit of weighing everyone else and finding them wanting. Ravenhurr saw in everyone else a lesser person whose best function was to be used by his betters.

Rodregas looked over the rooftop, following Ravenhurr's eyes. Most of the open flat roof of the tower was covered in various circles. The largest circle held all the others and was made of a glittering white sand-like substance. Its diameter had been drawn as large as possible within the limitations of the roof's edges. On the inside were sigils, runes, and small candles set out every few feet.

Rodregas knew enough of magic to understand that the purpose of this outer circle was to keep out unwanted magical influences. That could interfere with the spell casting inside the circle. Also, the circle would hold in magical power which a sorcerer could tap into spells that required unusual amounts of power.

Inside the large circle were four smaller circles.

Rodregas' eyes immediately went to the one on the north side made of blue sand, where inside sigils made of a yellow waxy substance laid a giant lion. This was not a normal lion such as those found in the nearby forest, but a giant beast.

Ravenhurr had been extremely lucky. He had bought a pair of female Dire Cats from the Immortalist Guild Dealer Taiga. With magic, he caused them to go into heat. It was exceedingly difficult to affect Dire beasts with magic, and his success had shown his power and accomplishment as a mage.

Rodregas had regretted not being on duty when the Dire Cats were staked out on the roof. Rodregas had heard from the other guards that the cats were in heat, and as Ravenhurr had hoped, on the second day of the Wild Hunt a Celestial Lion had sensed their presence. The great lion had spent the last night and day doing his best to impregnate both of the female beasts. The whole keep could hear the wild rutting going on.

Ravenhurr then had goats released on the roof and the Celestial Lion had gorged himself on them when he had finished rutting. The well-satisfied beast lay limp, sleeping, confident in his Celestial power, and oblivious to his surroundings. He lied unbound, as required by the ceremony. Rodregas assumed some subtle trick had been used to influence the beast to sleep in just the right spot.

The unlikely success of having an actual Celestial animal as part of the ceremony had put Ravenhurr into an exceptional good mood. Using one of the Dire Cats in the ceremony would have been good, but an actual Celestial animal would provide much more power.

Rodregas' hands clutched into a fist at his side as he could not help thinking the last thing the world needed was for Ravenhurr, or any of the Immortalists, to acquire more power. Rodregas knew there was almost no opposition to the Immortalist left, but futile as it would probably be, Rodregas could no longer go along with their immoral acts.

The two female Dire Cats that had been used to lure the Celestial Lion to the tower had fascinated Rodregas since Ravenhurr, at the expense of an enormous part of his fortune, had purchased them from the Immortalist Guild Dealer Taiga. When Rodregas looked into their eyes he had seen a greater understanding than that possessed by mere animals. When they growled, it felt like the earth trembled.

When Rodregas had seen the Dire Cats in their cage, he could not imagine a more powerful lion, until he had seen the Celestial Lion. The Celestial Lion was not just breathtaking, at almost twice as large as the Dire Cats and even more powerfully built. It was not size that set him apart. It was a way of moving, a grace that spoke of perfection.

To look at a animal from the Celestial Realm made Rodregas wish he could write poetry like some noble in one of the high western courts. It made him struggle for words he did not have. And what did this marvelous beast do? Rutted, gorged, and then fell asleep ready for the slaughter. Rodregas could not help but shake his head at how life can show you miracles that made you want to live again and then using the same miracle drives home the fact that there is truly no justice to existence.

Rodregas pulled his thoughts back to the roof. He would only have one shot at this. In a fair fight, no mortal was a match for one of the Immortalists. "Luckily," thought Rodregas, "I have no intention of playing fair."

His eyes jerked back to Ravenhurr, as the sorcerer made a sharp upward motion, rising from his sky tube. "Now," he said and quickly repeated in his smooth voice, "NOW!"

Lord Captain Poir, the leader of Ravenhurr's local Eternal Guards, had stepped out of the shadows and approached the prisoners, but Rodregas stepped forward first and grabbed the half Ælf maiden's arm. With a quick twist of the key, he removed her iron shackles but grabbed her arm hard so she could not run.

"This way," Rodregas said to her. As he separated her from the male prisoner and the other guards, he whispered to her, "If you want to live, do nothing until your circle is about to burn, then I will throw my club at the other guard. Run and make sure you get out of the circle."

She jerked towards him as he spoke, and her amazing eyes struck him again. He forced her forward, hoping that she could think on her feet. Rodregas carefully led her over the outer white circle and into a yellow circle across from the Celestial Lion. Lord Captain Poir led the male prisoner into the pale green circle that was the closest to being in the exact middle and was most strongly interconnected to the other circles.

As Rodregas crossed into the main circle, the sense of power almost made him stumble. He knew his own magical power was minimal, not much above average, but his few years of training as a boy had opened him up to magic more than the other three guards on the tower roof. Rodregas knew that if Ravenhurr had ever thought he had any magic training, he would long have been reassigned to a duty far from the ceremony. The very air seemed to strum like a string instrument with the gathered magical power.

Rodregas could not help but think about how out of his depth he was, trying to interfere with the ritual ceremony. However, as he forced the beautiful half Ælf forward, the woman whose name he had refused to learn. He knew he would try. "I will do it this time," Rodregas thought to himself, "This time I will not choose my survival over others."

His life was not worth living if he did nothing again. He wanted to feel at least a small measure of being the man they had raised him to be. "Celestial Gods, please let my life be worth something in death, if not in life," he prayed quietly.

Lord Captain Poir and Rodregas carefully put the two prisoners in the middle of their circles and then stepped out. They each picked up small wooden clubs. Dale and Junnit the other two Eternal Guardsmen stood across from the two of them holding matching clubs. The ceremony required the prisoners to stay in each circle unbound. The job of the guards was to remain outside the circle but make sure that the prisoners stayed inside. Metal would interfere with the magic, so the guards held simple wooden clubs, and wore only linen clothes with no metal fastenings.

As Rodregas pushed the half Ælf into her circle, making sure not to disturb the bluish sand covered in swirls of colorful small crystals, it surprised him at how vulnerable he felt without his armor but readied himself for the task at hand. He quickly reached out to the woman and pulled off her gag, as even that would count as a binding and would interfere with the ritual.

He wanted to whisper to her as he removed it, giving her a hint of the desperate gambit that he was about to try, but he knew that it was not worth the risk of others overhearing. Both of their lives depended on her doing what Rodregas had told her.

If he succeeded, she would know what Rodregas had done. If he failed, well, he was familiar enough with that feeling, and she would not be worrying about anything at all.

He saw her lips forming something under her breath, probably a spell, but she did not have time to execute a spell of sufficient strength in the time left her. Magic took too long to prepare to be useful so quickly.

Ravenhurr stepped into the last circle. This one made entirely of what appeared to be fresh blood and of symbols made from the careful placement of living organs.

Rodregas breathed in deeply, trying to settle himself, and almost gagged from the smells. The stench of fresh blood, the scent of fear from the prisoners, the smell of power, and other smells that he could not identify. Rodregas closed down on himself, "duty," he thought. "My genuine duty this time, the one they raised me to follow. Focus on the next step. I can do this."

As Rodregas raised the club, he kept his eyes away from the half-blood Ælf woman, not wanting to give himself away to anyone watching.

"Gods," Rodregas quietly prayed. "You have never answered my prayers. I have never had much to give you as an offering to your temples, nor have I done great deeds in your names, but if any of you hate these life-stealing Immortalists as I do, then let me know your favor."

Rodregas could not help but add a selfish plea to his desperate prayer. "All-Father Grímnr, if I live, I swear an oath that I will make it my duty for the rest of my life to fight the Immortalist." Rodregas doubted his prayers would do any good, but if nothing else he was a practical man and when you are pushing the odds, it never hurts to call in divine favor.

Rodregas knew things would start moving quickly now. Ravenhurr had been preparing the circles for months, feeding them with unearthly energies. Ravenhurr had not wanted the prisoners up on the tower roof until the last moment, lest their fear lead them to take desperate action.

The Sorcerer spoke the final words of the spell, setting off months of careful preparations. Rodregas knew sorcerers use ancient languages so that others who might watch cannot understand what they are saying and guess their intent beforehand. During the practice walk-through the week before, Ravenhurr had spoken the same words that he uttered now.

Ravenhurr's deep, melodious voice whispered, but the words were easy to hear, "Spitualu seperatia orgirgia turia," and the middle, pale green circle burned. Rodregas could not pronounce the ancient version of the Eastern Common language that Ravenhurr was using, but he thought he understood the gist of the meaning.

Rodregas could not believe the male prisoner did not battle his way out. The Lord Captain and Dale were both large men, but it would have been very difficult to keep such a gifted man in the circle, even with clubs, if he was determined to escape. However, he was young and lacked battle experience. He seemed unsure of what to do.

Then it was too late. The blue flames of the circle rose high, then inward, and engulfed him. The man split in two. The physical man stood there unharmed, but as he watched, another ethereal version, the man's spirit, his very non-corporal essence, was suddenly pulled from his body, and then whipped around and out of the burning circle.

Rodregas was not sure, but as this ethereal version of the man was pulled apart, Rodregas thought he could hear him screaming.

Rodregas pulled his eyes away from the horrifying vision as the corporal man went from looking confused and unsure to having no expression at all, like an empty piece of meat. Rodregas's eyes flinched away from the terrible sight as he felt he might scream in horror and fury at what was happening. This was far from the first ascension ritual that Rodregas had seen, but each time the horror grew.

Then Ravenhurr yelled out, "Spirea faira podia turiana," and the circle holding the Celestial Lion burned in the same blue flames. The blue flames that make up the creation forces of life that can only be called up when the Celestial and Infernal Realms was close.

Suddenly the sleeping lion looked up in surprise and growled, and then he burned. Rodregas had seen enough of lesser versions of the ritual to expect it, but to watch it with a Celestial animal was a sight that hurt the soul. The circle blazed with an intense heat that blasted his face and the magnificent creature inside blazed with blue creation fire. It was a sudden and violent and primal process.

The great lion started to stand up and then simply fell apart into blazing blue energy. That energy surged out of the circle and swirled around inside the larger outer circle. Every hair on Rodregas' body stood at attention. Then the blue flaming energy was sucked into the pale green circle. There the prisoner, now empty of his own self, stood perfectly still. The blazing blue energy was sucked into his body, and the corporal body suddenly seemed more solid than before.

Once more Ravenhurr yelled out in his melodious voice the trigger words for the next part of the ritual, "Mana faria podia ricoria." It was now or never for Rodregas to strike. Rodregas raised his arm up and threw his club forward with all his strength. There was no time to see if his club hit Junnit, the other guard, or if the half Ælf maiden ran.

Rodregas half ran, and half jumped to the next circle where Ravenhurr stood with raised arms.

Ravenhurr was focused on his magic ritual and was not prepared for his own guards' sudden action. Rodregas grabbed Ravenhurr's arm and his belt and using his weight and momentum against Ravenhurr, threw the sorcerer back into the circle of colorful crystals where the half Ælf maiden had stood.

Ravenhurr, in an amazing act of balance, almost caught himself. He seemed to defy gravity as he hung in the air. Rodregas tried to reach out to push Ravenhurr into the circle, but before his hand touched the sorcerer, Ravenhurr lost his fight with gravity and fell into the nearby circle.

The moment that Ravenhurr crossed into the circle, he burned. His body twisted in pain as he burned the same blue fire of creation that he had called forth to rip apart a man's soul and steal the physical essence of a Celestial Lion. The flames he had called forth to steal the Ælf maiden's magical abilities now burned him.

The timing had been near impossible. The spell calling forth the flames of creation could only burn one life. But the timing was perfect; Ravenhurr called forth the fire, and then he was in it. The flames consumed his body in seconds and flaring from the circle went the multi-colored energy of his magic, the one element that the circle was designed to protect from the flames. His magic power shot out of the circle and started orbiting the larger circle. He was completely gone.

Rodregas excitedly thought, "Victory!" He had done it. He had killed the Immortalist Sorcerer Ravenhurr. His betrayal had caught the sorcerer by surprise, and the creation fire had give him no chance to fight back.

The multi-colored energy of the dead sorcerers' magic swirled around the outer circle and sucked into the empty vessel of the muscular prisoner. The magic energy throbbed, and Rodregas could feel the ritual screaming for the ultimate release of the magic.

There was no way to save anyone else. Rodregas and everyone on the rooftop would die in the next few seconds in the magical backlash of the failed spell. If the spell Ravenhurr had called forth was not completed the immense power would explode and probably destroy the whole tower and everyone who lived in it. But Rodregas thought he had understood the meaning of the last trigger words used in the rehearsal.

He now stood in the very circle that Ravenhurr had been standing and Rodregas' years of rejecting his early upbringing made him embarrassed to say the words, but he reached down into that nearly empty place where his little bit of power still sparked. Rodregas reached deep and pulled that spark of power up until he felt the tingle and inner sensation that he always inelegantly called 'my itch.'

Rodregas filled his words with the power and the intent

behind them. "My mind," he said. "My soul, my body to be made one through the flame," he whispered, and then the circle of blood and living organs that he now stood in burned and he burned. He burned so intensely that no scream crossed his lips. He felt every fiber of his being burn. Rodregas wanted to scream, but no sound could pass his lips.

CHAPTER 2
FROM THE ASHES

When Rodregas awoke he was confused. Why he was lying on the floor? As he opened his eyes he was alarmed to see Lord Captain Poir looking down at him with a confused and worried expression. Lord Captain Poir said, "Master Ravenhurr?" It was a question.

Rodregas wondered why his captain would think he was the Master. And then suddenly it all rushed back to him, all the details of the final terrible ceremony.

"Oh, my gods, I burned!" Rodregas said in alarm. He quickly raised his hand to his eyes. But, instead of his scarred, wrinkled hand, that should have been seared by burns. There was a powerful, smooth hand. Rodregas reached up and touched his face.

"Dear Gods," he thought in amazement, "the trigger words had worked." He had done what he had learned to despise and hate most of all. He had switched into the body of an innocent man. "I am an Immortalist," thought Rodregas in dismay.

It had been his only shot at survival, and the young man had already been dead in all the ways that mattered, but still it was an act of incredible repugnance to him. He thought, "Once again I have done what I needed to survive."

As Rodregas lay on the floor, he looked up at the stars and the looming figure of the Lord Captain. He had to think quickly. It was instant death for anyone to interfere with an Immortalist Ascension ceremony. It was the most stringent rule enforced by the Guild of the Celestial Path, and therefore the most enforced rule in the Eastern Kingdoms.

"Ah, thank you Captain, I am fine," Rodregas said. He instantly realized the captain would know that all was not well. Rodregas felt exposed without his armor and said the first thing that came to mind. "Please, if you can get me my clothes." Rodregas waved over to where the sorcerers robe was folded on a small table next to the stairway.

As he looked over, Rodregas saw that Junnit and Dale had re-bound the half-blood Ælf maiden with iron and replaced her gag so she could not use magic on them. While they guarded her, they also kept her at a distance as if she was somehow strange now. To them she was supposed to have been consumed by the ritual, and they seemed a little put off having the Ælf maiden standing there. Both were watching their prisoner but also throwing quick concerned glances over to where Rodregas now crouched on the tower roof.

Lord Captain Poir looked hesitant, but then nodded. He walked over to the table and gathered up the robes. "Damn," Rodregas thought, he had said "please." Master Ravenhurr ordered something done. He did not say "please" to his guard captain.

As Rodregas stood, Lord Captain Poir held the robe open and Rodregas clumsily put it on. His movements were awkward in this new, larger body. His angle was wrong, Rodregas felt like he was standing on a crate.

"Should I order the birthday celebration milord?" asked the captain. The coming celebration had been the talk of speculation for months and the object of more than a little betting among the guards.

Rodregas nodded, his thoughts swirling as he realized that he could use the celebration to his benefit. Without looking at the captain, he walked toward the stairway, and the captain followed close behind him.

At the door Rodregas took a deep breath and said, "Captain, that ceremony did not go smoothly, but the gods once again proved to favor me, and I wish to be generous with the birthday ceremony. Tell the purser to pay everyone an extra month's wages today and give everyone a week off to spend as they wish. Make sure you tell Purser Stevents to be generous. I want all staff rewarded, even the kitchen drudges." He finished, hoping it did not sound as halting and made up as he knew it to be.

"Yes, sir," replied Lord Captain Poir, his expression going from a guarded concern to enthusiasm. He seemed reassured when Rodregas mentioned Stevents. He must have thought either Ravenhurr had been a bit damaged by the ritual or that the man whose body he now inhabited might still be alive and faking it. Obviously, the man who had just been a prisoner would not know about Stevents. It must not have occurred to him that his senior sergeant, who had burned, might now inhabit the body.

The Ælf maiden twisted her body against the guards and tried to meet Rodregas' eyes, and he realized that only she had the magical background to have realized what had happened.

"Just two things, sir," said Captain Poir in a hesitant voice.

"Yes?" he asked, trying to act calm and in control.

"We might lose some guards and probably some kitchen drudges if they have money in hand and an entire week off. Also, we leave ourselves open for theft if we don't keep at least a minimum of guards at the front gate."

Rodregas relaxed at the mundane nature of the questions. "True, but I will not stint in thanking the gods for a favorable ceremony. Keep a few guards at the gate, but only the minimum needed. But that reminds me. Release any remaining prisoners and make sure they are fed and clothed and allow them to make their way back to their homes."

"That has some danger to it," said Lord Captain Poir hurriedly. His expression returning to a look of concern.

"True," he replied. "But do as I command," Rodregas stated in his firmest voice.

Lord Captain Poir nodded and immediately said, "As you command, master."

Rodregas opened the door to the stairway when another thought hit him, and he turned back to the captain, and said, "I need time to adjust. Make sure I am not disturbed in my quarters tonight but tell Adept Korin that before he leaves to celebrate, to come up to my room for some last-minute instructions."

Lord Captain Poir responded with his very military, "Yes sir." Before turning to order the other guards to gather up the remaining prisoner. Rodregas had to admit that while most of the guards were no better trained than a ruffian off the street, the Lord Captain, who was the only greater sigil warrior among Ravenhurr's person guards was highly trained.

Ravenhurr had liked to recruit his own guardsmen, but his Lord Captain who commanded his personal Eternal Guardsmen had been trained in the Capital. Thank goodness he did not understand the simplest things about magic.

On the other hand, the beautiful half Ælf clearly had some ideas. He was glad she was gagged and not able to speak, and the guards knew better than to release a mage from her bindings until they had to.

As Rodregas made his way down to the next level, the personal level of Master Ravenhurr, he closed the door to his suite of rooms that covered the entire floor. He listened as the other guards made their way down the tower. He leaned against the wall and took a deep breath.

That had been close. It shocked Rodregas he had gotten away with it, especially after he had commanded the release of the remaining prisoners. He had been twice as generous as he thought Ravenhurr would have been, and Ravenhurr was too practical a man to release the prisoners as part of his celebration.

The only prisoners in the keep's dungeon were beings that were held for potential use in the ceremony. That meant they were of impressive power or talent. The prisoners were too dangerous to release, after Ravenhurr had so pissed them off by their imprisonment. But people did not question the order of the sorcerer and master of Raven Keep, so it should work.

He dared not stay longer in the tower than he had to. Rodregas did not believe that he could fool Ravenhurr's guards and servants for long. Ravenhurr was a powerful sorcerer who used magic quite casually. It would become obvious that Rodregas did not know how to use magic.

As soon as the keep emptied for the birthday celebration, he would make his escape. If he missed this opportunity, he was not sure when he could try again. It was exceedingly rare for an Immortalist to leave his tower, and if he were behaving oddly, the Guild of the Celestial Path would send someone to check on him soon. They were careful in their control of the kingdoms, under their influence.

For a while, Rodregas just leaned against the icy stone wall. Not thinking of anything, there was too much to think about to even start. So instead of thinking he simply felt the cool stone wall and it slowly, truly, hit him. He was alive. For some time that simple awareness was enough.

He was alive, and in a stronger, younger body. With the physical essence of the Celestial Lion now part of his new body, and the magic of the sorcerer Ravenhurr. He would be an extremely gifted person.

That everything had gone so well was a god-sent miracle. He had rescued the maiden and killed the sorcerer. Of course, the man's body he now inhabited own soul and intellect had been destroyed and a Celestial Lion from the realm of the gods itself had been destroyed. It was far from a perfect victory, but Rodregas knew there were never perfect victories.

He had had more luck in the last half hour than in his entire downtrodden life. Then, the next revelation hit him; maybe the Celestial Gods had answered his prayers. He had sworn a life oath to All-Father Grímnr that if he lived, it would become his sworn duty to take down the Immortalists. Rodregas' new heart seemed to stop for a moment at that thought and a chill ran down his body. Sure, of his impending death, Rodregas had casually sworn a life-oath to the All-Father. If he broke it, he would damn his own soul.

There were well over two hundred Immortalists in the Eastern Kingdoms, each one incredibly powerful. That did now count their apprentices and adepts, each more powerful than a normal mortal Magi. What had happened today was pure luck and unlikely to be repeated. Trying to tear apart the Immortalists and their powerful Guild was a near impossible task.

Not to mention that the Immortalist Sorcerers controlled the Eternal Guard made up of lessor and greater sigil warriors and the most feared military force in the world.

Ravenhurr had been a powerful Immortalist, but nothing compared to the Immortalist Guild Dealer Taiga. He had been slowly rising in power for centuries on the path to true godhood. It was a surprise that he had not yet followed other legendary Guild masters into achieving godhood, the singular focus and purpose of the Guild of the Celestial Path.

Every time that either the fall or spring equinox came like today, and the Infernal and Celestial Realms were close, they rumored it he would make the final ascension. Only a few Immortalists had ever succeeded in this task. The first was the legendary Accerntorino. He was said to have created the Immortalist ascension ritual and to have been a genius without equal.

The first Guild Dealer Accerntorino was also known for his ego. Within two decades of his accession to the Celestial Realm, he challenged the All-Father Grímnr for control of the Celestial Pantheon of the Gods. Accerntorino claimed he could better lead them to victory over the Daemon Lords of the Infernal Realm. But Grímnr quickly and soundly defeated the upstart Accerntorino. What still caused whispers almost 400 years later was his fate; the All-Father had destroyed him.

Everyone knew stories of various gods that had challenged Grímnr over the millennia. The punishments he had dealt some of these rivals were horrible and some funny or embarrassing. A few times he had even driven Gods to temporally ally with the Daemon Lords in the Infernal Realm.

But the All-Father did not permanently kill any of these other challengers. It was his duty to protect the Pantheon, even when they betrayed him. Yet Grímnr reaction to this newly created god, this incredibly powerful, magic-wielding new god, was to destroy him; and that was the end.

Centuries later, when the next Guild master had ascended to the Celestial plane, she kept her ego in sharp check. The new Goddess Blodeuwald was known for how helpful she was to the rest of the Pantheon, especially All-Father Grímnr. Rodregas had always assumed that this had been the point of killing Accerntorino. If mortals would become Celestial, they would do so on the Celestials terms.

He raised his hand up again and touched his unfamiliar face, feeling its strong, smooth, square jaw. The teeth were not the sore, crooked teeth that he had had to be so careful to chew with this morning. They were now strong and straight. His familiar balding head was now covered in thick long curls, too beautiful for a man in his opinion. Rodregas would cut the hair short when he had a chance. Ravenhurr had looked for the most perfect physical specimen that he could find and Rodregas was now him.

Over the years, Ravenhurr had "collected" many very gifted men. They were local royalty and 'of the blood' being Celestial Born, descended from dalliances with lustful gods loose in the natural realm during the Wild Hunt. These men had won athletic contests and were known for their physical talents, good looks and sharp wits. Ravenhurr tested them for strength, reflexes and dexterity. Those that succeeded were further tested for the sharpness of their senses, their intelligence and ability to learn unknown languages.

They rewarded the winner of these tests with having his soul and mind ripped out and made into a piece of meat to be filled with the mind, personality, and the very soul of Ravenhurr himself. However, this time, instead of Ravenhurr, his old guard sergeant had ended up as a new powerful Immortalist.

As the cold of the stone chilled his back, Rodregas thought about his promise to the Celestial Gods that if he could kill Ravenhurr and live, then his new duty would be to fight the Immortalists. When all and everyone else had failed him over the years, only his duty had kept Rodregas alive. He no longer knew what to do without it.

His back straightened, and he pulled away from the wall that he had slumped against. Rodregas lived instead of the unnamed man whose body he now lived in. He had seen the tragedy of a gifted person after gifted person be torn asunder by the Immortalists. Rodregas hated the Immortalists for their casual destruction and use of people.

Could he now live in one of these stolen bodies unless he had a reason? The Immortalists and their Guild were evil and needed to be opposed. The gods had given him a new duty. He stepped away from the wall. It was time to get to work.

CHAPTER 3
THE RAVEN TOWER

Rodregas stepped into the master's bedroom for the first time in his twenty years of service in Raven Tower. He was unarmed, unarmored and needed to get as far away from the keep as he could before someone noticed that he was not a sorcerer.

He needed money. Money would buy him what he needed to start his new life. He had spent too much time on the road without money, and he would not repeat the experience if he could help it.

Unfortunately, Ravenhurr had not been interested in material wealth, and what money he had, he spent on materials needed for his magical ceremonies; still there should be something that he could use.

The bedroom was not large, but this floor also held Ravenhurr's study and a water closet. The far wall held a four-poster bed covered by a richly colored duvet. To the left of the bed was the door to the water closet, and to the left of that a wardrobe. Along the connecting wall, the fireplace calmly burned. To the right of the fireplace was a dresser with a compact mirror and at the foot of the bed was an ornate trunk that matched the wardrobe. On first glance, there was nothing of much value, except for perhaps the candleholder on the dresser. It looked like silver, inset with semi-precious stones.

First, he went to the dresser, and started dumping clothes on the ground. He was hoping to find some hidden wealth, stashed in the drawers. He ended up with a pile of clothes. Some were fancy, but none would be of much use on the road and none were worth selling. Next, Rodregas went to the wardrobe, which was engraved with the shape of trees, and made of a sweet-smelling wood. Rodregas thought it was much more likely to hold something of value.

He opened the doors to see brightly colored robes, and there on the left hung a suit of shining chain mail. Rodregas could feel his own wide smile at the sight. Armor! He reached in and pulled it out. The chain mail was light and seemed to flow around his fingers. The links seemed to be made of silver and he recognized it as Mithril.

Ravenhurr had a suit of Mithril chain! Rodregas could feel his heartbeat in excitement. Mithril, a rare magical metal that was stronger than steel but much less heavy and made one of the best light armors.

Ælves, who are not physically as strong as other people, loved the metal. It was also commonly worn by the regular Eternal Guard who could afford the high cost and wore it along with their night bronze helmets and breast plates.

Rodregas held it up to himself and then, as excited as he had become, his heart sank as he realized that the suit was both too short and much too slim for him to wear. While there were straps to adjust it, his new body was very large and he would never wear the beautiful armor.

He threw the armor on the bed. It might not work for him to wear, but he could get a sizable amount of money selling such fancy armor. It was the first item of actual worth that he had found.

On a shelf above it was another small pile of the silver chain. When he pulled it up, he saw that it was a helmet, a solid Mithril skullcap with sides of chain mail designed to connect at the bottom. He reached up and tried to pull it on over his head, but even his head was too large for the Ælf style mithril armor. It quickly joined the suit of armor and the candleholder on the bed.

On the bottom shelf he found a nice pair of boots of Ælf make but sized for a human. Attached were matching greaves, armor designed to protect the lower leg, and a pair of armored gauntlets to compete the set. All ended up on the bed. Nothing else of interest was in the wardrobe. Though the two fanciest robes, both heavily embroidered and of Western Silk, also went to the bed.

Next, he went to the trunk which was made of a rich cedar wood that matched the enormous wardrobe, but was much more portable. Unfortunately, the only items of use in it were several blankets of excellent quality wool. The remaining contents comprised drawings, pictures and other personal items.

Rodregas dumped the trunk contents on the floor, sandwiched the armor in the blankets and loaded up the trunk. How he would cart the trunk out of the tower he did not yet know.

He went to the door and listened; it seemed to be getting quieter. It was the middle of the night and the stir from the ceremony seemed to have subsided. It was only hours until dawn, when everyone would head out to celebrate the new 'birth' of Ravenhurr. Not a true celebration for most; as their lord and master, 'he' was more feared than loved. Rodregas locked the door to prevent a surprise. He should have done that before; it was sloppy of him not to take such a simple precaution.

Asking Lord Captain Poir to send up Adept Korin had been unplanned. He had been dreaming of killing Korin for all the twenty years that he had served in the tower. The Sorcerer Ravenhurr had been an immoral monster that used those around him for his own selfish desires. But Adept Korin was of a more casual evil. He never passed up the opportunity to hurt those around him, physically or emotionally.

Ravenhurr had existed in the same body for the full twenty years of Rodregas' service and was hundreds of years old. In all his years serving in the tower, Ravenhurr had only tried to hold the ceremony three times, each time abandoning the attempt due to the lack of a Celestial animal. A Celestial animal was extremely rare, but required as part of the ceremony for Ravenhurr's next step up in power.

In contrast, his assistant, the Adept Korin, had been going through bodies constantly. Worse, he seemed to take great delight in letting people know what fate awaited them. Rape and torture of the victims were common occurrences with Korin. And Rodregas had dreamed of killing him almost from the start.

Rodregas had hated Ravenhurr and knew that his Master could have stopped his assistant's actions with a word. Ravenhurr had been too powerful for Rodregas to dream of destroying. He was stronger, faster, and smarter than him to where even dreams of fighting him had never crossed his mind until this past week. However, his assistant Korin had only been an Immortalist for a few decades; his victims and his power were still purely mortal.

Rodregas had known that in a fair fight he could kill the Immortalist adept. Korin was no warrior, and his actions spoke of cowardice when Korin hurt those who had no chance in a fight against him. Rodregas had been trying to get him alone, where he could kill him without blame, for years.

Rodregas reached down to grab the bottom of the heavily made bed and almost fell over when the bed lifted far more easily than expected. The sound of wood screeched as weight switched to the back legs of the bed and then moved at his awkward action, and the top of the columns smashed against the plaster ceiling. Rodregas carefully lowered the bed back down. As the bed settled back to the floor, a light dusting of plaster from the damaged ceiling covered him.

Was Rodregas really that strong? Or was the bed just lighter than it looked? He went back over to the trunk and lifted it up. He lifted the solid-built trunk easily, and it felt strangely light. Next, he went over to the dresser.

Rodregas had known that the physical essence of the Celestial Lion was in his body and that his physical attributes would be improved. But Rodregas had never heard of Immortalist being this strong. You just heard that they were long lived and never got sick. Rodregas guesses that they just used magic against their foes, not swords. He had never heard of one getting involved in a physical battle.

Rodregas had known that in the Eternal Guard the most loyal and powerful of their officers were occasionally given new bodies by the Immortalist. But he thought their physical power lay in their greater sigils and magical equipment.

His new body was very large and very muscular, and much stronger than he would have guessed without even a lessor sigil.

Rodregas lifted his right arm and curled it into a tight

muscle. He felt the biceps with his free hand. The texture under the skin felt like bundles of large, powerful cables.

He felt his face break into another smile. He had seen this face smile when its previous owner had been a prisoner. The smile the prisoner had worn was an incredibly open, charming smile.

The smile he felt on his face now had little resemblance to the one he remembered seeing, though without looking in the mirror he had no way of knowing for sure. "Come on up, Korin. I have a surprise for you," Rodregas whispered under his breath.

He went around the room one last time poking around for anything else of note and, finding nothing, went over to the door to the water closet. Inside, the first thing he did was test out the plumbing, finding the experience both new and familiar. He also had a chance to examine his own plumbing and was pleased with the results. His new body was large and powerfully built, even in places that most people would not see.

The only thing of use in the water closet was a shaving kit, which Rodregas added to the trunk. Next, he went to the study door only to find it locked. He looked for a key, but there was nothing. He guessed that it was locked by magic and required a magic word or incantation to open the lock. He pushed and pulled on the door, but it was solidly made and there was nothing to get a good hold of to test his new strength.

He looked around for something to use as a pry bar; next to the fireplace was a poker. He grabbed it and forced it into the crack where a normal door would have its catch. He got it wedged in good but then stopped and went over to the outside door and opening it, listened for anyone nearby before going back inside the room. He carefully closed the door behind him. The sound of him breaking down the study door would ring loud in the predawn silence, but his need for money was too great.

What he had found would be worth some good coin but finding a trader that would give him its worth would take time. He needed to find silver and gold. Rodregas muffled the door with a blanket the best he could and then, with a violent shove and twist of the fireplace poker, shattered open the study door. He held his breath. Everything was silent. He listened but heard no signs of approaching guards. They had probably heard something, but none would question master Ravenhurr, or at least the person they thought was the master.

He pulled his way in through the shattered rest of the door; in the middle of the room was an enormous round table with several books and papers spread out on it. Next to the open windows was a very nice desk with a very comfortable looking chair. Next to the fireplace were several larger overstuffed and even more comfortable looking chairs. There were not as many books as Rodregas had thought there would be. They covered only one wall in shelves and miscellaneous piles of scrolls and other items. Next to the desk there was a second fancy set of shelves with glass covers to protect them.

He went over to the glass-enclosed shelves. The books looked richly made but old. Books of sorcery would sell very well. The glass covers were locked, so again he muffled the sound with the blanket and forced the cabinet doors open. With each cabinet door, the glass broke. He tried to open the cabinet doors without breaking the glass. But whatever magic locks were in force were just too secure. So, he had to use brute strength to shatter the doors one by one.

Several of the books fell during his struggles with the cabinet. Rodregas reached down and grabbed a couple of them and then dropped them right back to the ground in shock as evil licked his hand. He shook the feeling off his hand and went back to the water closet and washed it in the water basin. He knew there was nothing physical on his hand, but he also knew that water was a natural purifier and disrupted many magical influences. What he had felt was disgusting. Why would a book, no matter what its contents, have such a feel to it?

He walked back to the book and got down on the ground. Without touching it, Rodregas slowly ran his fingertips along the binder of the book. While the feeling was not as strong as when he had held it, the feeling of what could only be described as evil emanated from the book. Was this feeling coming from the book or was this some new ability of his new body to sense the nature of the book's contents?

Rodregas got up and walked over to the bookshelf. He closed his eyes, and trying not to touch, lightly ran his hands close to the row of books. Quickly he realized that with some books he felt nothing. Other books seemed to buzz with energy but gave off no nasty feelings. Still others had an awful odor of decay or foulness that made him want to cover his nose and pull away. In truth, there was no smell, but a feeling.

Rodregas made a quick decision to trust this new ability and to act on them. He had the impression that these foul books were of the most evil soul-stealing magic of the Immortalists. He opened up the fireplace. Rodregas chucked all the evil books into the fire with the poker. The ones from which pure magic radiated he placed into the trunk; true books of magic would sell nicely. Sorting the books and then getting them to burn took several hours, and he felt how long it had been since his new body had slept.

The sound of the tower was changing, the first sounds of the kitchen crew getting ready for the morning. Still, he kept at it, though there seemed to be nothing else of wealth in the room. He was determined to see the evil books burn. They held the secrets to the Immortalist art and other evil magic. Leaving them would only lead to another person rising in Ravenhurr's place. Several of the foulest books seemed to refuse to burn, but the flames eventually consumed all, just as they had consumed Ravenhurr.

Finally, the last of the evil books of magic burned, and the few remaining books that felt of magic but lacked the evil stench of the others were packed in the trunk. Only six volumes had been free of the stench, while over forty were burned.

The sun was now streaming into the room, and he was feeling the lack of sleep. He decided that it would take a while for the keep to empty as everyone went into town to 'celebrate' Ravenhurr's new birthday. He stretched out on the big four-poster bed. He had thought he would struggle to sleep, but immediately found deep sleep. In what felt like only a few minutes later, he struggled from deep within his dreams to the sound of a polite knock on the door. He looked around for a second, confused by his surroundings until memories returned.

The sunlight through the windows was now indirect, so he guessed it to be mid or even late afternoon. Again, came the polite knock. No one would dare such persistence without direct orders from Ravenhurr. It had to be Adept Korin. He nearly leaped off the bed and looked for a sword, but there was none.

He stepped in front of the bedroom door after first doing his best to close the broken study door. He quietly unlocked it and stepped back and said, "enter." And waited for the Adept to come inside. Korin came into the room with a relaxed step that showed him to be much more comfortable than Rodregas was.

The Immortalist Adept was a good-looking young man. It was always weird with him. He changed bodies so often that you always felt like you were meeting someone new, but it was not long before you realized that it was Korin. He wore a slim male body that was well-built, not much over 20 years old, with blue eyes and blond hair.

Rodregas was not sure what to say to the man, so he stood there looking at him. He would appear to be the Master and it would not be surprising for Ravenhurr to keep him waiting for a few minutes. Korin waited patiently, seemingly at ease with what Rodregas would assume to be strange behavior by Master Ravenhurr.

"Are you ready to leave and celebrate my new birth?" Rodregas asked him.

Adept Korin nodded politely and said, "Yes, Master, the gods favor your desire to imitate their celestial glory."

Rodregas nodded back in acknowledgement and said, "And have you found any new bodies who you would like to... wear?"

That question seemed to surprise the adept, but Korin smiled and said, "No, Master. I have been too busy working on my studies."

Korin now looked at him with a bewildered expression, with an eyebrow slightly raised. Rodregas wondered if he had said something wrong. While he had seen the two interact for some years, he really did not know what was appropriate for him to say in such a circumstance.

Rodregas knew that he did not have the skills for pretending he was an Immortalist sorcerer, so he said, "How many people have you killed during the past year, Korin? And how many others have you raped or tortured?" he asked, trying to keep a calm voice.

Now Korin looked incredibly surprised, and he started looking around. Rodregas saw that Korin noticed the study door, though he was working hard to not show it.

"How many?" Rodregas repeated his question.

"I am not sure," Korin said. "For us to truly become divine we must develop our skills."

As Korin answered the question, he took a step back. Rodregas quickly stepped forward and pushed him hard against the wall. Korin hit with a hard smack and slid to the ground. Hurt, but not badly.

Rodregas slammed the door closed and re-locked it. Then he quickly reached down and covered Korin's mouth, pulled him up, and slipped behind him.

Rodregas saw Korin's bulging eyes as he tried to get a better look at his captor. Korin struggled, but not as if his life depended on it. He was probably confused. The image of the day that Rodregas had started to hate him came back.

They had taken a family of Ælves prisoner; they were only common Ælves with no magic. Korin was interested in the father, a good-looking man. The wife was equally beautiful, and they had a boy named Jorin. Rodregas had taken Jorin under his wing. He had only been working at Raven Keep for a little over a year at the time and was still learning the names of the prisoners.

Rodregas had thought Jorin was a pleasant lad, well behaved and bright, and his eyes were eager for signs of hope. Rodregas brought him extra food and words of reassurance. Ravenhurr had no need for him nor his mother, and he had seen other prisoners who were not of use set free. Ravenhurr never showed mercy, but neither was he needlessly wasteful. Rodregas had thought they would set Jorin free in time.

Two months went by and Rodregas had developed a strong fondness for the boy. A few of the guards made jokes that Rodregas had a new pet. But Rodregas was used to the rough humor of soldiers and let such jokes roll off.

The night came when the father was taken for the ceremony. Rodregas was on guard duty when Korin came down in his new body. The poor lad had stared at the man who had been his father, saying nothing, but tears ran down his cheeks.

The apprentice Immortalist had then taken the mother out of the cell and raped her right in front of the prisoner cells. The Adept was rough, and the act was pure violence. Korin, in his new body, clearly enjoyed the violence more than the sex act. The boy had screamed and pleaded for the sorcerer to stop. After Korin had finished with the mother, he had the guards release the boy who had run over to his sobbing, bleeding mother.

In a fatherly gesture Korin had kissed the boy on the cheek and wrapping his hands around the boy's head in a slow loving gesture, made a quick yank and broke Join's neck. The next day the guards released the young Ælf widow.

Rodregas had helped drag her beyond the gates. She lay there, not moving, limp. Though alive. She was dead in every way that mattered. Rodregas had gone back into the keep without looking back. He never knew what had happened to her after that.

After dreaming every night about killing the sorcerer

since that distant day, Rodregas now had Korin in his grip. It was time to end Korin's vile pestilence on the world. Rodregas got behind him with his right hand covering his mouth, and with his left hand took a firm grip on the top of his head.

Rodregas leaned over to his ear and whispered, "You probably don't remember, but you killed a boy named Jorin by snapping his neck, and today you receive your judgement for that."

Snapping a grown man's neck is hard. Rodregas had never done it; he had learned that there were better ways to kill a man than trying to break his spine with bare hands. But with the memory of Korin breaking the adolescent boy's neck, adrenaline pounded in his new arms. This was justice long overdue.

With a quick movement of his arms and the haunting memory of the sounds of crunching and popping from all those years ago, he twisted Korin's head nearly all the way around. Rodregas held his body as it spasmed wildly for a moment. Then the sorcerer adept went still and limp. Rodregas dropped him to the floor.

Korin's' body hit the floor and emptied itself. "Gods," Rodregas thought and asked out loud to no one, "What did he eat this morning?" He grabbed the body and dragged it into the water closet and dropped it into the small bronze tub.

Rodregas started to leave and then saw Korin's purse. The Adept was dressed for travel and Rodregas had yet to find even a single coin in the master's chambers. He reached down and took the purse off his belt. Rodregas opened it to find only a few silvers. He knew Korin should have more. He opened the man's shirt and, as he suspected, another purse hung from his neck. It was of flat leather and inside it was twelve pieces of silver and a small book.

Rodregas tentatively touched the book, and it buzzed slightly of magic. It held no foulness, so he tossed it into the trunk. He added the coin purses to the robe he was wearing. He still needed more hard money and some decent clothes.

Rodregas looked out the window to see a few people leaving the keep grounds, and a few still hanging around the yard. He knew he could not leave without everyone seeing him. He searched the rest of the study in the daylight. He found nothing of actual use until he pulled a drawer completely out of the desk and found a false back to the drawer. He found it was holding a purple silk purse containing eight pieces of gold and two of silver. Now he had the money he needed to be on the run. After forcing himself to wait until the last visible person left the front gate, Rodregas grabbed the trunk and went to the stairs.

He listened quietly, and hearing nothing, he set the trunk down and tiptoed down the stairs. The next floor housed the laboratory. The door was locked, and he did not want to break it down until he was sure everyone had left.

The next floor down was the main floor; He stepped out to the main hall and listened. He heard nothing but his stomach rumble; he was starving and knew that he should eat. He was already in the main hall; the room to the right was the kitchen.

He stepped into the kitchen but then came to a sudden stop. Standing next to one sink was an ancient, very dirty kitchen drudge slowly peeling a potato. She looked up at him in surprise, and with a hint of fear. Rodregas raised his hand up in a peaceful motion. She probably had nowhere else to go.

He ignored her and went to the cabinets and the cold

box. He got out cheese and bread, found some fruit and had an enjoyable, simple meal. He would need to pack as much food as possible for his journey. The old kitchen drudge was still peeling the same potato when he left the kitchen.

Freshly fed and feeling better for it, Rodregas went across the main hall and entered the door opposite the kitchen into the barracks section of the small tower keep. The place was about as messy as he had ever seen it; the normal tidiness demanded by Lord Captain Poir had apparently been put aside in excitement over the chance to take some time off for the celebration.

His personal bunk and trunk were a mess. His good blanket was missing, as was his spare pair of boots and most of his other belongings. The rest of the guards had thought him dead and made free with his stuff.

Rodregas reached into the trunk but all that was left in there were a few bits of trash, a few candle stubs, some scraps of paper and a bit of cloth. He reached down and picked up the piece of cloth and held it up. He stared for some time at the design sewn into it and then stuck it into his outer purse.

He had a powerful urge to clean up his bunk and leave the area in the order it deserved, but that would be too big of a hint of what had happened. So, he was careful to leave it as it was; the longer they thought he was Ravenhurr, the better.

He then walked past the rest of the wooden cots of the barracks to the back where the captain's room was. The Lord Captain's room, unlike the outer barracks, was spotless and in perfect order. He searched through the captain's pair of trunks and found some clothes that fit him, though tightly.

The captain had been a sizeable man, but not as large as Rodregas now was. Still, the soft linen shirt of light brown, which he knew had been loose on the captain, was much more comfortable than the wizard robe he had been wearing. Unfortunately, none of the pants would fit. Poir, though a large man, had skinny legs.

Rodregas felt ridiculous wearing only a linen shirt and his coin purses as he stepped to the armory door.

The door was built of massive slabs of iron oak with hinges of night bronze.

Rodregas reached up and pulled the emergency key from the crack at the right of the door. Because of his status as a senior sergeant, he knew where the key was kept. Once the door was open, he stepped inside.

Immediately, his eyes looked for the corner where the Lord Captain kept his personal suit of full plate armor made of night bronze. They only allowed a greater sigil warrior either a Lord Captain of the Eternal Guard or a Lord Knight of the Order of the Soaring Stars to wear such armor. To no surprise, but to Rodregas's disappointment there was no sign of it. The enchanted armor was too precious for the Lord Captain to go anywhere without it.

Neither was there any sign of any regular guardsmen's armor of any actual value. Apparently, the Lord Captain had sent the Guards out in armor, in case there was any trouble. Even Rodregas's personal gear had been reassigned.

In resignation, he now looked over to a long side bench where several pieces of armor were piled up. These would be more recent pieces not yet sorted or sold off. They had been deemed of no use to the guard. Captain Poir had a tendency to leave some equipment there for lengthy periods, just in case they might prove useful at a later date.

Most of the armor was average civilian crap, but he found several sizeable pieces of leather scale armor that were his size. The armor was braided leather with steel scales attached. He quickly tried it on and found it to be a perfect fit. He surmised that it had been the property of the original owner of his new body. It was probably custom made and was solid, if unspectacular, quality armor.

The braided, lacquered leather reinforced with the steel scales provided decent protection for most fights. This style of armor was vulnerable to a highly skilled swordsman, and useless against a warrior in chain or plate armor. But for someone who wanted protection from the dangers of the road, it was better than most civilian armor. There were matching pants and even boots. He quickly dressed and felt much better once armored. He had spent most of his adult life in armor. He just could not relax when he wore only clothes.

Rodregas then looked around; the keep's armory had casks of arrows and spears, and some older, used short swords and bows on the wall. There were only two powerful weapons like those used by proper members of the Eternal Guards. The premier soldiers that enforced the rule of the Immortalist Guild of the Celestial Path who ruled all the Eastern Kingdoms, but neither of these weapons were kept in the armory.

He looked over to the short swords laying on one table and picked two of them up; they felt a little weird. The swords were too light, and the balance seemed off as he took a few practice strokes. There was a large two-handed great sword, a weapon that was difficult to handle if you were not very strong, and its sheath matched the armor he now wore.

Rodregas picked it up and took a few swings and

found that it was not as clumsy as he thought it would be. It was of simple steel and of average make. He did not like such large swords. The weight provided a lot of momentum and power for a strike, but if you missed it was hard to recover and extremely easy to leave yourself wide open for a counter strike from your opponent.

It looked like the guards had gone to celebrate "his" birthday by taking most of the better armor and weapons with them. Rodregas grabbed a shield, and a barrel of the best-looking arrows, and carried them to the front entrance.

There was probably money in the purser's office, but he knew that the door, and the room, was rigged with poison needles and other traps, both mundane and magical. Rodregas had the impression that Ravenhurr had spent most of his wealth of late on the Dire Cats. After Rodregas' recent generosity to celebrate his birthday, he did not want to take the risk of dying for a nearly empty treasure box.

He looked out of the entrance, over to the gate and up to the top of the wall where a small tower provided cover. There, one of the few guards left should be watching the front gate. Also kept in the watch tower were two of the nicest weapons Rodregas had ever seen: a pair of recurve bows of Wood Nymph created black yew. There was no way they would have been taken. There were standing orders to kill anyone who tried to remove them. Rodregas was not a very good bowman, but he would definitely try to bring them with him.

He peeked out of the main doors and looked around the open keep. The stables were to the left, and the gate was to the right. The courtyard was not large. He could see no one, but he knew there would be at least two guards left: one at the gate and one in the watchtower over the gate.

In front of the stable was a large bony horse, dappled

in brown and white. Rodregas thought her name was Tory or Torin, he could not remember which. She was an older horse, in her early twenties, and known for her mild manor. She was saddled and ready to go, evidently, she was Korin's planned mount.

Rodregas took a deep breath and calmly walked out of the keep and over to the stables. It was not large, ordinarily holding only about a dozen horses. He looked around to find that they had emptied it out, except for the two carriage horses. Both hefty horses were of a gray color with dark manes and feet. They must have been left in case Ravenhurr wished to travel, which would be unlikely with all his guards and servants scattered over the town, but dutiful servants did not take their master's transport from him.

In the open central area, he saw both the small carriage and the supply wagon that Ravenhurr used for traveling and for carrying supplies back and forth to the keep. He looked at it and smiled. With the carriage horses and wagon, he could strip a lot of useful items out of the keep.

He went next door to the smith's and started gathering up tools and loading them up into the smith's travel trunk. The nicest tools were in a cabinet, and with a grunt (it was heavy even for him) he picked it up and loaded it into the cart, along with some other useful implements.

He would need to carry as much food as possible. He quickly went back into the main keep and wrapped up the mattress from Captain Poir's bunk and started carrying barrels of flour and other foodstuffs to his pile next to the front entrance. The drudge stared at him with a strange look but did not question his actions.

He then remembered that he should go up and check out the laboratory for anything else of value and check out the dungeon to make sure they had freed all the prisoners. He had brought a proper crowbar from his visit to the smith's and made quick work of the laboratory door. The room had several large circles in the floor and tables and shelves along the side. The shelves held bones and bowls of strange fluids and other items whose uses he could not imagine.

Anything that felt foul he threw into the fireplace, after getting a good flame going. Several books and strange containers ended up in the fire, though he found two books that felt of magic that he kept. He also found a small statue of a strange green mechanical frog that had that magic tingle to it. He could not imagine its use; it appeared a simple toy, but he put it in his pile to take.

There was a heavy oak cabinet in the corner which he forced open. Inside were large pottery containers, which he had seen before. They held some of the magic powders used to make the circles that were so important to many of the most powerful of the Immortalist's spells.

He checked the powders for magic, and several gave off potent feelings of evil, so he added them to the pile. Two came off with the foulest feel yet even worse than the books in the studio. He could not burn them but knocked them into the middle of the room and then added a couple of the other non-magic powder containers.

In his last action before he left, he used the crowbar to shatter all the containers, and mixed the contents together. He hoped that would make them impossible to use.

After moving what he wanted to take with him to his pile at the entrance of the tower, he headed down the stairs to the dungeon. Rodregas did not want to go down there. Some of his worst memories had taken place down in the dungeon. Too many terrible deeds had occurred there, not that he had done many of them himself, but he could not stop them.

That was not true, he could have tried to stop the terrible things that had happened, but he had chosen to survive instead. He knew the depth of his lack of true courage from his years of failure to act before now. He went through the guardroom and was happy to see that Lord Captain Poir had followed orders. There was no sign of the eight or so prisoners, including his rescued half Ælf maiden.

He stared at the problem in the largest cell. There, sprawled on the floor, were the two female Dire Cats that had been used to trap the Celestial lion.

Rodregas swore as soon as he looked at the cats, they were already looking at him straight in the eye. The large green eyes demanded something of him even as the animals lay in apparent complete relaxation, sprawled on the stone floor. He had to let them out, but how was he going to do that?

If he opened the door, they might tear him apart. Rodregas thought the cats may also attack the guard at the front gate on their way out. He looked around and realized that the other side of the hall had a door that opened in the same direction as the door leading to the cage. He opened it up and thought that if he opened the Dire Cats' door, he could block them from this direction, while keeping himself safe behind the two doors.

He knew the guards at the gate would be curious about what he had been doing, but they would do nothing to challenge the man they thought was the Sorcerer

Ravenhurr. He also knew that he would have to get them out of the way of the Dire Cats. At least that way he could also claim the black yew bows.

Rodregas walked back up the stairs and he thought it would be an excellent idea to feed the Dire Cats before setting them free. But he did not have time to grab a couple of chickens in the coop next to the kitchen. The sooner he was away from the keep, the better.

As Rodregas walked up to the watchtower gates he once again wore the sorcerer's robe that Captain Poir had fetched for him, but this time he wore it outside of his armor. He climbed the inner stairs until he stepped into the watchtower room at the top. He played it boldly, walked up to the staring guard and signaled him to turn around. Then Rodregas gagged and bound him. The confused guard did not even struggle.

Next, Rodregas went to the front gate and repeated his actions with the lone guard at the gate; he then picked him up and took him to sit with his friend at the top of the watch tower. He made sure both were securely tied up and blindfolded and took off their weapon harnesses and kept them; their two short swords were nicer than the ones he had taken from the armory. Both men also had purses with them that jingled with their bonus money in a promising way.

He then headed back to the dungeon, stopping at the chicken coop to let out the chickens. They quickly spread all over the yard. It would be better for the town folk who lived so close to the fort if the Dire Cats were not starving when they left. On his way into the dungeon, he left all the doors propped open so the way out would be clear, and he made sure that all the other doors were closed.

Luckily, the kitchen drudge had already locked

herself in the kitchen. Rodregas then went back to the dungeon level and opened the opposite door and the Dire Cats' prison door and watched. He had expected them to either bolt for it or stay in the perceived 'safety' of their room. Instead they both casually got up and walked out, as if they were guests in a fancy inn, with all the time in the world.

As they walked out the door, both cats gave him a casual glance as he held the two doors firmly closed together bracing for their weight if they threw themselves at the doors, but they just walked by and headed up the stairs. He wanted to follow, but Rodregas held himself back, patiently waiting until it was safe. They might look like lions, but he knew they were smarter than any beast, and they could be setting him up. Finally, after waiting what seemed like forever, but was probably only about twenty minutes, Rodregas slowly made his way back up through the keep.

When he poked his head out the entrance, there was no sign of Dire Cats or chickens, but he noted a few stray feathers in the courtyard. Other than a few alarmed sounds from the chicken coop, it was quiet.

Rodregas felt of relief at the idea that the lions had eaten. Still, he double-checked the keep and the courtyard carefully before bringing out the cart and the horses and loading up all his booty. The cart groaned with the load. After a last check for Dire Cats in front of the keep, he headed out and away from both Raven Keep and away from his old life.

CHAPTER 4
A FRESH START OR AN OLD PROBLEM

Raven Keep, unlike many fortifications, was not located on a high spot. In fact, it was perched half-way down a gentle valley. Farther down the valley, only a few minutes' ride away, was Raven Town. Even the kindest of folk would admit the town was not much more than an inn, a stable, the homes of the people that supported the local farming community and Raven Keep.

Many of the keep employees and their family members lived in Raven Town. Luckily for Rodregas, there was a turnoff almost immediately that let him circle around the edge of town and then head out of the valley. He went north toward the town of Cruet. As dusk was falling, there was little traffic. Luckily this part of the road was clear and open, and the horses were fresh so he made good headway even as it became dark.

He pushed hard until he reached the fork that headed west up into the hills. It was seldom traveled by anyone except fur trappers. Rodregas pushed on through the night and into the sunrise of the next day until even the horse that had been Korin's ride, which he had tied to the back of the wagon seemed to be tired and ready for rest. He stopped and let the animals take a break next to a small creek.

Rodregas was not sure what would happen when the relief guards went to the tower and found the other guards tied up, apparently by Ravenhurr himself. His assistant had been killed in the master's own room. They would find the keep partially pillaged. He knew Lord Captain Poir would probably do one of two things: either come after him immediately or head to the Celestial Path Guild Hall in the capital.

If Lord Captain Poir headed immediately for the Guild Hall to report the strange happening, it would give more time for Rodregas to find a place to lie low. However, it would be better for him if Poir went looking for Rodregas himself instead and spread his men all over the countryside trying to find him.

There were only twenty Ravenhurr guardsmen. If they were sent in every possible direction, especially in pairs as was proper procedure, there was an excellent chance that he would come across only two of them at a time. If they were still confused about whether he was or was not Ravenhurr, he would have an excellent chance of overcoming them. Unless the Lord Captain found him himself, as a greater sigil warrior in night bronze plate, Rodregas would have little chance against the warrior.

On the other hand, if the forces of the Guild came after him, it doomed him. The guardsmen of the Immortalist guild, know as the Eternal Guards, had the reputation as the premier fighters of the realm. If they found out what had happened at Raven Keep, there was not much chance for Rodregas' survival.

After a simple meal, a good rub down for the horses and a few hours of rest, Rodregas got the wagon back on the road. If he could keep this pace up, he could be well hidden before any forces could find him.

At the end of the second day, before he had come to his last turn off, he realized that he would have to get some sleep. He was feeling exhausted. His body might be surprisingly strong and quick, but apparently it still needed to sleep.

As soon as the horses were fed, rubbed down, hobbled, and left to graze, Rodregas unrolled Captain Poir's mattress and collapsed into it with a welcome sigh. Sleep came to him almost instantly.

In Rodregas' life he had experienced several very unpleasant ways of waking up, but this was the worst: a searing hot pain stabbed into his stomach! He reared up from his mat, but he felt hands holding him down onto the mattress. It was dark, but he could see in the dim light of the moon that someone was shoving a knife into his belly.

He knew that in the next couple of seconds, his actions would decide his fate. He was bleeding, so he would be losing strength. Whoever his assailants were, they had him trapped. Rodregas violently kicked out with one leg, but his stabbing attacker avoided the blow. He let up on the knife for a second though. Instead of following up, Rodregas used the momentum of his kick to swing his body sideways.

Skilled, close fighting was all about leverage. Instead of resisting the attacker's strength, Rodregas pushed down on the earth with his hands and lifted his body up and to the side, curling the leg he had kicked out underneath. He planted his foot under his body. His attackers seemed confused, grabbing him and trying to counter his change of position. Rodregas only had one leg under him, but he pushed off with it with all his strength and thrust himself up. It should have failed with all the men holding him down, but he now had Celestial strength, and even with the knife wound he was strong.

His attackers backed off, confused by the fact that he had gone from being their prisoner to surging to his feet. The person pinning Rodregas' left arm got too far away. This gave Rodregas the leverage he needed to pull the arm free. He punched his assailant hard in the face. The attacker flew back and Rodregas jumped sideways to get more space.

Rodregas rested his right hand on the knife blade still sticking out of his stomach. It relieved him to feel that it was not too deep. He had not taken off his armor. Although the knife had pierced the leather weave, the tip penetrated only an inch or two.

Rodregas gritted his teeth and pulled the knife free. From the feel of its balance, it was not a proper fighting weapon, but only a simple utility knife. Rather than try to use the unfamiliar weapon that was slick with his blood, he threw it into the dark. Rodregas knew he was in a fight for his life.

He backed up from his confused opponents and gave himself more space. It was the middle of the night and there was only a sliver of moon, but he could still make out the forms of his attackers; there were four of them. No, a fifth stood away from the others and watched. The one who had stabbed him had the most aggressive posture. He looked tall and strong. Rodregas knew he had to take him out quickly, so he moved in hard.

None of the attackers seemed to wear armor, nor did they have any weapons, other than the largest man, who was farthest away and held what looked to be a garden rake. Rodregas charged, bulling his way into the lead attacker and knocking him down. The assailant fell, being surprised by Rodregas' actions. Rodregas grabbed him by the hair with his left hand and hit him full in the nose with his right fist. The man crumbled.

Two others closed in with a group tackle. The one on the right came in too close, and Rodregas gave him a good hard jab with his elbow in the stomach. Rodregas heard his attacker's entire breath exit at his blow, and he collapsed to the ground.

Rodregas followed up with a roundhouse kick and laid a good blow into the kidney area of the other man. Rodregas realized that his attackers were not trained fighters. He felt himself relax as he realized that they posed no genuine danger to him now that he was on his feet and aware.

Just as Rodregas relaxed from the heart pounding life or death moment that had awoken him, the enormous form of the man holding the rake stepped forward. Rodregas realized that he was even taller and bigger than the first one. The attacker swung the rake right at him with all his weight behind it. Rodregas was too close to dodge, and the rake hit his wounded gut straight on with the full brunt of his attacker's momentum.

Rodregas swooned in pain as his fresh wound took the blunt of the blow. He had felt like he was faster and stronger than everyone else and had not been expecting the power of the blow. Rodregas went flying back down to the ground, moaning. He rolled with it and came back up. Rodregas thought about the swiftness of the strike and realized that this man would be a challenge.

Judging by the distance his attacker kept and how he was keeping his center of gravity low and balanced, Rodregas knew this opponent was well trained. He was not just bigger and stronger; he knew how to fight. A skillful fighter knows you do not let an opponent recover.

His attacker came in hard and fast. Rodregas never saw the blow to his face, but luckily it was not a direct hit as Rodregas was already moving in close. Before the attacker could deliver another blow, he was inside his opponent's swing.

Getting close is not always the best strategy on a powerful, larger opponent. His attacker's large hand reached for his face. Rodregas turned into his weight and tried to use his momentum to drive the enormous body off balance. But the attacker was built like a bull: broad and full of muscle. Rodregas' push against him had little effect.

Something felt odd about this last attacker; his body felt

wrong, not human. Rodregas thought, "maybe an Orqui?" That would explain the muscular build, but that did not seem right either. The two fighters separated. Sometimes there is a mutual agreement during a fight, especially when both are not sure who has the advantage.

The two of them started circling, and Rodregas tried to keep an eye out for the other men, but they seemed disoriented in the dark and appeared to be keeping their distance. Rodregas thought he saw other movement, farther out, but it was more animal-like. It surprised him any wild animals would be this close to the noise of a fight.

Rodregas waited for an opening, but it was hard to know exactly what was going on in the dark. He was bleeding from his belly wound and decided that he could not wait. Rodregas pulled his short swords from the harness on his side and rushed in on the big guy.

The large attacker was big and powerful, but his rake had shattered and Rodregas had his short swords and wore armor. His attacker appeared to not have a backup weapon.

Then a voice rang out, "Stop, STOP, it is not him! It is not the Sorcerer Ravenhurr." It was a woman's voice.

Then a much deeper voice, one that seemed half growl, responded, "She is right. This is no sorcerer we fight."

The voice was from his present combatant, the only one who had proven to be dangerous to him. "She is right," Rodregas said to the group, "I am not Ravenhurr."

"We don't know that," challenged another voice from the dark. As he stepped forward, he recognized the shape of the large aggressive man that Rodregas had first thought was the leader. "If he is not Gerald, then he must be Ravenhurr."

There was a silent response to that statement, but finally one of the other men lit a torch and held it up. Rodregas quickly realized that in front of him were five of the eight prisoners who had been held in the dungeon.

"How did you track me here?" Rodregas asked. The one with the torch waved it over toward the lone female of the group, the half-blood Ælf maiden from the tower.

"I am afraid you are not much of a woodsman, not that it is easy to hide wagon tracks," she stated, her voice hinting disapproval at his skill. "Still, it was far too easy, even though my people do not count me as one of their better trackers."

Rodregas thought of asking her if she was referring to her Ælf or her Nymph heritage as her people, but decided it was best not to ask. He had to admit she had a delightful voice to go along with that athletic body and unique look.

There were three human men, all large and well built, the half Ælf maiden, and whatever the gigantic man was. The guy he had tagged as the leader was nearly as tall and well-built as Rodregas' new body. The other two men were also very impressive. They were all men that Ravenhurr had been testing for use as replacement bodies. Rodregas' present body had 'won' as the most gifted human male that Ravenhurr could find.

Rodregas knew that the exceptionally large male was something else an Orqui and 'of the blood', but not Celestial Born, but descended from an Infernal Daemon, one of those known as Hellborn.

The Hellborn was a good head taller than even Rodregas, and even more broad and muscular. In fact, his chest was so broad that it looked almost deformed, and something bulged in the middle of both of his shoulders, though the cloak he wore blocked the details of the strange bulge. His face was blunt, except for sharp cheekbones, and his skin had a reddish-brown hue. His head was crowned with a pair of horns like a ram's. The horns were curled into his black bushy hair, which was long, very thick, and very wild. It was sticking out in weird ways from his head.

It had confused all the guards why Ravenhurr had kept

the Hellborn, as it was against the Guild rules to use any of Infernal blood in the ceremony. The Immortalist were trying to become Celestial gods, not a member of the Infernal realms. It was a rule not of the Guild but of both the Gods and Daemons. The only rule that Rodregas knew was agreed upon by both sides, known as the First Rule. Everyone knew you did not break it.

Rodregas assumed that using the Hellborn in an ascension ritual could not be Ravenhurr's motivation, but then why keep him and possibly bring down the wrath of the Guild if not the gods themselves? Not that any of the guards would mention it to anyone.

"Who are you?" asked the man that Rodregas had tagged as 'the leader.'

"I am not sure who I am," Rodregas responded. "And I think I will keep any answers I figure out to myself for now."

"You are not Gerald though, are you?" asked the Ælf maiden.

"Not to ask a dumb question," Rodregas asked in a curious tone "but who is Gerald?" Silence followed his query but finally he got an answer.

"He is the man that you appear to be, whose body you now… have," responded the half-blood Ælf.

"And what are you five named?" Rodregas asked. There was a pause at his question. He knew this was an important moment because once people say who they are, they are much less likely to do violence. Rodregas did not understand the reason, but he knew that to be true.

"I am Imeraldä," said the Ælf maiden.

Then came the Hellborn, "My name is Doi'vanmorian, but humans usually call me Doi'van," he stated in a slow careful way in a very deep, deep voice.

The leader, after a pause, said, "I am Audrian of the family, Corin." The other two men identified themselves as

Brit and Eagor.

Geor was the one with the torch and was blond, and like the other men, unusually good looking and well built. Brit said little and was of black hair and light skin. Offhand, Rodregas thought he looked to have come from the northern Kingdoms.

"Gerald was a friend of ours, we went through a lot together in the Raven Keep dungeon," explained Audrian. "If you are neither him nor Ravenhurr, who are you? Only another Immortalist sorcerer should have been able to steal a body from Ravenhurr," Audrian finished.

It was a good question, and one Rodregas was asking himself. He wanted to spill the story, but he did not really trust these men. He had spent hard years on the road and knew not to trust people you have just met. You especially do not trust people who try to kill you while you sleep.

And as long as people thought he might be Ravenhurr, maybe a little crazy from a spell gone wrong or something, the less likely the Guild of the Celestial Path would send the Eternal Guards against him.

So Rodregas said, "Let us just say I am trying to figure out who I am. You can call me...," he thought for a minute, making it obvious he was making up a fake name. He did not want to use his actual name. He thought to himself, "Who do I want to be?"

"If I'm going to fight against the Immortalists, then I need a name fit for a Celestial Paladin, or maybe one fit for an Infernal Adversary," he thought to himself with a smile. The only way he could have survived the ceremony would have been divine intervention, so he said the first thing that came to mind, "You can call me Sir Paladin, that will work for now," he said it with a smile and a slight snicker at his own joke.

"Just what kind of Paladin would you be?" Imeraldä asked him.

"Why, it should be obvious to you more than anyone," Rodregas said with a slight bow to the beautiful half Ælf. "The heroic Paladin that rescues beautiful maidens in distress and who sets free innocent prisoners from the dungeons of evil sorcerers."

Rodregas could not help but smile at his own line. He had always found that an excellent joke was like a good insult. The best always had enough truth in them to sting. Geor smiled, but the others seemed not to have appreciated his little joke.

The Ælf woman just looked at Rodregas quietly and thoughtfully. The Hellborn Orqui smiled, but with a look that said he did it because the other men smiled. Rodregas had a feeling that Doi'van lacked much of a sense of humor. The other three men simply shook their heads at his idiotic statement.

Rodregas was sure everyone here had lost a loved one, at some point, to an Immortalist. But no Paladin of the Gods had ever come to their rescue. The truth was that even if one of the gods had chosen Rodregas as their champion. It was more likely to be some god who was pissed off at the Immortalists. One looking for a champion for their own selfish reasons.

As a child Rodregas had dreamed of being such a champion, but Paladins were always chosen from the ranks of the Order of the Soaring Stars or other powerful sigil warriors, and while Rodregas had once served the Order as a squire he had never come close to achieving knighthood.

"All right, Sir Paladin, I have to admit I have talked to the Sorcerer Ravenhurr a few too many times, and you definitely don't seem to be him. We are taking your wagon and your supplies. We will let you go in peace in the morning," said Audrian in that tone of voice that implied that he expected people to follow his orders.

"Hand over the shorts swords," Audrian continued,

gesturing at the two blades that Rodregas had sheathed at his side. "We will return one in the morning." Rodregas smiled and nodded and pulled the two swords out simultaneously. He was thinking his new body was ambidextrous, equally comfortable with both hands. That could prove useful but would require some additional training to take full advantage of during a fight.

"Actually, since I was kicking your ass barehanded, even with a knife in my belly. How about this instead, I won't kill the bunch of you if you keep your distance, and leave my camp at first light?" Rodregas' tone was casual. "And, if you ask nicely, I will even leave you a few supplies to get to the nearest town if you promise not to tell anyone that you saw me. And you will promise that in the name of the All-Father, or you will die at my hand." Rodregas did not smile now, nor did they.

"So, you think you could kill all of us? Put your sword down now!" demanded Audrian.

Rodregas stepped forward and buried just the tip of his right-handed short sword into Audrian's chest, hitting the ribs but not shoving the blade through the bones and cartilage. Audrian gasped in surprise and stared down at his chest.

"Swear you will keep my secret and you live, do not and you die. Choose!"

Audrian just stood there looking at him. Then he nodded and said, "In the name of the All-Father Grímnr, Lord of Stars and Sky, I swear that I will keep your secrets."

Rodregas nodded and relaxed slightly; few would dare break a promise to the All-Father.

Rodregas decided that Brit and Geor were like pale shadows as they quickly followed suit. When he turned to the last two, he saw that they were extremely interested in what he was saying.

"Where do you go, Sir Paladin?" asked the Hellborn

showing no sense of humor at Rodregas' little joke about being a Paladin. Rodregas hoped Doi'van had not taken him literally. "Traveling as far as I can, is my primary plan. The Guild of the Celestial Path will be looking for me. Let's just say I don't wish to be found anywhere right now."

"And if they find you? And they will in time. Will you react more like an Infernal Adversary instead of a Paladin?" asked the Hellborn.

Rodregas flourished his short swords and smiled and stated, "Let's just say that it should be interesting."

The Hellborn nodded thoughtfully at Rodregas reply. The half Ælf had followed the conversation between them with obvious interest and quickly followed Doi'van's' lead in swearing the oath to the All-Father. But with the two of them the oath seemed different, more easily said and with no need for threats. Rodregas was not sure why, but he decided it was something to think about when he had more time.

The rest of the night passed quickly as Rodregas did his best to bandage his stomach wound. He did not think the knife had cut into anything too important; at least it was not bleeding too badly. It surprised him that he was not more tired; maybe his new body handled such things better and could make do with less sleep.

He was usually a light sleeper and was incredibly surprised that they had been able to get the drop on him. His guess was that the Ælf maiden had cast some spell on him to mask their approach, and he kept a close eye on her to make sure she did not repeat the effort. Of course, she was also genuinely nice to look at, so he did not need much of an excuse to enjoy the view.

In the morning, he pulled out some supplies and bundled them. He tried not to show how much it now hurt. The wound might not kill him, but every movement hurt. He also handed Audrian a few of his coins. It was not much, but it would get them started. They were lucky he was being so generous. Rodregas could not blame them for their actions, if he had been in their place, he would have tried to kill Ravenhurr.

The three human men were eager to get started back to the main road. He noticed that the Hellborn Doi'van and Imeraldä seemed to hang back. As the three men headed down the road Doi'van walked up to Rodregas and stated,

"I would rather travel with you." That was it. The Hellborn just stood there like some immense tree after that simple statement.

Audrian seemed as surprised as Rodregas was. They both spoke at the same time, their thoughts strangely in agreement. "Are you crazy?" asked Audrian at the same time as Rodregas said, "That is crazy."

"Look, the Guild will be after me," Rodregas stated. "It will not be safe to travel in my company," he added.

"I know," stated the Hellborn in a voice that was so deep it was like stones grinding. "But even so, I would travel with you." Again, he made the statement and showed no interest in explaining his action.

"Actually," added Imeraldä, shaking her long curly hair behind her as if to clear the way for her decision, "I was thinking the same thing. I am not safe from the Guild anyhow. My natural magical talent is extraordinarily strong, and until I am better skilled in it, I am very vulnerable," she stated. "While Audrian, Brit and Geor are very brave to let me travel with them, I fear that I put their lives in danger. You, on the other hand, are in more danger than I am, and should be even more motivated to stay out of the sight of the Guild." After saying the brief speech that she had clearly been practicing in her head, she added, "Joining you makes sense."

Rodregas hesitated, but she had an excellent point, and turning away such a beautiful young woman was a tough thing to do. She had sound reasoning, and he had a reasonably safe place to hide that he had been heading toward. So, even if he headed out on a raid of the Immortalists, she should be safe enough. The human men would be of least interest to the Guild and the easiest to blend back wherever they had come from.

On the other hand, while Hellborn were feared and disliked, the Immortalists should not be interested in Doi'van. He was also a gifted warrior and between the two of them they would make a dangerous duo. However, the Hellborn were feared because of their daemonic natures. They are rumored to have hungers and urges, and famously bad tempers. Doi'van could be just as much of a danger as help. Rodregas had to admit though, that in the little time he had dealt with him, he kind of liked the big guy.

It looked like Audrian would argue, but Rodregas just cut him off and stated, "Very well, you two may travel with me, but let's get on the road. Audrian, make sure you and the other two do not forget your oaths. I will expect no one to know that we head for the Northern Coast."

Audrian looked like he would say something. Rodregas thought the loss of the Hellborn did not bother him, but the beautiful half Ælf was another matter. However, her point about how she put them in danger made him hesitate.

Rodregas just headed for the wagon and got it going. With a last confused look from Rodregas, Audrian and the other two headed back towards the nearest town.

The three talked little as they traveled. Rodregas set a hard pace and Imeraldä sat in the back of the wagon. Doi'van weighed too much to ride in the overburdened wagon or to ride the horse, so he jogged next to the wagon. He had impressive endurance.

Right before dark, Rodregas who was watching the ground carefully found the faint signs of the rocky trail that he remembered. He turned the cart onto it, and after going down the path a bit he came across a suitable place to camp for the night. As Doi'van and Rodregas set up camp, Imeraldä went back, doing her best to erase their tracks. After dinner they all took turns sleeping and keeping watch.

Rodregas took the first watch and several times he thought he saw something. It was not the men they had left behind, but some animal that never came close. It seemed to hang on the edge of the camp.

"A wolf maybe?" Rodregas thought. It seemed to be watching the camp, but it was not doing anything aggressive.

He remembered thinking he had seen an animal during the fight. "Maybe we were in a wolf pack's territory, and they were just making sure that we were not disturbing their young," he thought.

Happily, this night proved to be more restful and peaceful than the last.

CHAPTER 5
A PLACE OF PRIDE

Rodregas drove the wagon with Imeraldä sitting next to him; Doi'van continued his impressive show of endurance next to the wagon and had no trouble keeping up. As the trail was more of a hunting path than a proper road and they were traveling on an upward incline, the wagon was struggling to make much time.

It was not until their midday stop that the three had any proper conversation. "So," asked Imeraldä, "where are we going? I assume it is not the Northern Kingdoms as you said to Audrian. For one thing that would be stupid, and for a second you seem to be climbing ever higher into the Arida Mountains and that is hardly the best way north."

Rodregas nodded. He hoped to make it to his hideaway by nightfall, so he decided it did not hurt to share his plan at this point.

"You're right; we are not going to the Northern Kingdoms. A long time ago a few companions and I were hiding out in the Aridas. In one of the higher hollows I found an old farmhouse. It has been abandoned for a long time, but it is well made and there is water and lots of fruit trees and berry bushes that must be left over from an old orchard."

After a moment he added, "I always thought if I ever needed a place to hide out that it was ideal. It will be rough there. Outside of what we bring, there will not be much. But it will be a wonderful place to rest and..." he said gently patting his stomach, "heal up. We should be there by nightfall."

"Not bad," said Imeraldä. "Sounds like a place that will be hard to find, but is this not territory infested with wild Dire animals?"

"Yup," Rodregas said, "another reason I think this area is usually hard to find; most people stay clear." He continued after a pause to let them think of entering territory known to be the hunting range of feared predators, "I saw no sign of any Dire beast in the hollows when I was there, but they probably know of the place. Still, I would rather handle a pack of Hellhounds than The Eternal Guards." Neither looked pleased at his logic, but both nodded in agreement.

A few hours later it was getting dark as Rodregas recognized the spot and turned the wagon left for the final hard assent. At this point there was no trail, and common sense would have argued against the path. It was hard work.

The horses had to be hand-led around rocks and trees and pulled up. Doi'van and Rodregas had to manhandle the wagon around a few corners which was easier to do than it should have been, but Celestial and Hellborn strength together made quick work of it.

Then, as they finally leveled out into the small little valley of the hollow, the hair all over Rodregas' body suddenly stood up on end and his skin shivered. Rodregas was expecting it but was a little shocked by the strength of his reaction. All those years ago he had had to struggle to feel it. Now he almost swayed in the currents of the magic stream of energy.

The wagon halted as Doi'van stopped pushing it up the incline. He just stood there, his wild black unkempt hair seeming to blow in an invisible wind. Imeraldä looked equally surprised and caught up. That was interesting. Clearly Imeraldä would have the power to sense the stream of magic, but Doi'van had seemed equally effected.

She turned to Rodregas; her eyebrows arched high in surprise and said, "A ley line and powerful? I knew there were several going through the Aridas, but your little abandoned farm is next to a ley line?" she asked.

"Actually," Rodregas said, "it is right in the middle of it, and there is even a slight undercurrent suggesting that another weaker one crosses at the farm."

Rodregas explained, "I had been on the run when we found this place. It had worried me that those tracking me were using magic. So, to keep them off my track, I traveled in and out of ley lines to throw off the magic scent. This one runs underground before coming out in this small valley. I was trying to find the ley line again. That is how I found the old farmhouse."

Ley lines are like rivers of magic energy that encircle the world. They locate most major Immortalist keeps and other magic locations either on one, or where two of them cross. Magicians love them for all the free magical power just flowing by to use. But while there is plenty of power, it is difficult to use. The power is naturally full of disturbances and chaotic energies.

The horror stories of magicians having terrible accidents with spells gone crazy on ley lines were legend. So Immortalist used circles to manage the power. Raven Keep was on such a ley line, but you could not feel it because of the powerful circles built into the tower. It was why Raven Town was not closer.

"Come on," Rodregas said. "Let's get to shelter before dark." As he headed into the hidden hollow, the orchard became clear. He was sure that at one point it had straight rows and a pattern to it. But the orchard had been wild for an exceedingly long time. While there was a bunch of fruit trees and berry bushes, most were the descendants of the original orchard and it was hard to find anything that resembled a straight row.

The apples trees were in fruit, and they all started grabbing a few of each to eat as they went. Rodregas was not much of a farmer and did not know what the unfamiliar types were named, but he liked the small green ones with the yellow splotches; they were sweet with a wonderful tang.

"You know," said Doi'van, "Hiding on a ley line definitely makes sense for keeping the Immortalists off our back and these apples are delicious."

Rodregas stared at him as he ate. Humans ate around the core, but Doi'van was eating the whole apple as he talked. "And I love the feel of all the magic. My body was meant to live in a place that has more magic than our world does, but the lines are chaotic. It is hard to sleep on a wild line. It will be hard to stay here for long." Doi'van's deep voice had the tone of making a simple observation, not conversation.

Rodregas nodded; he had been waiting for the comment, but he had thought it would be Imeraldä who brought it up. "True," he said, "unless you have a way of smoothing it out." Rodregas waited for a few seconds as the three approached the main farmhouse building.

The walls were of thick-cut stone and it was built on an impressive scale for a farmhouse, though worn-looking. There were no signs of a roof, doors, or windows. As they entered the yard, the feeling of the hair standing up on their bodies settled down and instead a feeling of fullness replaced it.

The horses had been acting up and Rodregas hoped that with the energy smoothing out, the horses would stop fighting their lines. Contrary to his hope, the horses seemed to be getting more agitated.

As the magic smoothed out Rodregas smiled and said, "The ley line would be as much of a problem as a help. Unless they make the farmhouse of Nymph stone."

Rodregas expected the sound of pleased surprise but heard alarmed, in-drawn breaths from them both. He saw that they were looking to the right, where he suddenly noticed movement.

Two female Dire Cats stepped out of the orchard and made their way to the farmhouse. They had a relaxed, bored look. He thought they gave him a casual nod, but he could not see any movement. Rodregas simply knew that these were the two Dire Cats that he had freed from the Dungeon. "Did everyone from that dungeon follow me?" he whispered to himself.

The three stood there fighting to keep the horses from running and watched as the Dire Cats stepped through the main door for a moment but left after only a brief time. The Dire Cats then circled around to the far edge of the main house and then disappeared.

Rodregas said, "I think they just went into the cellar of the home. The entrance is over there. Come on, let us get the horses over to the old barn and get them set for the night before it gets too dark."

"Are those the two Dire Cats from Raven Keep?" asked Imeraldä. As she spoke she shook her long auburn hair behind her, something he was realizing was a nervous gesture.

"Yes, I think so," Rodregas said. "I freed them from the dungeon before I left, and then I thought I saw them yesterday. Apparently, everyone in the dungeon is following me," he said with a chuckle.

"You saw them?" asked Doi'van.

"Not exactly," he said. "I saw movement a few times. I just thought it might be them. I did not know for sure," he explained.

Doi'van asked Imeraldä, "Did you know they were tracking us?"

"No, I had no clue." she said looking embarrassed. She then added, "I am a Forest Nymph but not really a skilled tracker. I mean, our Paladin was easy enough to find, but tracking Dire Cats through the forest, that would require true skill."

"But you did not sense them at all?" asked the Hellborn again.

"No," she shook her head. "Why?" she asked, her voice curious about his repeated questioning.

"Because I am wondering if our 'Paladin' has a connection to the Dire Cats. I know they used a Celestial lion in the ceremony. Whoever our Paladin is I assume he now has its essence, and the Celestial lion took these two as his mates." Imeraldä and Doi'van looked at Rodregas.

Then she slowly added, "and what was one of your first actions? You freed them from the dungeon. Dire Cats are smarter than regular lions; they might see you as an ally or part of their herd. No wait, I think with cats you call them prides. But I wonder how they see Doi'van and me?" she asked. Neither Doi'van nor Rodregas had an answer to that question.

"Well," Rodregas said, "we need to find shelter and if

they meant us harm, they would not have shown themselves. It's getting dark. Let's get the horses into the barn. If they have been tracking me since I let them out, they don't seem to want to eat us."

With that, Rodregas got out of the wagon and pulled the horses into the barn. Their noses were flaring, and he had to pull them almost to the opening. As soon as they got close, they both went charging in. The horses sensed the barn was shelter to keep them safe from the Dire Cats.

Like the farmhouse, the barn was also built of the same impressive large cut stone. However, while the stone was in great shape, all other materials seemed to have fallen apart. There were several small trees and bushes growing in the barn. The floor was also stone, and there was not enough dirt and debris for them to grow very large. They had to clear a path to get the wagon in. Imeraldä ran her hand over the stone with a gentle caress.

"It is Nymph stone, right?" Rodregas asked.

She nodded and said, "Yes, I am half Forest Nymph, and this is beautiful work." All Nymphs have a specific attachment to nature such as forest, stone or water. There was a lot of variation among the Nymphs, but they could do amazing things with their element.

A connection to stone was much sought after by the Immortalist and other mages. The stone could not store magic like the circles but it could smooth out the high level of magic available on ley lines and make it more comfortable to use, not in the big way of the magic of circles, but for using magic in small ways. And, of course, only homes made by nymphs could make living on a ley line comfortable.

"This home truly is a find," said Doi'van, "and now I see why the Dire Cats showed themselves to us."

"What do you mean?" Rodregas asked.

"Dire Beasts seek such places to lair," answered Doi'van. "Whether their ancestry is Celestial or Infernal, they instinctively seek a place that has a higher level of magic energy. But they find ley lines like this irritating as much as we do, unless there is some way to smooth out its turbulence. This is especially true of pregnant females. The strongest dire animals are not just those of nearest descent, but also those who come to term in high magical environments." Rodregas nodded, he had heard bits of this, but he had not really thought about it.

Doi'van stretched his hands up and up to an impressive height, and a smile spread across his face, the first one Rodregas had seen on the Hellborn face. It was good to see, though it was also a little scary as his teeth were more pointed than Rodregas was used to seeing. His teeth had more in common with the Dire Cats than himself or Imeraldä.

"I know this first-hand as it is the same for us Hellborn. We will not grow strong if we don't spend most of our childhood in a place rich in magic. This place feels wonderful. The last few years, the only time I was in a place rich in magic, I was also a prisoner. It is good not to hunger for magic and be FREE!"

Rodregas was curious about the Hellborn's background but had been hesitant to ask. You do not want to piss off one of the Hellborn.

Hellborn were not necessarily chaotic and sadistic beings, like actual daemons. At least they weren't unless they voluntarily became one of Hell's Chosen Adversary's. Rodregas did not think even one of the Immortalist would mess with one of Hell's Chosen. Hellborn on the mortal world were welcome among the Orqui, much like those of

Celestial blood were among the Humans and the Ælves. The Orqui mated with Daemons and their offspring became its races noble house, just as the blood of Celestials flowed in the noble houses of Humans and Ælf.

Here in the Eastern Kingdom true ruler ship was not by the Celestial Born of the noble houses anymore but by the Immortalist and their Guild of the Celestial Path. Often those of Celestial blood, instead of being rulers, were hunted by the Guild to fuel for their rituals.

Rodregas decided it was now or never if he would ask Doi'van of his past. "So," he said, "was your mother in a place of strong magic when she was pregnant with you?" He held his breath, worried that his question might be impolite.

But Doi'van's smile continued, and he nodded, "Yes, my mother is a princess of the Farisa tribe across the Long Sea. There the Orqui are torn between following the Celestials and the Daemon Lords of the Infernal Realm. My family and the Farisa tribe follow the Celestials. The Daemon Lords love to tempt all those of Celestial blood. I was born a bastard from an illicit affair of such a temptation. While the shape my father had taken had been fair, I came out, well let's just say my paternity was not in question."

"This is an old game among my people," Doi'van continued "and while my birth was awkward for my mother in my clan, they kept me in the palace and I grew to adulthood in its strong magical confines and to my full strength."

"So, if your mother was of Celestial blood," Imeraldä broke in, "are you of both Infernal and Celestial blood?"

Doi'van seemed hesitant to answer for a moment but after a lengthy pause said, "Yes, but most choose not to see it that way. You are either Hellborn or not. After I grew to manhood, I decided my authentic place was among one of the other clans, one that follows the lordship of the Hellborn." He spoke this slowly, each deep rumble of his tone dragged out. "I was wrong though, and quickly realized that those who follow the Lords of the Infernal Realms were even a worse fit for me than at home, though they saw me as royal blood and not tainted."

Doi'van added, "I eventually decided to start somewhere new and took a ship across the Long Sea." Doi'van paused at this and shook his head, his hair flying wild, as he seemed to want to shake out a memory from his massive head before he continued.

"I am afraid I did not ask enough questions. I just wanted to get a fresh start. I was in Guild Dealer Taigas' Menagerie to be sold within a week of my arrival." He finished, his smile fading at the memory.

"When was that?" Rodregas asked.

Doi'van looked at him for a second and said, "two years ago."

"But that makes no sense," Rodregas said, his voice angry though he did not know why. "The Guild is trying to make their Immortalist members Celestial. Why would they hold you for two years?"

Doi'van nodded, but then shook his head. "Trust me, I would like to know that answer more than you." Doi'van's smile was now long gone, and with a shrug of his huge misshapen shoulders, he changed the subject.

"So, Imeraldä, the stone here still seems strong and like new, though it has been long after the construction of this place."

She was looking at Doi'van strangely and it seemed to take her a moment to shift gears and answer his question. "Yes, stone enchanted to absorb the power of the ley lines becomes stronger over time. Stones formed like this will last as long as the ley line does not move, which happens only rarely and over centuries. What is strange is this is not a farm designed by Nymphs. The design of the home and barn is human, yet it would be strange for a simple farmer to afford to have his building built of Nymph stone. Not to mention having it built way up here in this remote place," she said.

"Sir Paladin," Doi'van asked, "You said you traveled here the first time with friends. Might they tell folks of this place?"

"No," Rodregas answered, "they were not exactly friends, and they both died long ago. Plus, they had no magic and did not even realize this place was on a ley line, and I never told them. They just saw an old farm-house in bad repair."

"So, what now?" Doi'van asked.

"Well," Rodregas said, "I think we should just sleep here tonight. We can try the house in the morning. But I don't want to disturb the Dire Cats during the night." They both nodded. They had come to the same thought already.

"Oh," Rodregas said, "here." He pulled out one of the extra short swords and its harness from where he had it stashed in the wagon and handed it to Doi'van. "If you guys promise not to stab me in the night, it makes sense for you two to be armed. Though, I do not think that harness is big enough to fit you without some work."

Rodregas held his last unclaimed short sword up and said, "And here is one for you, Imeraldä." She picked it up, but he could tell she did not know how to handle the weapon. Doi'van looked comfortable enough, but the handle was almost too small for his enormous hand and it looked more like a large dagger in his hand than a sword.

"You don't have a bow hidden in that wagon, do you? I do not understand how to use one of these pig stickers, but I am very good with a bow," said Imeraldä. She said it, expecting him not to have anything.

Rodregas had a bow. He had two very nice bows wrapped up in the wagon. But, while the short swords he handed them were dangerous, they were common and easy to replace. On the other hand, the Black Yew bows were rare and powerful.

He also thought about the chain mail that he had found in Ravenhurr's wardrobe. While it was way too small to fit him, it would fit Imeraldä just fine. But to give this woman he barely knew such fine armor and weapons was not something to do casually. It made sense sitting there on the foothills of the Arida Mountains, worrying about animal attacks or Eternal Guard patrols, but they were a magnificent gift. No one had ever given him such a gift.

"What?" she asked Rodregas. "You are looking at me like I asked you for your first-born child," she stated in a surprised voice.

"Last night you two tried to kill me, I thought I was being very generous to share my hideout and give each of you a sword. Frankly, I am worried that you will both give it back to me when I am sleeping tonight." Imeraldä looked guilty, Doi'van looked... well, Rodregas could not guess what the expression on his blunt reddish face meant.

"Look," said Imeraldä, once again shaking her long hair behind her, "I feel terrible about that. I told Audrian that I was not sure you were really Ravenhurr and that the spell did not go as planned. By the Infernal Rivers, if the spell had gone as planned, I would have burned in creation fire and my magic would be inside of your body right now."

She caught him with those large amazingly green eyes and said, "I had a theory on what happened, but was not sure how to explain it so Audrian would understand. He was adamant, and I couldn't argue with his logic. As he had said to you last night, logically you must be Gerald or Ravenhurr."

"But you aren't," she continued, "And well, you seem nice, and you can handle yourself in a fight. I was just joking about the bow. You have been generous. I was just talking. You two can both wrestle a bear barehanded and probably win. Hell, Audrian stabbed you with a knife last night and while you are bleeding a bit, you are getting around well considering. Now you are showing us trust by giving us weapons. I am sorry," she finished. From her expression she meant what she said, but Rodregas did not think she was happy to say it.

Doi'van just looked at Rodregas for a moment with a thoughtful expression; he was considering it.

"I am not sorry for my actions last night," the Hellborn said. "We did what we thought was right. You appeared to be an Immortalist Sorcerer, and I have grown to hate the Immortalist. When it became clear that you were not, I stopped trying to kill you."

He paused at this, and then Rodregas could tell he made a decision. "You have given me a sword, if a small one, and among my people that is a powerful gesture. I will not lie to you, I have left my old life behind and over the last few years I have learned to truly hate the Immortalists. I travel with you only because the others would go back to their homes, and I have no home to go back to," Doi'van seemed to finish, but then added, "Last night you pointed out that the forces of the Immortalists would be after you and you would fight them. And you also proved that you can fight."

Once again, the Hellborn paused. He was a man that liked to think before he spoke. "I am using you as bait. When they come for you, I will kill them. Fighting together we will kill some of their vaulted Eternal Guards."

As Doi'van finished, he gave a low growl and shook his horned head. His thick mane of wild jet-black hair was almost as distinctive as Imeraldä's auburn flowing locks. But with Doi'van the gesture spoke of defiance and challenge, like some magnificent bull lowing his horns and getting ready to charge.

Until now he had seemed very thoughtful, almost careful in the words he spoke, but when he spoke of killing and shook his head in defiance, his mouth widened. To say he grinned would not be accurate, what he did was show his teeth. This man was a predator and looked forward to the hunt.

There was something extremely dangerous about this Hellborn, something that reminded you that this creature was the spawn of Greater Daemons. While he might not have chosen the side of the Infernal hells, there was a very dark and dangerous side to him. Rodregas could almost smell the fire and brimstone.

Rodregas met Doi'van's smile with a smile of his own. He reached out, and grabbed Doi'van's forearm and gripped it in the handshake of warriors. Rodregas said, "you have spoken to me honestly. I will honor that with my own honesty. I don't know exactly how I ended up in this body, but I know that I killed Ravenhurr, and I killed his bastard assistant, Korin. The Immortalists are a sore on the world. Their use of others' bodies and power and their very way of life is abhorrent."

Rodregas looked Doi'van in the eyes and said, "The name I was born with is Rodregas. When I decided to kill Ravenhurr, I swore a life oath to the gods that if they let me survive, I would take on the duty of killing the Immortalists. It is a duty that I know will end in my death. There are hundreds of Immortalist. Some almost as powerful as gods, but it is a good death and one I have chosen."

Rodregas paused and looked at Doi'van's features. They were brutish and rough by human standards, but his instincts said that this man was honest, and he added, "If for a while you wish to share my duty and fight at my side, then we walk a path bathed in the Celestial light."

Rodregas had spoken slowly and so Doi'van would understand the depth of what he said. They stood there gripping each other's forearms and then Doi'van nodded and replied, "Then let us walk this path together." He was speaking in that deep voice; his statement had a finality about it. It was a wonderful moment, one of those moments when two people realize that they will share the same path in life and possibly death.

It did not last long for as they broke their grip Imeraldä said, "All right, you two are tough and all, but don't expect me to join in this crazy crusade. Do you know how many thousands of wannabe heroes have died over the years trying to stop the Immortalist's preying on the rest of us?"

She seemed to shiver for a second and then took a breath and said, "I won't join you in your crusade, but I will try to help you as I can."

Rodregas nodded and said, "fair enough," and then reached out to her with the same forearm grip. The grip of one equal warrior to another. She seemed surprised at his gesture.

Rodregas said, "help as you can, not as a warrior, but as you see fit, and travel this way with us for a bit. If nothing else, it should prove interesting."

She hesitated for a moment, then gripped first his arm and then repeated the gesture with Doi'van. She said, "Ok, let's give that a shot."

Rodregas then made a gut decision. He had decided to no longer live safely but to live as he wanted to live. He had never been given magnificent gifts, but that did not mean that he should not give grand gifts to others. Doi'van's help would be priceless; he was a powerful warrior. Imeraldä would also walk this path with them. He would never get what the armor and bow were worth on the black market.

Rodregas reached down first and opened the trunk and said, "Well, if you will be traveling with us for a while, this won't fit either of us guys. It makes most sense for you to have it."

He started handing her the Mithril chain armor. Her eyes grew bright at the sight of the silver chain and she went, "Oh, my god, you bastard! You had Mithril chain mail in the wagon. Do I really get to have it?"

Rodregas smiled and said, "As long as you are sharing the journey with us."

She took several moments to appreciate the armor and tried it on; Rodregas waited, enjoying her appreciation of his stolen gift.

Just as she calmed down, he said, "Oh, and didn't you say something about wanting a bow?" And quietly, he handed her one of the Black Yew recurves. She reached for it with a smile and as soon as she touched it she just stared at it. Her expression of wonder made his old dried up heart smile.

He was not sure how to feel, like a pleased father giving out mid-winter gifts to children, or like an inexperienced lover giving flowers to a new crush. Rodregas was unsure which reaction was proper now, and which she would want him to feel.

Doi'van had watched the complete show with the thoughtful expression that he was starting to believe was his normal face to the world. "And do you have a full suit of Night Bronze Plate Mail for me and a blue steel battle axe as well?" he asked in his careful voice.

"I am afraid that if we want any proper armor for ourselves, we will have to take it off some Eternal Guard's corpse. But I have one other Black Yew bow, and a bigger sword that probably makes more sense for you to use than me, since I have used nothing but short swords for a very long time."

Rodregas then pulled out the two-handed great sword that he had found at the keep and handed it to Doi'van. On Doi'van it was more a hand and a half sword, but as he flourished it around a bit, Rodregas could see he was pleased.

"The steel is simple, but the balance is good. I am starting to be thrilled that I helped pull this wagon up the hill," Doi'van said with a deep chuckle which sounded like distant thunder.

Rodregas nodded and said, "I am afraid other than a few items to sell, everything else is food and blankets for us... and the horses and tools that I stripped out of Raven Keep. I figured I would need the tools to fix this place up and make it livable."

Rodregas continued, "It is dark and late. Let's make

camp in here. In the morning we can start seeing about getting this farm in order." With that they all worked together to get the barn organized and clean. There was no more talking. Each had plenty of their own thoughts to mull over.

Rodregas was feeling good, dangerously positive. He had learned long ago that the better you felt, the harder came the emotional fall. He knew this was all too good to last. But knowing that it would not last also made it more important that he enjoy the moment.

Rodregas was free. He was being hunted; but hunted because he had finally dealt out justice. He had killed two monsters, two evil creatures who wore faces not their own. He felt no remorse for killing them. Rodregas had finally escaped to his quiet place in the mountains to rest and, best of all, with two companions who seemed to be honorable people.

Clearly, Doi'van had a dark side, and he knew little of either of his companions. But it had been a long time since he had wanted to know more about anyone. Rodregas had a new strong and powerful body. He owed a great debt of guilt for that and would have to do much to repay it.

He had been able to free prisoners and give them a second chance at life. How many times had he dreamed of that while the prisoners had pleaded with him? He had long ago turned a stone face to the prisoners. He had refused to learn their names and had just survived by doing his duty.

Rodregas pulled out the captain's mattress, he hesitated before walking over to where Imeraldä was spreading a blanket and with a smile but no words he pulled up the blanket and unrolled the mattress and laid the blanket on top. She just watched him. Rodregas knew she was wondering about his intentions.

Did he want to share the mattress with her? He did, of course, but this was a time of new beginnings. Rodregas would live and die with the honor that he had always meant to.

He walked back to the wagon, grabbed another blanket, and put it down far enough away from Imeraldä to show his honorable intentions. But not too far in case there was trouble. With an enormous smile, he laid down and slept. His dreams for the first time in a very long time were not a nightmare of his failures, but the dreams of a righteous man.

CHAPTER 6
LUNCH WITH THE ENEMY

The Immortalist Vandret climbed up the stairs to the rooftop solar of the Guild Dealer Taiga's tower palace, with an eager stride. To dine with the great Immortalist was an honor that excited him. He followed a servant dressed in expensive silks of a drab brown color through the well-lighted passageways and stairs, nervously straightening his own expensive wardrobe.

As they approached the top of the tower, the servant stepped aside without a word and with an open palm waived Vandret forward. The top of the stairs had a small platform where two massive Lord Captains stood in their glittering night bronze armor. At first, they showed no signs of movement, though Vandret could feel their eyes on him, weighing his right to enter the private solar of their master.

The two guardsmen in their full plate looked to be more statues than actual men, something that was not beyond the magic of the man whose door they guarded. The double doors to the private solar was also of night bronze, but the door was covered in intricate wards and symbols, while their armor held only an engraving of their sigil animals. The guard on the right had an engraving on his Pauldrons over his shoulders of The White Stag, while the man on the left wore the sigil of The Mountain Bear on his breastplate.

After a moment that seemed to stretch longer than was polite, the Lord Captain to the right slowly nodded and, with no hand touching it, the two massive doors opened to welcome him into the sanctum.

Vandret hurried through the open doors. He normally found the sight of the Eternal Guards reassuring. The talented sigil warriors sworn to the protection of Immortalist like himself, but he knew these two would cut him down like a common pauper if they sensed he was a danger to their master.

There was a short hallway leading from the doors, with slim white columns on each side. In between each column were magnificent pieces of art; paintings, sculptures and even a small wall hanging with amazing vibrant colors of a strange abstract design. Vandret was a man of some refinement and appreciation for art and he wished he dared to stop and inspect the pieces.

They had to be some of the greatest artwork in the kingdom to be on display here. Where only those invited to a private meeting with Taiga would see them. But Vandret dared to do nothing more than glance at them as he hurried forward. It would not be smart to make the Guild Dealer wait for even a moment.

Guild Dealer Taiga was not such a common man that he did his work from a desk. His desires and commands came during parties and social events, and if you were truly honored though personal invitations to dine with him in his personal solar overlooking his city.

As Vandret stepped through the arch into the solar its bare simplicity struck him. The city known as the Menagerie of the Sky, which Taiga ruled, was a lush place full of pleasures and growing things. They said anything that could be found in the world was within its gleaming walls and exotic gardens.

But the private place where its Master worked, was a stark contrast. Its marble columns and arched ceiling spoke of sophistication and understated power and more accurately reflected the nature of its owner. A stark contrast to the over the top shows and pleasures of the city that he ruled.

Two small intricate waterfalls softly trickled down each wall to the side, providing a soft soothing sound, the back of the room was an archway leading to the terrace, overhead the incredible crystal ceiling let in the natural daylight of the late afternoon sun and would illuminate the top of the tower during the night.

In the middle of the room was an enameled silver table set for two, with Taiga lounging in his throne-like chair on the other side. Vandret hurried forward and fell to his knees, his head lowered; he did not say a word until Taiga spoke.

"Please, my friend, there is no need for subservience here. Let us enjoy a meal together. And if you don't mind, I have a few thoughts I would share with you over the food."

"Of course, my lord," said Vandret as he stood up. He dared to focus on the Guild Dealer for the first time. Taiga wore the form of a High Ælf male that was slim and graceful as was most of its kind. His hair and eyes were a striking pale violet color. His skin a light nut color that made a striking contrast. The similar colored silk toga that he wore highlighted the contrast. He wore no rings or accessories. His outfit was pure sophistication.

Vandret suddenly wished he had thought to dress simpler for the occasion. His green and emerald outfit, with its gold trim, seemed garish in comparison. His lean human male body that normally seemed attractive and robust seemed ungainly and drab in comparison.

Taiga's manner continued friendly but inquisitive as the conversation started politely, a discussion on recent spells that Vandret was working on, his thoughts on the recent political and economic tensions with the Romig Empire.

Wine and food appeared on the table. Vandret never saw it come, or the empty plates go; it simply was. The food, like everything in the tower, was of the finest quality, grilled silver salmon, greens from the Northern Kingdoms, small pastries from the Korin Islands. Taiga seemed in no hurry to get to any point, Immortalist had nothing, if not time. Finally, Taiga brought up the point that Vandret believed had gained him the honor of joining Taiga in his solar.

"So, I understand that you journey to the Cathedral of the Heavens for this year's open tourney?" Taiga asked, his voice as melodic as one would expect from a Ælf, but just a tad deeper than one would assume.

"Yes, my lord, I leave in the morning," Vandret replied.

"Excellent, keep your eyes open for potential talent worthy of the Eternal Guard," Taiga stated.

Vandret nodded, that was one of his chief responsibilities, but it could not be why he had been invited up to Taiga solar.

"I would encourage you to be careful on your trip over. You heard about what happened to Ravenhurr?" asked Taiga.

Vandret almost felt his eyebrows rise, "of course, but what should I watch out for? I heard it was just some sort of accident. I was not aware that any of the Knights of the Order were implicated."

Taiga smiled and waved a hand in a dismissing motion. "Oh, don't misjudge my words. I did not mean to imply any misdeeds of our valiant Knights of the Soaring Stars. I am not aware of them doing much of anything, much less kill an Immortalist."

"Then what should I keep my eye out for?" asked Vandret. He was becoming even more curious to the direction of the conversation.

"You, my fine Vandret, are more in the world than most of us. You are out traveling and adventuring while most of us Immortalist just sit in our towers. I have always thought our one weakness was our isolation. It is hard to know what is exactly happening when we are not out to see it." For a moment Taiga paused, looking up at the crystal roof overhead in apparent contemplation of the implications of their isolated natures.

After a moment in which Vandret waited patiently, Taiga continued, "You are one of our best, and yet you are also in the world. The tourney draws the magically powerful and those who wish to take a sigil. I would simply suggest that you keep your eyes open. Your mind a little more focused on what is happening around you, both on your journey, and at the Cathedral."

Taiga's tone almost dismissed his own comments as a simple chatter of no import. Except Vandret had been invited to have lunch with the most powerful person on the planet to drop the suggestion. The great Immortalist clearly concerned that something unexpected might be happening. The rest of the dinner quickly wrapped up and Vandret soon found himself caught up in his own thoughts, as he journeyed down the several floors. The Great Hall that served as the gathering place for the other Immortalist in residence in the city. A woman stepped up to his side and rudely interrupted his questing mind by asking him, "so did you ask him?"

"Ask him what?" Vandret asked. The Immortalist sorcerer, who was in the form of a tall athletic human female with spectacular long red hair and blue eyes, gave Vandret a silent glare before responding.

"Last night at the arena party you agreed to ask Vandret where all the night bronze is going," She replied in a clear clipped voice.

"Actually," Vandret responded, "I said that my visit to his solar would be a perfect opportunity to ask him if he knew the location and purpose of all the missing materials."

"So why did you not take advantage of the opportunity? If anyone knows where it is all going it is Taiga,"

"My lovely Gracella, you are an Immortalist of impressive power and intellect, but we are Immortalist, time is on our side. I have known that something very large was under construction for just a few decades. But it is clear that it has been going on for much longer. It is not unusual in our history for one of Taiga's power and ambitions to have some great undertaking. I admit it is unusual for such a monumental undertaking not to be reported to the senior council. Still, there is no need to be in such a rush to ask questions."

"Vandret don't play your word games with me, you know and I know, that this is not a normal amount of night bronze and magical material for it to be used just in some new fortress or magical experiment. Not with one of the great cosmic alignments coming in such a scant time. It would surprise neither of us if Taiga was getting ready to make his ascension, but then he would have called a concave and have the eager support of all members of the Guild."

"You're not suggesting that Guild Dealer Taiga is involved in some foul play or doing something against the wishes of the senior council?" asked Vandret his tone equally outraged and surprised.

Gracella almost physically jumped at the suggestion and could not help herself from a quick glance around the hall before responding. "I don't think Taiga has any interest that is not in the interest of the whole Guild of the Celestial Path. I am just concerned that proper protocol is not being taken," she said.

"I think whatever Taiga is up to shall be entertaining, and that soon enough he will ascend to the Celestial Heavens, laughing at us for our doubts and questions."

Gracella nodded, but Vandret knew her thoughts were the same as any Immortalist at the conversation of Ascension to the Celestial Realm. The final ritual was the hardest, no matter how many centuries you practiced the art. If you succeeded a new God walked the Heavens. If you failed, then you were quickly forgotten and dismissed.

"So, what did he want?" she asked.

Vandret hesitated for a moment, not sure if he should respond. Gracella was an impressive Immortalist and a rising star in the Guild. She had been Taiga's own Adept when she was young, and as a favored member of the Guild her friendship could prove important someday. "He wanted me to keep an eye out when I travel to the

Cathedral of the Heavens," he responded.

The two of them were slowly walking back to his suite of rooms, through the gleaming marble corridors, with their wide windows and their breath-taking views of the city below. They both shared polite nods to other Immortalist, mostly 'young' Adepts who lived in the city. She did not respond to his answer at first, finally she asked, "Does he want you to keep an eye out for anything in particular?"

Vandret nodded and said. "He mentioned Ravenhurr as a concern."

"But, he went mad after a failed ritual. That is not uncommon," she said with a voice laced with surprise.

"Actually," said Vandret, "it is exceedingly rare for a Master of Ravenhurr's level to go mad. I am not sure if you ever met him, but he was good, no more than that he was exceptionally good."

"Then in that case we had better all keep our eyes open," she said thoughtfully.

CHAPTER 7
A TIME TO PREPARE

Rodregas woke up first, at dawn. He stayed in his bed just thinking and reviewing all that he had gone through in the last few days; it was a lot to adjust to. When the others got up, they ate some of the supplies, including the last of the fresh bread. They had plenty of cheese and an endless supply of apples.

Rodregas had an idea about how he wanted to start this new day. "Doi'van, Imeraldä," he said, getting their attention. "As a teenager I served as a squire of the knightly Order of the Soaring Stars."

At their nod he added, "they never raised me to knighthood. I had neither the noble lineage nor the martial prowess. But my life as a squire was a wonderful life, one I appreciated more afterwards than when I was living it."

He could not help smiling at the second chance at the life he had been given, as he added, "The knights and the squires always started off the day with a prayer to the Celestial Gods. I have not done this in over forty years, but I will start again this fine beautiful morning, and you are welcome to join me if you would."

The two looked at Rodregas. They were very different people, but they both seemed unsure what to say to his request.

Doi'van nodded at Imeraldä and said to Rodregas, "It has been too long since I have prayed. It would be good for the soul. Please lead us in prayer." Imeraldä said nothing, but she nodded and followed the two of them outside.

Rodregas knelt in the grass facing the sun, the sign of the All-Father in the Celestial heavens. He reached out and wove his fingers together; he pulled his thumbs down and opened his woven hands in the ancient symbol of opening oneself to the gods.

"Dear Celestials in the heavens, we open our hearts to you, and we accept our duties as your warriors here in the world." Rodregas prayed, "Let your courage fill our hearts and your strength fill our arms. May we know the guidance of your twin principles, Honor and Justice."

He then knelt down on the grass and pulled one of the two short swords from his weapon harness. He crossed his arms and laid the blade across his own upper arms. It was possible, only with great concentration, to do this without dropping the sword or cutting himself. His instructor had taught the squires this simple prayer. It guaranteed that the squires stayed focused during meditation.

Doi'van and Imeraldä looked at him as he knelt in the grass with the sword naked on his bare arms. Both were clearly not used to this form of Celestial prayer. Rodregas spoke carefully so as not to tip the sword and said, "It's called sword meditation. My instructor would start us out with the prayer and then we would meditate on our duty."

"For how long?" asked Imeraldä.

"Until you are sure of what your duty is," Rodregas replied, hearing the voice of the old knight who had led the drills. All the instructors had been retired knights who enjoyed teaching the squires. He did not think the two would join him for this, but both pulled their weapons and imitated his position. Doi'van with his large great sword balanced on his powerful arms. Imeraldä grabbed her bow instead of the short sword, which with her lack of training was probably an excellent idea.

Rodregas focused inwards and resumed his meditation. It felt good to do the morning sword meditation again. Rodregas had a lot of wonderful memories from his life as a squire, before everything had gone wrong. Part of him felt uncomfortable for doing this again, like he no longer had the right. But if they raise you from Page to Squire, as he had been, you always got to keep the title of Squire.

Squires, who are not raised to knighthood, were much sought after for other positions. Their martial training and education, especially in law and etiquette, were a great foundation for many careers. As Rodregas knelt on the ground balancing the sword across his arms, and the sun warm on his face, he thought back to that time when he had used his Squire title to get into the officer academy in the neighboring Ramig Empire.

Though giving up his dream of becoming a Knight of the Soaring Stars had been hard, Rodregas had thought he would become a successful officer in the army. Unfortunately, things had gone far amiss. His life had taken a darker turn.

Rodregas shook his head. He was focusing on the distant past, not his duty. That is what this meditation was all about, so what was his duty now? Killing Immortalists was not something that he, or even the three of them together, could just start doing. The problem was not just the individual Immortalist. Many an angry town would have killed the local Immortalist Sorcerer after having their people taken.

Anyone that struck back at an individual Immortalist would face the wrath of the Guild of the Celestial Path, which included not just the god-like power of the Guild Dealer and his various sorcerers, but also the army of the Guild known as The Eternal Guards.

While not the largest army in the world, they were the most feared. The leader of The Eternal Guards was Lord General Sigoria. The stories of the Lord General were living legend. A mortal son of a Celestial God, he was a rare Blood Prince and the only living man known to have two greater sigils to enhance his natural powers. Lord General Sigoria had been the Grand Marshal of the Knights of the Soaring Stars that had also trained Rodregas before the great betrayal.

The Order was unique in that it trained not just in the martial arts but also in the magical. The Order recruited those who had magical power. But lacked the temperament or intelligence to be a sorcerer. Instead of working toward developing their control of sorcery, they gained a magical enhancement but lost the versatility of magi.

Gaining knighthood was only for those who both had the martial skills, and enough magic, to gain either a lessor or greater sigil. The Guild outlawed such sigils except for their own warriors within the Eastern Kingdoms. The Order of the Soaring Stars was an exception as they were the traditional source for the God's Paladins. The Celestial Guild had never dared to anger the gods by interfering with the Orders use of sigils.

Sigoria had been one of the greatest of the Order of the Soaring Stars, but he had grown old and his health had failed him. When tempted by the Immortalists with a new body as strong as his old, he had accepted. Even though such action was anathema to the very teachings of the Order. He had become an officer of the Eternal Guards, and eventually their leader. Several of the most powerful Knights had followed a similar path over the centuries, with many members of their officer core being previous members of the knighthood. These former Knights traded their honor for near Eternal life as long as they served in the Guards.

The Eternal Guards were all sigil warriors with one or several magical enhancements. They also had the best resources of the entire Eastern Kingdom, including the most powerful enchanted armor and the best weapons. Their officers rode Dire Beasts for steeds.

Taking on a sigil warrior would be a monumental challenge for Rodregas, or at least he thought it would be. He was still unclear of how strong and fast he was. His stomach hurt from his wound, but not as bad as it should. The first step in his duty was to heal up from his wound and relearn how to fight in his new body.

When he got up, Imeraldä was already standing, but Doi'van remained kneeling in thought. He nodded to Imeraldä, and she quietly followed him back into the barn. About ten minutes later Doi'van joined them and they planned how to clean up the farm.

There was the matter of the house, which was a more natural place for the three of them to shelter, but Rodregas was unsure of the Dire Cats. They spent the rest of the morning cleaning up the barn for the horses. After lunch, Rodregas would see if he could figure out the intentions of the lions.

With the three of them working, they cleaned up the barn quickly. While they could move the dirt and debris out, it was still just bare walls and stone floors. After a brief meal, Rodregas headed over to the main house.

Rodregas admitted to himself that he was nervous. The Dire Cats were magnificent beasts. He had no desire to hurt them, and less to be killed by them. He was also unsure of how they could share the farm with such dangerous predators.

Like the barn, the house was made of perfect cut stone that looked almost new; everything else had gone back to nature. Rodregas circled around to the back where the stone steps led to the cellar. He was sure that originally there had been doors covering the entrance, but they were long gone.

Rodregas smelled what he would find well before he came around the corner. Next to the entrance was the corpse of a gigantic bear which had recently been killed and partly eaten. It had been a magnificent creature, the largest of the local black bears that he had ever seen. Rodregas realized that it had been a Dire beast, drawn here by the safe magical energies.

Next to the dead bear were the two Dire Cats. Rodregas had gone around the corner thinking they were in the cellar but found himself only twenty feet from them. He froze, the two cats seemed to expect him. They both watched him with steady eyes. One reached out with a huge paw and dragged the dead bear's body closer. Did it think he was here to steal it?

The danger of the Dire Cats was crystal clear. He had not even heard them fighting, and yet they had killed a Dire Bear while Rodregas and the others slept! The good news was that they both seemed very full and had a sleepy look to them. Rodregas guessed that he had awakened them from a nap.

Rodregas had to remind himself that he needed to

develop an understanding with the lions. Predators like them worked on a very simple alpha relationship; the strong ruled. They were Dire animals, but he was the equivalent of a Celestial animal. He was alpha; pound for pound, Rodregas would be stronger and quicker than even these two beasts.

Each animal seemed to weigh almost twice as much as he did. Still, Rodregas knew with sudden clarity that he needed to establish himself as the one in charge. If he did not establish his leadership, the next time the Dire Cats were hungry they would try eating one of his party, or at least a horse.

Rodregas walked over to the bear corpse and as he approached, both cats seemed to fully wake up and took on a crouching stance. He pretended to ignore them and pulled one of his short swords out casually.

Rodregas kept his focus on the bear. He knew that the lioness in prides do most of the hunting and the alpha males ate after the kill. He cut away a sizeable chunk of the bear's haunch to take back to the barn for their dinner. One lioness growled and bit down on the haunch near to him. His heart stopped for a moment. Rodregas thought she would take his hand for a second.

With his free hand, he made a fist and slammed the side of her head. Not with all his strength, but still a serious hit. She grunted and let go, growled and stepped over the bear's body. He slowly reached up, and using the full strength of his body, pushed hard on her muscular chest, pushing her away from the bear's haunch. He then ignored her and went back to cutting the haunch loose. He waited, but the two lioness seemed to have gone from aggression to napping, with him missing the transition.

Slowly, Rodregas got up with his bear haunch and

took it back to the barn. He met the surprised look of Doi'van and Imeraldä with a half-smile, "I hope you like the taste of bear?" As he was unsure of how old the meat was, he immediately started a fire and cooked it. As he worked on preparing the fire, he explained what had happened.

"Are you suicidal?" asked Imeraldä in an angry voice. "I know you felt they were not a danger, but to walk up and take the food from two Dire Cats? That is just asking to be killed." Her voice was unusually high pitched, and she was shaking her head in disbelief.

"The Dire Bear must have been living in the cellar," said Doi'van. "I bet they had to go in, and kill it there. We probably did not hear the battle because it was underground. They probably dragged it out after. It is said that Dire meat makes you strong. Not sure if that is true." His voice, in contrast to Imeraldä's, sounded normal.

"Don't you care that he did something so stupid?" asked Imeraldä.

"Well," Doi'van replied slowly, "the cats are connected to him because of his Celestial lion essence. He freed them and now he has found a rich place for them to rear their young if they are pregnant from the mating. With beasts like that, you are in charge, or you are food. I think he probably did the right thing. No way to know for sure, but they did not rip him apart, so we will say he was very brave and not idiotic."

Then he added, "but, if you had asked me beforehand, I would have said that taking food from a Dire Cat was an idiotic idea." He finished with a smile full of sharp teeth, almost a match for the lions, and in a casual movement lowered his horned head in what Rodregas thought might be his equivalent of a shrug.

The next morning, they repeated the Morning Prayer and meditation ritual. This time while Doi'van joined in, Imeraldä mostly watched. Afterwards Rodregas said to both, "I have been thinking we will probably be here a few weeks, while I finish healing up from the knife wound and our trail goes cold. I want to make the most of the time."

Doi'van said, "I have a feeling that you have something in mind."

Rodregas nodded and said, "I have developed some dreadful habits the last few years; I know my technique is rusty and now my timing is all off with my new body. I am not sure what your training backgrounds are?" he asked, waving at Imeraldä. Who was holding her Black Yew bow close, with an intimacy that spoke more of a caress than holding a weapon,

"Imeraldä likes the bow." Rodregas continued, "Even though Imeraldä plans to stay out of the middle of things, learning some basic hand-to-hand and sword fighting is an outstanding idea. Doi'van and I can spar with each other, which will help us get used to fighting against the sigil warriors of The Eternal Guard. I wanted to suggest that we should practice every morning until noon, then work to get the farm cleaned up during the rest of the day. At dusk we can work again on our fighting or relax."

Doi'van nodded and said, "before we battle a group of Immortalists or The Eternal Guards, we need to get some decent armor and weapons. They will have the finest equipment that the Guild sorcerers can make or buy. While the two of us might be a match for most of the sigil warriors' one on one, their equipment will make them hard to beat."

"I agree that has to be something we figure out," Rodregas said, "but, I am thinking decent horses might be more important first."

"Horses? How will that help us in battle?" asked Doi'van. Rodregas responded, "a trained war horse can help directly, but what I am worried about is escaping after an attack. Even if we have a successful raid against an Immortalist, we will need to be far away before a sizeable group of The Eternal Guard can track us down. The Eternal Guards, or at least their officers, use Dire Steeds. If we are mounted on regular horses and they come after us on Dire Steeds, well, they will catch us and that will be that." Doi'van nodded at that. Rodregas had the impression that he had not thought of anything but the actual fight.

Imeraldä said, "Ok, that is all fine. You two need to find Dire Steeds and armor and weapons before you fight the Eternal Guards. Good luck finding that up here in the mountains. What I need, and I think you two do as well, is to practice magic."

Imeraldä smirked at their expressions. She continued, "I am partly being selfish. Once I have sufficient control, they cannot steal my magic. So, while I don't disagree that it would be a splendid idea for me to practice some fighting skills, I also think we should all think of practicing magic."

She paused and said in a flat tone that highlighted her seriousness, "the ranks of the Eternal Guards are full of sigil warriors, who have sacrificed their ability to cast magic spells for one or more permanent enhancements. We need some counter to this advantage. If we practice our magic every day, we should make a little progress even without any teachers or books." She finished with a toss of her long hair.

She seemed to think Rodregas would challenge her statement and argue that they should just focus on the martial training. However, Rodregas had been a squire of the Order of the Soaring Stars, one of the few orders that required magical learning of all its pages and squires to strengthen their magic before taking on a lessor even a greater sigil.

The permanent inscription of either a lessor or greater sigil into one's magic permanently reduced the amount of magic you had to cast spells. They gave sigils only to those who made knighthood. Still, one had to have enough magic to make the inscribing possible and that early training to try to grow his natural magical talent he had.

"I totally agree," Rodregas said. "I know only what they teach a squire of our Order, but that I am happy to share. Hopefully, we can learn the basics from each other. I also have a few books that I took from Ravenhurr's library. I was going to sell them, but if you want to look at them later and see if they might be of use, you can check them out," Rodregas said.

"Really, you have books on magic?" she asked with an eager tone. "Can you show me now?"

Rodregas hesitated; he did not want to show her the books right away. Instead, he wanted to see what kind of training Doi'van had. But he could not turn down the request from the beautiful woman. "Sure," he said walking back to the barn and the wagon. Rodregas jumped on the back, making the wagon squeal at his sudden weight, and opened 'his' trunk and pulled out the last blanket left in it, the one he had wrapped the books up in.

Rodregas unrolled the blanket on the back of the now mostly emptied wagon, showing the dozen books that he had saved from Ravenhurr's collection. Imeraldä reached out for one of the closest, but then stopped as her fingers touched them, as if a spark of lightning had hit her.

Obviously, she could feel that same power Rodregas had. That was interesting.

She then ran her hand from one to the next until she had touched all twelve books. Then, she looked up and her expression reminded Rodregas of some girl who had gotten the perfect mid-winter gift that she had been dreaming of.

"These are not books on magic," she said. "These are magical Grimoires, several of them of impressive power."

"Really?" Rodregas said, "I was a squire who learned a little magic, but I really can't say that I know the difference between a book of magic and a Grimoire."

Imeraldä looked surprised and said, "oh, you guys must depend on the oral tradition. That is a hard way to learn. The symbols and geometric figures that form a powerful spell are often too complex to learn from just the spoken word."

Rodregas cut in and clarified, "I mean, in the order we read books on magic theory and history, but I never felt energy from them before."

Imeraldä nodded, "Let me explain. First, you have a lot more power now, and power calls to power. So, you are a lot more sensitive to the power that the books have. But what separates Grimoires from other books is that they are made like the stone walls of these buildings, by Nymphs. The original reason was to have books that would not rot over a period of centuries, but the nymph-created paper and leather can hold a faint imprint of magic."

"Each time that a sorcerer cast a spell from the book, that spell pattern is lightly engraved into the page. A mage can sense the previous patterns engraved in the book. The ability of such books to show the pattern of the spell means that even a mage who knows a spell by heart can cast it faster by using such a book. It also means that such books are much sought after and never given up freely. Grimoires are never sold unless the owner dies."

She made sure that both men were both following her meaning and then continued, "While the Grimoires are a brilliant tool for quick and accurate casting of a spell, it is even more potentially useful for someone trying to learn magic. Reading a regular book with the spell written down and trying to keep all the symbols and shapes just right in your head, even as you fill the complex shape with power, requires years to learn. But a powerful Grimoire can quickly show you the shape and help you learn new spells in weeks, instead of years."

"Also, sorcerers, like all people learn in unique ways. Some can quickly grasp a written idea where others will struggle to learn from a regular book. Or a magician who is also a gifted musician will understand the flow and pace of the spell much better, like a piece of music. The most powerful Grimoires have had multiple users who are very different in their learning styles. Books like these will allow you not to just learn the spells, the best way for you, but in a much deeper, complex way. Spells learned this way can be much more powerful than spells learned from either a regular book or the oral traditions."

"How powerful and complex are the spells in the books we have?" Rodregas asked.

Imeraldä smiled and seemed hesitant before saying, "I am not sure. I have touched Grimoires, but my education in celestial magic ended before I ever got to use more than the simplest ones."

"Really?" Rodregas answered in surprise. "Well, looks like we will have to use these books and find out," he said.

Doi'van was listening, his enormous body still, but

he had said nothing. "What do you say, Doi'van, are you ready to learn some magic? I saw how you reacted to the ley line; you have some power."

Doi'van tilted his head to Rodregas and said, "really, do you think so? I feel something now and then, but they have never tested me. We expect Orqui of the royal households in the Burning Lands to be warriors, not Magi. People see me and how strong I am. They just assume I would not be good at magic."

"Wish I had that problem," Rodregas said. "I mean before, people always used to assume I had neither brawn nor brains." With a smile he added, "what do you say? Shall the three of us set some time aside, to teach each other what we know of magic, and see what we can learn from these magic books of Ravenhurr's?" he asked.

"No," said Doi'van. "I mean, yes, I would like to learn what you can teach me. I like to learn," he said slowly but carefully. The big guy was embarrassed. The Hellborn added, "My people are not big readers. I learned to read some ancient Orqui for ceremonial functions, but I never learned how to read the common tongue." The last words he added slowly, but then quickly added, "But if you can teach me some basics from the oral techniques that Imeraldä mentioned, I would like to learn some magic if I can."

Rodregas looked at Doi'van. There was something about his expression, a yearning. "Do you want to learn to read the common tongue?" he asked.

"What do you mean?" Doi'van asked, stepping away from the other two like he was uncomfortable.

"Just what I said, would you like to learn to read?" Rodregas said in a carefully casual voice.

Doi'van responded, "We don't have time for me to

learn to read. You should practice with these Grimoires. It makes no sense to teach me to read when we are likely to see battle too soon for it to be helpful." Doi'van's voice, which was always deep, seemed to have gone down several octaves, such that the earth almost seemed to vibrate. Somehow, while the conversation on magic Grimoires had interested him, learning to read the common tongue seemed to terrify him.

Rodregas knew the feeling of wanting something so much that you are afraid to accept it when offered, for fear of failing.

"Well," Rodregas said, "I think it might come in handy to have you able to read. If we survive the summer and are holed up here all winter, you might start reading some of these books by then. I fear that I am not a talented teacher, but I have taught a few soldiers over the years who wanted to learn."

After both nodded their acceptance, Rodregas added, "after our noon meal, let's plan on making it book time. We don't have a decent lamp to read by, so we will have to do it during the day. We can start by teaching each other any basic magic we know. Then I will work with you on learning to read while Imeraldä goes through these books to see if any of them have some simple stuff that we can work on." Rodregas finished in his best sergeant's voice. It held a tone that let everyone know that a decision has been made.

Imeraldä was glued to the books, eager to explore their secrets, but Doi'van and Rodregas went to work on cleaning up the rest of the barn. They could not do much more without getting some timber. They all worked or read until it was too dark and then they fell asleep quickly.

The next morning, after they had finished Morning

Prayer, Rodregas said, "all right, are you two ready for a little fighting practice?" At their nod he added, "It is always good to start with the basics. I thought we would go over some fighting forms. Are you two familiar with learning forms, also known as Kata?" he asked.

He was expecting Imeraldä to shake her head but was a little surprised when Doi'van did. The great Orqui Hellborn clearly knew how to fight, but his training in the Burning Lands must be different that Rodregas had as a squire.

Rodregas explained, "forms are a series of motions that simulate fighting, but also give you an opportunity to work on balance and to visualize and understand your actions and responses to different fighting situations. While strength and speed are important for any kind of fighting, whether it is hand-to-hand or sword fighting, excellent technique is all about balance and center of gravity. What you want to learn is to keep your center low and your balance strong, even when you are tired and exhausted." Doi'van had his normal interested expression, but Imeraldä looked unconvinced.

"Ok," he said, "time for an example. Imeraldä stand tall," Rodregas stated. She put her shoulders back and stood with a rigid posture which caused her firm bust to thrust out. Rodregas didn't think she meant the gesture to be sexual, but he hesitated at the sight of her superb shape. Rodregas ignored his own rush of hormones, and pushed her high on the shoulder, and she stumbled back before catching her balance.

"Now," he said, "lower your center of gravity. Bend your legs and keep them loose." She followed his instructions, and he thought this would make her beauty less striking. But she just went from a statuesque dancer to a crouching feline. He breathed in through his nose and tried to ignore his newly youthful hormones.

This time when he pushed her shoulder, she went back but did not stumble. "See, you stayed in control. You stumble in a fight, and you are dead. With your center low you have control." Rodregas explained. "You are ready to dodge and to strike back as needed. Plus, you have leverage. If you develop exemplary foot work and keep them moving, you will win against stronger but less-disciplined fighters."

They both nodded, now understanding the lesson. "Now watch and try to learn this basic form." Rodregas stepped into position; his knees deeply bent, his hands loose but raised just below his shoulders. He stepped forward and raised his left arm in a sweeping block, and then he took another step and struck out in a swift blow to an imagined attacker with his right hand.

While he followed a set form in his mind, he also saw his invisible attacker and he struck like he was there. His blow stopping only when they met the invisible attacker's form. After sharing a few basic blocks and strikes, he stopped and faced the other two again, and said, "Now, I will repeat that and then you two can take a turn."

Learning to fight through mastering one's own form was new to both, and they struggled to follow his example. Doi'van often over-reached with his punches against the imagined opponent. While Imeraldä's movements had little real strength or violence behind them. She also kept dropping her hands and leaving herself open to attack.

He restarted, slowly going over the first form's footwork, even the slight moves caused his stomach wound to bleed lightly and he guessed he probably needed to wrap it tighter after he was done.

Rodregas kept repeating the most basic form until he felt they were getting their center of gravity under control, but keeping their feet free to move and their hands up ready to block. He was enjoying teaching Kata, both for himself and because they were both eager students and learned quickly.

Once again, he found himself smiling. The smile felt almost uncomfortable on this face. Rodregas realized that it might be harder to relearn what it felt like to enjoy living, then to relearn how to fight in the new body he had stolen.

CHAPTER 8
THE TEST BEFORE THE TEST

Over the next few weeks, Rodregas, Doi'van and Imeraldä fell into a routine. It quickly became clear that while Imeraldä might not be a trained mage, she was far more knowledgeable than Doi'van or Rodregas in magic. So, while Rodregas often led the training in the morning, she led the afternoon.

Rodregas thought Doi'van was learning far more quickly than any of the squires he had trained with. Doi'van looked like a daemonic nightmare, and he loved to test his strength in battle, but he was a quick learner both with the forms and with the books. Even though Doi'van could not read the common tongue, Rodregas would read him some of the Grimoires, since they were the only books they had. His insights and questions were insightful. Rodregas realized that Doi'van's raw intellect was greater than his own.

Two weeks into the routine, the three were getting into the rhythm. They had moved into the old house and for not having a roof; it was comfortable. Though they had all claimed rooms of their own, they were all still sleeping in the living room, partly because of the fire they kept there and partly for the company.

They were surprised with visits by the two Dire Cats on a regular basis. The first evening, when they were settling into the night, the two cats casually walked through the door. The three of them froze while the two cats just sprawled out in casual comfort close to the fire.

One cat (Rodregas could not tell the two apart yet) stretched over and rubbed her chin against Rodregas' leg. The power behind its head was such that it almost knocked him over. He had seen small house cats make similar gestures, but it was disconcerting to have two powerful predators such as the Dire Cats being so friendly.

"I guess this means we are part of the pride," said Imeraldä, slowly reaching over and giving the other cat a tummy rub. Rodregas held his breath, as the cat responded with its paws by stretching out, its claws popping free with the stretch.

They showed no signs of aggression, but looking at the size of their claws, and then at Imeraldä, made Rodregas want to jump over the Dire Cat and put his body in front of her. Rodregas was fully aware of how one swipe of those claws would kill her.

Unlike the house cats that he was familiar with, Rodregas could see a kind of intelligence in their eyes. He had the feeling they both knew to be careful with a fragile mortal, and they thought it was funny that he was so worried.

This scene repeated itself almost every night, and several times the cats also brought game they had killed into the farmyard. Rodregas made a point of always taking a piece of the kill, as he felt they expected this as part of their adopted group. Plus, it added fresh meat to their diet without the three having to go hunting. He started to take the presence of the Dire Cats for granted and stopped worrying about the danger.

Several days later came the first night where neither the cats nor Doi'van were in the room. Doi'van was out messing with the well. They could get fresh water out of it, but it had a lot of debris in it. Imeraldä was reading one of the magic Grimoires by the fireplace. Rodregas was supposed to be reading as well but had lost his focus on the complex diagram and was just looking at Imeraldä.

She was so beautiful, slim yet curvy. Some of those curves were smooth muscle, and some were pure female. She seemed to have brought together two of the most attractive parts of the Ælves and the Nymphs: the slim body of the Ælf with the athletic curves of a Nymph. Her skin had a smooth, light golden-brown color that often shined with sweat during their practices and looked so soft that it was hard not to reach out and touch it.

"Did you need something?" asked Imeraldä. Rodregas had not realized that she had noticed him watching her. There was a tease to her voice and an expression that said she knew what he was thinking and that she did not mind.

Rodregas was an experienced man, but he was not sure if he had ever seen a woman as beautiful as her, much less thought he ever had a chance with such a woman. He had to smile, amused by his own reaction. He felt his heartbeat speed up and a rush of heat. He had not felt such hormonal surges in a long time.

He made a decision. He had carefully been a gentleman and had tried nothing with the beautiful half Ælf, but her teasing expression left him an opening. He took advantage of it. He spoke slowly and carefully, letting her know that he knew what he was saying. "Actually, I was looking at you, you are beautiful. Your incredible eyes and hair, you are breathtaking." Rodregas looked at her, his eyes going slowly over her entire body as he spoke. Then he shifted his gaze toward Imeraldä's large green eyes.

As their eyes held, he slid over to her, running the back of his hand across her cheek. "Your skin is so soft," Rodregas said. "You are beautiful, intelligent, brave." He reached down and placed his finger below her chin and raised it up to be equal in height to his sitting form.

"I have wanted you since I first saw you," and with that straight-forward statement, he reached down, and holding her face steady with his single finger, he slowly, softly kissed her.

For a moment she tried to pull away, but he kept the pressure of his finger steady and firm so she could feel his desire. He made his lips eager but light, not too forceful. He was strong and he let her feel his strength, but he also gave her plenty of leverage so that if she wanted to pull away, she could.

He was making his desire clear, but the decision was hers. He was also determined to walk the path of righteousness and was trying hard not to be too eager. He was determined to be very careful.

A younger man would have been in a hurry. But Rodregas was lost in the softness of her lips, the look of her eyes, and the beauty of her spirit. He wished he could make this moment last forever.

Rodregas believed that most women did not know if they were interested until a man made his move. It is something instinctive. There is a single moment when either it clicks, or it does not. The moment held unmoving; the dice were rolling. She responded to his kiss but did not sink into his arms. She was making a hard decision. Rodregas felt good that she must feel something to hesitate; the moment seemed to go on forever.

He drank in her smell. Like her, it was unique, something between a honey blossom and a ripe apple. Like many things in life since he left Raven Keep, he cherished the feel, the taste, and the smell.

Then she broke away and whispered, "I am afraid." Imeraldä spoke so quietly that he could barely hear. "I want to," she paused and then continued her light whisper, "But being a half Nymph, half Ælf means, it is not easy to become involved with me, for a human. I don't want to hurt you."

He missed her taste as she pulled away, and he was surprised by what she said, but he also knew that he no longer wanted to live in fear.

"Shhhhh, it is all right. With me you never have to worry, you never have to be afraid." He was going to tell her he would not hurt her, but since she seemed afraid that she would be the one hurting him, he held the comment back.

He just pulled her close again, but instead of a soft kiss, he kept himself from touching her and simply looked deep into her eyes. He thought about how much he appreciated her. Rodregas let her feel how much he thought of her. Only after he saw her eyes make a decision, did he slide his hands down her body and cup the small of her back and pull her into a kiss, but this time he let more of his passion and need show.

With his kiss, her resistance evaporated, and she went from hesitant to eager. Her hands started pulling at his leather armor, eager to get him naked and feel his skin.

At her action, Rodregas felt awkward. This was not really his body that she wanted to touch. He was not really this young, handsome man that she felt attracted to. He wanted to pull away but did not let himself. He had initiated the intimacy, and it would not be fair of him to pull away because of his personal doubts.

"Easy," Rodregas said, "I want to go nice and slow and enjoy every step." They kissed again, this time eagerly exploring each other's mouth and lips. He ran his lips down the line of her chin. Though he was trying to go slowly, they quickly found themselves naked.

He thought if he had let her, she would have jumped right on him and slid himself inside her. Rodregas knew that Nymphs were legendary for their enjoyment of sex, but he was a little surprised at her eagerness.

She ran her hands and lips across his chest, fascinated by 'his', powerful musculature and smooth skin. Once again Rodregas pulled away from her touch. He had never really had a woman that eager to touch him before. Her eagerness to touch his body made him feel a little put off. It was good to be touched, in fact, he craved it. But her eagerness highlighted to him that the body she wanted to touch was not really his. It was the body of Gerald, not Rodregas.

Her body was everything that he had thought it would be, both wonderfully hard and lush. To say she was the most beautiful woman he had ever enjoyed touching was a ridiculous understatement.

Imeraldä reached up to his neck and pulled herself up on top of his lap. She wrapped her legs around him and hoisted herself up like she was climbing the trunk of a tree. He had wanted to take his time and explore her with his hands and lips, but she was in no mood for foreplay.

Rodregas was in no mood to stop her now that his own passion was building, and there was no reason to think they would not be repeating this experience. There would be other times to explore her. Now was time to give in to their most primal needs.

For one last moment he held her back, slowing her movements. He was a little worried that she would have trouble handling his size, but she literally started bouncing on his lap, and his own groans joined hers. He stopped thinking and gave himself to the pleasure of the moment.

Afterwards, well… after several afterwards, they were curled up on her mattress. Rodregas was very happy he had salvaged the mattress from Lord Captain Poir. He had had no way to know that the mattress would come in so handy.

He lay there with Imeraldä's head laying on his shoulder, her body half draped on his own, and half on the mattress. He was thankful that Doi'van had heard what was going on and given them space. Rodregas assumed he must have slept back in the barn. Doi'van walking in unaware of the situation would have been very embarrassing. Rodregas had suggested to Imeraldä that they should stop in case Doi'van walked in, but she had shown no signs of caring and quickly took the thought away from him with her actions.

Rodregas wanted to ask her what this encounter had meant, but he knew that while such questions were natural, they were never helpful. Two people fresh from their first lovemaking were in no place to talk about a relationship.

Rodregas had made a promise to the gods and though she was the most amazing woman in the world, still he would do his duty. He tried to find the right thing to say. Rodregas looked down at her with her head on his shoulder and her pile of auburn curls spread equally over both their naked bodies. Her long hair covered a lot of the two of them but really hid nothing.

He met her large green eyes and said, "you amaze me. I knew you were brave and courageous, but now I know where your true magic talent is..." He looked at her eyes as he spoke and even when he smiled at his own words, he let her see the sincerity of what he said.

Rodregas had learned that the fundamental rule of flattery with women is to never lie. It was a lesson taught to Rodregas by a lost love, and one that had served him well over the years. Most women can always tell a lie, especially in such a moment of connection as the talk after wonderful sex. Luckily, even with far more normal women there is always something good you can say; with Imeraldä he could have gone on for hours.

Imeraldä's eyes lit up in pleasure and humor at his words but, he was careful to say nothing of the future, nothing of love. Such talk would serve no purpose and would likely ruin the moment. To his surprise, she also kept such thoughts to herself. The rest of the night, the two lovers spent quietly connected and at peace, but they shared few words.

In the morning after meditation, Doi'van pulled forth two wooden staves that he had cut and said with a smile and an exaggerated wink. "Apparently you are healed from your wound now, so I think it is time to stop with these making of shadows like children and time for more physical training."

As the Hellborn finished speaking he tossed Rodregas one of the staves. "With my people we teach our children to fight using the staff. It is hard to kill someone by accident with a staff, but you can still deliver pain. The avoidance of pain is an impressive way to teach someone to be nimble. My war masters at the palace would say you two are too old to learn the staff, but it is the way that I know."

"Sir Paladin," he said to Rodregas, using the unearned honor title. "I assume with your training from all your ex-knights that you know how to use the staff?" As Doi'van spoke he looked at how Rodregas was holding the staff. His expression made it clear that his hold on the staff was all wrong.

"Fight with a staff?" Rodregas responded in surprise. "No, can't say that I ever have. The weapons of the Knight are the sword, the mace, the lance and the bow. Those are the weapons of a warrior," he stated.

"And what do you do when facing a warrior in full plate armor?" asked Doi'van. "Even chain mail can stop an arrow or the edge of a sword. And while a mace is great against a chain, crushing your opponent and breaking their bones, such tactics takes a long time against plate armor."

Rodregas was not sure what to say to that question. The mace or the warhammer was the weapon of choice against all well armored opponents. Doi'van was right, edged weapons were not of much use against a full set of plate armor. That is why knights or others who could afford the cost wore all that metal.

Rodregas had to shrug; he had no answer other than an extended fight with the mace that rarely ended until one or the other was too tired and battered to defend themselves.

Doi'van nodded at Rodregas expression of confusion, "My clan is known as the greatest warriors of the Burning Lands beyond the Long Sea. We are victorious against heavily armored opponents because we are masters of the halberd. With a halberd we can quickly dismount an armored warrior, knock him to the ground and then, with the leverage provided by the halberd..."

Doi'van swung his staff and acted like he was holding down a foe with his left foot. He made a savage two-handed thrust downward, "we can pierce his armor and win the battle quickly."

Rodregas nodded. He was not sure what this 'halberd' was. Rodregas assumed it was some sort of a spear from the way Doi'van was holding the staff. Rodregas did not see how a spear could do what Doi'van was suggesting, but since Doi'van had been up for learning the Kata, Rodregas would learn how to fight with a lengthy piece of wood.

Doi'van then stepped forward and started swinging the staff with such mastery as to make it beautiful. The staff was but a blur as it whirled in one hand and then the other, behind his back, over his shoulder. It was a dance. Rodregas had seen a few sword masters fight; and it was like this. The staff moved faster and with more control than one's eyes could follow.

Doi'van finished the exhibition with the staff swinging over his shoulder and with a savage swing downward movement, ending with perfect control where it would have connected with a fallen opponent. Rodregas almost pointed out that he was doing Kata, practicing against an opponent only seen in your mind, but decided that this was the time for him to learn and Doi'van to teach. Rodregas had long ago learned that it was hard to learn if you were talking.

Over the next hour, Rodregas regretted his decision to learn. Doi'van was a master with the staff. Rodregas could not help but feel impressed. In the Eastern Kingdoms, and every other kingdom that he knew of, the staff was a peasant weapon. As many lords only allowed swords for their soldiers and nobility.

Farmers and crafts people could not own edged weapons of war. Though Rodregas had known such rules to be broken by non-noble families. It was done discretely, usually under the pretext of keeping a family heirloom. During the harvest fairs that most rural areas had, fighting contests were common, but they were always contest of wrestling or bare-knuckle fighting. The only weapons allowed by the local workers were the staff and sometimes the bow.

Rodregas had always regarded the staff as a primitive weapon which no true warrior would bother with, but to watch Doi'van with it was breathtaking.

The staff whirled around him in a blur, and the length of the weapon made full use of his height and size. But the Hellborn also had complete control of the weapon as he highlighted that morning by whizzing past Rodregas' clumsy blocks and bruising every part of his body until even the smallest movement hurt.

Rodregas was used to being better trained than others, but with the staff he was starting from scratch; even holding it properly was new to him. Doi'van showed him how to keep one hand at the center of the staff and one hand between the center and the end. One always gripped the staff in thirds. When it was held horizontally in front, the right palm faced away from the body and the left hand faced the body, enabling the staff to rotate. The backhand pulling the staff held the power for generated strikes, while it used the front hand for guidance. When striking, you twisted the wrist, the same as when one turned the hand over when punching.

Rodregas' eyes were quickly opened to the weapon, and it was fun to learn something so new, but he was much worse for the lesson. After lunch he limped over to the great oak which they sat under most days for their magical training and reading. Imeraldä was off in the trees taking care of nature's business. As the two settled down he broached the subject on his mind.

"Doi'van, are you mad at me? Is this something to do with me and Imeraldä… getting together last night?" Rodregas asked.

"What do you mean?" Doi'van asked, clearly surprised. "No, I can't say it is a good idea. Mixing more than casually with Nymphs always leads to problems, but it is not my problem. In fact," he said with a careful glance around him. "I would have jumped at the chance myself."

"I am probably too ugly by both Ælf and Nymph standards for her to be interested. Then again, you know Nymphs; they are naturally polyamorous and very sexual. It is a shock that she was not already sexually involved with one or both of us already."

Doi'van added, "Maybe her Ælf blood means she does not have as strong a sex drive as most Nymphs since Ælven marriage bonds are always monogamous. By the Infernal Rivers, she is half Ælf and half Nymph, who knows what to expect. Humans and Orqui are both in the middle of their two extremes and becoming emotionally involved with either always ends with heartbreak."

Doi'van's deep voice was just stating a fact, if an unpleasant one.

Rodregas nodded, he agreed, but he was not the inexperienced man he looked. "I understand that, and I expect nothing from her." He smiled and said, "but I plan to enjoy what we have for as long as it lasts."

"And when she takes other lovers?" Doi'van asked.

Rodregas responded with the only answer he had, "I will do my best to handle it and not get jealous," he said. Rodregas knew it would be hard, but he was a hard man and he would have to manage.

Doi'van nodded, then glanced over to see Imeraldä walking over with several of the Grimoires and he added, "I was not angry, in fact, by my people's standards I was being very easy on you. Since you are human and can't handle pain like an Orqui. But, without pain, you will not reach your potential for quickness and reflexes. On the practice field, such quickness means fewer bruises. On the battlefield such reflexes mean life and death."

Rodregas nodded, his words held the ring of truth, but he was not looking forward to days of practices and bruises.

The pattern of their days changed. Now after prayer and meditation came first the practice of the Kata, and then the staff, and then finally the books. The genuine change came in the evening. The nights were full of such pleasure and joy, such as Rodregas had seldom known in his life. The rest of summer passed as the most joyful that he had known, as the three learned together and grew close. After the staff they moved to the bow where Imeraldä became the master.

To use the magical Black Yew bows required learning a spell to merge the users with the bow. The spell was unlike anything Rodregas had learned. Imeraldä said it was seldom taught to non-nymphs, though Ravenhurr had known the spell, and taught a few of the guards with a touch of the talent.

Using the bows was a matter of sending your innate power into the wood and singing with it. Not singing out loud, but making the power vibrate and move in a rhythm that matched the wood. When that magical rhythm was reached, the bow suddenly became almost fluid and moved nearly of its own volition. The arrows flew with incredible force and accuracy. The only problem was that the three could not practice freely as the arrows sometimes shattered on impact, as they flew with such force.

Doi'van quickly mastered the spell and the use of the bow. Rodregas, on the other hand, struggled to learn the artistry of the spell. One afternoon, a few days after Doi'van had mastered the spell, Rodregas stood there with the bow, trying hard to both find the rhythm of the spell and shoot the weapon.

Imeraldä stood next to him, her hand lightly touching the bow, as she tried to figure out why he was still struggling with the mastery of the weapon. Rodregas reached down into himself, to that place that held his magic. Though Rodregas had never had much power, he had always enjoyed using his "itch" (as he had always called it) to do modest things.

Using his magic now was an extraordinary experience. Whereas before it had been calming, requiring him to focus, to be able to call forth his little bit of power, now he held a whirling tornado of energy. It was not a matter of having enough. It was a matter of having almost too much power that overwhelmed the simple spell. Rodregas breathed in, trying to keep his mind empty but for the shape and vibration of the magic, as he fed a tiny amount into the bow.

For a second, he had it. The bow responded, and Rodregas could pull the bow back, but the moment was quickly gone. The bow bounced back into its regular shape and his arrow shot up and floundered in the air before falling to earth. Where both Imeraldä and Doi'van had nailed the dead tree in the exact center, his arrow was closer to the barn than the target. Unfortunately, the barn was in the wrong direction.

Rodregas heard a few unkind chuckles from both of the others at his shot. "I don't understand it," he said. "Why do I have so much trouble controlling my magical power now? I know I have a lot more power, but you both have lots of power. I can't seem to control it." The frustration in his own voice was clear. "Could you feel anything?" Rodregas asked Imeraldä.

"No." she responded. "Your power is strong and untamed, in flavor more like Doi'van's power than a nymph's or Ælf's, but Doi'van can master the spell. I think the problem is, that for all of your life, your power was weak but easy to control. A mage born of power learns to control it at an early age. You never had to learn any control; your power was so weak that you always struggled to have enough power to do anything with it."

"Ok, I never learned proper control. The spells I learned as a squire were small, weak things. But can I learn to control my extra power now?" Rodregas asked.

"Probably," she responded. "But it will be harder and slower than if you were learning earlier in life. It requires relearning something that is almost an instinct at this point in your life. Part of the problem is that the spell to activate the magic in the bow is just vastly different from anything you have probably done before."

Rodregas knew she was speaking the truth. He had never thought he would be some powerful mage. That Doi'van had so easily learned the spell just reminded him of how many times in his life he had failed to have the ability to succeed in things he wanted. Rodregas' new body was very gifted, but it was still mortal and some things he would just not be able to do as well as others. In some ways this was reassuring, a connection to his past.

"Can I ask you a question?" she asked.

Rodregas smiled and said, "of course, what?"

"Have you thought of trying to become a sigil warrior? You are a powerful magician now. You could probably take one or even two of the greater sigils and still have more power than you had before, and as a warrior the enhancement from the sigil would make you an even more powerful fighter."

Rodregas nodded, "I have thought about it. In fact, I am sure given the opportunity that I would take on one of the greater or several of the lesser sigils. I am a warrior first, not a mage. Leaving a little magic left over would be great if I can, but you never really know until after the searing."

Rodregas paused and then added, "The problem is that only two groups in the Eastern Kingdoms have the knowledge to sear a sigil. The first is the Guild of the Celestial Path. I think we all agree they are not sharing it with me soon," Rodregas continued with a smile. "And the second is the Knightly Order of the Soaring Stars, who have the greatest collection. But they only let their knights take sigils. I don't think they will share soon either."

Imeraldä looked at Rodregas. She knew that the Order of the Soaring Stars was the Order that Rodregas had belonged to as a squire, but his taking on of another's body was anathema to the teaching of the Order. Rodregas was an Immortalist in fact, if not a member of the Guild, and he was sure most of the knights would kill him if they found out his story.

"But don't some Magi have the secrets for some lesser sigils?" asked Doi'van, joining the conversation. "I thought a lot of them used ones that help them not to grow old."

"That is true," said Imeraldä with a shrug. "A healing sigil is why wizards live so long. Most consider it to be the moral choice instead of the Immortalists' answer for long life."

"What about you Doi'van?" Rodregas asked. "Imeraldä says that you are almost as powerful as me as a magician. If we found a way, would you like to take on some power of the sigils?" he asked.

Rodregas had expected an immediate response, but a lengthy pause followed his question before Doi'van answered. Rodregas had learned that, Doi'van thought before speaking. "I am not sure. I enjoy learning magic, though I am just beginning. I would think I would take on a minor sigil or two. I am a skilled warrior, but I like to learn fresh things and I would like to have sufficient magic to learn spells."

Rodregas nodded. Doi'van's response would have surprised him before, but he had learned much of the thoughtful Hellborn in their time together. When one looked at him and how powerfully built he was, it was easy to imagine what he could do on the battlefield with a greater sigil added to his power. He would be a true daemon in battle. But while Doi'van loved his strength, he also loved his intelligence.

In comparison, Rodregas was less interested in

exploring and learning fresh things as he was about what he could do to enhance his ability to carry out his duty.

"Well," Rodregas said, "I don't think we will have any options for sigils for now. Let us continue to learn what we can of battle and of magic. If we are lucky, we can worry about more if we survive our first strike at the Immortalists."

The next morning, during his meditation, Rodregas realized that it was time for action. He realized that if they continued to hide out in the farmhouse, winter would come, and travel would be much more difficult. He knelt on the ground examining the new color of the trees; he knew that it was now time to strike.

CHAPTER 9
INTO THE FIRES

Six days later the three of them found themselves ready to cross the Old Princess Road. Imeraldä had been scouting ahead, and she signaled for the two men to stay back in the trees. As a half Forest Nymph, she seemed to be able to disappear into the forest. Rodregas quickly learned how she had tracked him from Raven Keep.

While she claimed that other Forest Nymphs had far better skills, Rodregas had seen no one to match her abilities. They had taken the three horses back up the trail where any sounds they made would not be heard from the road. Doi'van and Rodregas had found some cover that gave a superb view of the road.

They sat on the ground and waited until Imeraldä signaled that something was coming. Rodregas neither heard nor saw any activity, and his physical senses were far more accurate than when he had been a young man. His guess was that her connection with the forest had somehow warned her that something was coming.

Doi'van and Rodregas looked at each other as they squatted down in the shrubs. Doi'van had one of the Black Yew bows out, with arrows at hand. It would not be surprising if a patrol of the Eternal Guard would be on the road. The road was the principal route from the port city of Chrisana Stone to the Menagerie of Sky, the capital city ruled over by the Immortalist leader Taiga. But, more likely, what Imeraldä sensed was a trade caravan running a regular route from Chrisana Stone to any of several of the Eastern Kingdom's cities.

If it was a light scouting patrol of Eternal Guard with just two or three guards, it would be the best-case scenario for them. Give them decent odds to take on some Eternal Guards and gain better weapons, armor and horses. If it was a caravan, then they would sit and watch, as it would be suicide to do anything against a full patrol.

Rodregas heard a rustle in the brush and glanced over to make sure it was just a squirrel or the like. He jumped up as a humanoid shape appeared out of the trees until he saw that it was just Imeraldä. She seemed to pay less attention now to stealth as she was to speed. From Imeraldä's expression, Rodregas knew it was something more dangerous than a trade caravan coming down the road.

Imeraldä squatted down next to them and

whispered, "A slave caravan is coming. They have a score of guards. We need to back up before they get here."

"We have suitable cover here," Rodregas whispered back, "let's check them out as they pass. They will probably stop at Stallion's Perch." After much debate between the three of them back at The Farm that had decided that Stallion's Perch was their destination, a small keep that bred Dire horses for the Eternal Guard.

"We can't," responded Imeraldä with a whisper. "Besides their regular guards, they are traveling with a patrol of Eternal guards. I think there are only four, but scout patrols often have a warrior with a minor sigil of enhanced senses. He might spot us." As she spoke Rodregas noticed that Imeraldä had a strange expression on her face. She was scared, but also seemed sad.

"What kind of slaves do they have?" Rodregas asked in a gentle voice.

Her body jerked more directly toward him, surprise covering her sad expression for a second. "Mixed, human, Ælf and Nymphs," She said before adding, "Rodregas, among the Nymphs they have children. My father raised me, he is a minor lord of the High Ælf, but the Nymphs have been good to me and these are children. I wish we could do something."

Rodregas nodded his understanding and said, "I wish we could, but the three of us against a score, the chances of our success is far smaller than the chances of our death." He stated in the 'matter of fact,' sergeant voice that he knew people would follow.

Rodregas stood up and turned, but while Doi'van stood, he faced the road and he said, "I have been on this road before, though I did not know then what it was named or where it led. To me it was a road of sorrow." Doi'van was using that flat voice that he used when stating facts. "Rodregas, you said our odds are bad, but how long shall we wait for the odds to be good?"

Doi'van's voice dropped the flat tone and sounded like rocks groaning deep in the earth, as if a great earthquake was coming, "You believe that a god of the Celestials is behind your survival, and that this god wants to see us fight the Immortalists. I spent two years of my life in the Menagerie, I swore to myself that given a chance I would see no others be enslaved by the Lord Taiga."

Doi'van continued with the same tone as if the earth shook, "I know these caravans. The guards will be mostly badly trained human scum armed in leather and with weapons of simple steel. The Eternal scouts are another matter. They will be highly trained but still the lowest of the Eternal Guards, mostly with just one of the lesser sigils such as strength or one that gives a guardsman enhanced senses. Against the three of us, a Forest Nymph with a powerful Black Yew bow, a Hellborn Prince of the Orqui and a warrior empowered with a Celestial Lion, are the odds truly that bad?" Doi'van growled.

Rodregas stood still, surprised by Doi'van's words. He did not know how good or bad their odds were. He knew they were not good, but his mind did not spin with the odds. He focused on the rightness of Doi'van's words. Trying to raid an armed keep probably had far worse odds. And for what? So, they could steal horses; so they could better their odds to escape a future fight? Here, if they succeeded, the three would not be stealing horses, they would free people from slavery.

Rodregas looked into Doi'van's eyes. The Hellborn was resolute. Rodregas felt humbled at the man's bravery, at his passion, at his strength. Rodregas knew there was no such thing as a hero, simply people that sometimes do the right thing when it was a hard choice. There was no question for Doi'van. He stood quiet and ready. He knew what the right thing was, and he therefore was taking the right action. Rodregas was not Doi'van's equal in spirit, but he knew that he could not turn away from the Hellborn's example.

Rodregas then turned to Imeraldä. Her eyes told a different story. She both wanted to run fast and far, and she wanted to free the Nymphs. Simply stated, she was scared. She was young, barely more than a girl, and not a trained warrior. She was also more fragile than either Doi'van or Rodregas. A blow that would only stun either of them would shatter her.

Her strong magic power would do her little good in a standup battle. For all of that, she gave a nod to the two warriors as they looked at her. She was willing to follow their lead. If they wanted to free the slaves, she would follow them. How could someone so young be so brave? How could he not honor such bravery?

Rodregas looked into Imeraldä's eyes. She was watching him, waiting for him to take the lead. There was no need for words, no argument. They had made the decision. They only needed direction.

Any hope for success laid in playing to their strength. Rodregas said, "Doi'van, you stay here and use the bow. You start from the middle of the caravan and focus on the slavers. If you get a free shot at an Eternal Guard, take it, but we need to reduce the numbers against us."

"Imeraldä, you need to stay away from the close-in fighting. Get as far back as you can and still be able to see and shoot. You will focus on the front of the caravan and focus on the regular slavers. Don't start shooting until

Doi'van does, hold steady until they get close and then use your Forest Nymph skills to fade back into the trees away from the fighting."

Then he said carefully, so she would understand, "Don't get yourself killed. But if you can stop and turn, take a few more shots. If they again turn and charge you run and don't stop running. Forget the horses, you will be much harder to track without them."

He was about to ask Imeraldä how long until they would arrive, when Rodregas heard noises from up the road. The slave caravan had arrived.

Rodregas held a finger to his lips and waved Imeraldä deeper into the trees. With any luck, she would be safe. It was hard to catch a Forest Nymph who was trying not to be found in the trees. Doi'van stepped partly out of the shrubs, and got behind a tree, to give him cover against return fire.

There was a good-size tree not far in front of the two of them. Rodregas put his back to it and drew his two short swords and then did the most difficult thing he could do in this situation. He looked at Doi'van and not at the caravan. There was no need for the two of them to be peeking around the trees at the caravan, though he desperately wanted to get a good look at the caravan to establish their odds.

They had rolled the dice. Rodregas had been learning to trust Doi'van and knew his life was now in Doi'van's hands. If Imeraldä had missed something critical and they should not attack, it was for Doi'van to catch.

Rodregas watched Doi'van, watched for him to raise the bow and start the fight. When the guards charged in to stop the shooting, then it would be his turn to strike. Rodregas would have to take on as many of the slavers and

Eternal Guards as possible. It would do little good to get caught up in a one-on-one battle; the odds were too many against them. He had to use his extra strength and speed and go after multiple targets.

Rodregas focused on his breathing, he needed his body ready. He rested against the tree, trying not to tense up, and breathed deep and slow. Quicker than he thought, Doi'van's black bow came up, and he shot. The Black Yew bows were an incredible advantage. They had been the pride of Raven Keep and were among the most dangerous and rare weapons that the Nymphs used to protect themselves.

These bows had primarily been ornamental trophies for Ravenhurr. Rodregas thought they symbolized a previous victory. Only a few of the guards would have had the power to use them, and Ravenhurr kept guards with even minor power away from the keep.

Against the leather armor of the slavers there would be no defense against the bow, even if they had shields; the arrows would likely blast through anything they had. Against the Eternal Guard it was a different matter; their armor would stop the arrows. And their weapons would be enchanted and equally effective as their bows against his armor. Their blue steel swords going through his leather like butter if he was not fast enough.

Depending on their sigils, they were likely to be faster or stronger or both. But the actual problem with the Eternal Guards is that Rodregas' short swords would not cut their armor. It put him and Doi'van at an extreme disadvantage. As the arrows flew behind him, he could not help thinking of the other disadvantage of bows. They were dealing with a limited supply of arrows; once the arrows were all shot, they lost their primary advantage.

Rodregas heard the noise of the first soldier to rush from the road to stop the archery attack. Rodregas went low from his crouching position behind the tree and swung hard. Rodregas hit knee high and the man trying to run by went flying headfirst into the dirt. Rodregas knew from the feel of the blow that his sword had hit armor and bounced off. It was an Eternal Guard. Doi'van shot another arrow, almost straight down, into the back of the exposed neck of the downed guard. The man thrashed once and then laid still.

A second warrior flew by in a blur. With such swiftness, Rodregas knew that the man must have a sigil of speed. The guardsmen headed right for Doi'van and was behind Rodregas before he could do anything. Doi'van must have seen him coming, and he dropped his bow and pulled out his great sword.

The guard must have been thinking his opponent would be a Nymph, because of the archery attack from the forest. He was not expecting a Hellborn Orqui and was unprepared to be up close to such a powerful opponent. Amazingly the guard, with the speed of his sigil, blocked Doi'van's first attack.

The resulting blow had an unpleasant sound as the blocking enchanted blue steel cut right through Doi'van's sword. Unfortunately for the guard, Doi'van stepped forward and jammed the remaining broken half of the sword into his opponent's chest. The weapon did not pierce the armor, but neither did the armor protect against the strength of the blow. The guard flew into the bushes, and with a sickening crunching sound hit a tree.

Rodregas heard another of the enemy and spun into the sound using all his speed and strength, hoping to take a guard with either advantage. His target proved to be a slaver in armor no better than his own. He had a ragged beard and held a small battle ax.

Rodregas' sword blow was too fast for the guard to block, and he had used enough strength to stun a guard wearing regulation armor. His sword cleaved the guard in half, and a gout of blood and gore splattered him. Rodregas pulled his sword free and spun away from the mess.

As he came to a crouch, the sound of arrows stopped. Part of his mind knew that Imeraldä was backing deeper into the forest. As he cleared the mess he had made of the last slaver, Rodregas came face to face with a man in the red and blue uniform of Eternal Guardsman. Behind him were two more slavers.

The Eternal Guard wore the classic half plate of regulation armor: A suit of Mithril chain covered with a night bronze breastplate, leg guards and vambraces for the forearms. His head was covered with a half helm. His Mithril was shining in the sun.

The middle of his breastplate had the symbol of the Immortalists, an eagle soaring up into the clouds. In his left hand was a one-handed long sword. In his right he held a small round steel shield. The shield did not give much coverage against bows and arrows but was light and great for blocking hand-to-hand attacks.

Rodregas swung his short swords in slow circular motions and slowly backed up. The two slavers behind the guard apparently had been impressed with the violence so far and stayed in the safety behind the Guard instead of separating to each side of him.

One slaver was human, surprisingly the other was a small Orqui or maybe a half-breed. The human slaver held a long sword, the Orqui a mace. Rodregas tried to think of a trick, but nothing came to mind. He knew he had to strike quickly before the odds got even worse. He started his attack with the basics.

He stepped in closer and swung one sword in a slashing forward movement and followed up with a backhanded half slash that flowed into a half block. He meant neither attack to do anything but feel this opponent out. The small tight swings would allow him to bring them into a defense position quickly.

The guard swung to meet his sword with his own weapon in a similar defensive move instead of going after him. His sword had the glimmer of blue steel, an enchanted metal that made the best edged weapons.

Rodregas backed up, not wanting to see the results if he tried matching against a blue steel sword, as it would result in his short sword becoming shorter.

Then Rodregas stepped forward. He had to be careful. Though he was a good foot taller than his opponent, the guard's long sword gave him better reach. Rodregas swung at him and retreated. The two shared several blows, moving back and forth. The third time that he retreated after taking a blow, the Eternal Guard went for the kill.

The Guard extended his entire body out in a lunge, thrusting his long sword out to its full length. The guard saw Rodregas' braided leather armor and steel swords and thrust with the point. Seeing nothing that could stop his attack. The lunge was perfect; the guard went for dead center. Even though Rodregas had been waiting for a similar move, the thrust almost caught him off guard. The guard had only one problem, one that he could not have expected.

Rodregas had been taking easy swings, not revealing his true speed. Once the guard committed, Rodregas brought both of his swords down and met the lunging blade. Rodregas could not meet his sword edge to edge, but it was thrusting out, and he caught it and pushed it down and to the left. At the same time, he moved his body to the side and in close.

Rodregas then lunged with his right sword, as he kept his left engaged, pushing the blue steel sword away. Rodregas's thrust with his free short sword was with a speed the guard could not have expected. The sword went right through the guard's unarmored throat before his opponent knew what was happening. The man slid to the ground, dead.

During the fight with the Eternal Guard, the Orqui slaver had stepped in close with his mace. Rodregas had no way to block the attack, the mace was a much harder weapon to deflect. So instead he dodged the first swing of the mace, and then dropped his weapons to the ground, and bull rushed the Orqui.

Rodregas grabbed the slaver's weapon harness before he could react. With his Celestial strength, Rodregas picked him up off the ground. Before the slaver could react, Rodregas went from lifting him up to driving him down into the ground. Adrenaline was surging, and suddenly Rodregas had a broken mess in his hand. The guard was very dead; the Orqui shattered by the impact into the ground.

Rodregas let go of the broken body and stood quickly, trying to clear himself of the gore. The remaining human slaver looked shocked at what had happened and Rodregas moved quickly to pick one of his swords back up.

Rodregas turned to the last slaver and saw fear in the man's eyes. Rodregas looked around and saw that he was no longer facing just one remaining opponent. The sounds had drawn others and four others closed in, including another Eternal Guard and three more slavers. He had hoped they could pick off enough with the Black Yew bows to keep odds like this from happening.

Rodregas glanced to the ground, hoping to see the previous guard's blue steel long sword. It would do a lot to give him at least a chance against these odds, but it was nowhere to be seen.

The dead guard's small shield, though, was near his feet. Rodregas quickly grabbed it and switched his short sword to his right and the shield to his left.

This time the warriors spread out and circled. Rodregas took a chance before they got too close and glanced over at Doi'van. In one of those weird pauses that happen in battle, he saw the path between them was open. Two dead slavers and a guardsman lay around the Hellborn warrior. Doi'van was also backing up toward Rodregas, surrounded by two more slavers.

Rodregas scooted back toward Doi'van and said, "back to back." Doi'van gave a grunt of acknowledgement, and they faced in opposite directions. They were quickly surrounded. Both Guardsmen had long swords and small shields and were dressed in the mithril and night bronze half plate of the guard. Rodregas looked for hints at what their lessor sigil enhancement might be.

The five human slavers had mismatched armor and weapons. The men circled them, but did not seem eager to move in. During the pause Doi'van spoke in a low growl, "all this, and can you believe there is not a decent sized Eternal Guard in the lot. When we finish with them, I will never fit in that armor."

Rodregas smiled at the disgust in the Hellborn's tone and the confidence that it implied. "True," Rodregas replied, "but it is pretty. I would love to be facing them with one of those blue steel swords."

"Don't go lowering your standards, blue steel and night bronze half-plate? Good enough for the common soldier, but I fancy something a little more distinctive."

Rodregas was about to ask him what he had in mind, when they found out why the surrounding men had been waiting. Two more slavers came up with crossbows. They were going to take them out from a safe distance. Doi'van and he needed no words; they both knew only instant action gave them a chance.

Rodregas would like to have tried to take on one of the Eternal Guards first, but he had already noticed that the slaver with a mace, was a little too close and a little too far away, from his nearest companion. He was a skinny man with dirty hair and seemed to be having trouble holding his heavy weapon.

Rodregas jumped in close and the slaver swung the mace with surprising force, but Rodregas met it with his newly gained shield and knocked it aside. Rodregas moved with too much speed to be blocked. He slid the short sword into the slaver's stomach and gutted him in a quick and vicious movement.

Doi'van had immediately launched himself at a slaver coming from the opposite direction, slamming his opponent's sword away with an ax he had taken from one of his fallen foes, and chopping him down before he moved.

Rodregas went for the nearest Eternal Guard, trying to keep the momentum. He followed up with the same move he had used with the slaver, stepping forward and slamming his shield forward to either knock his opponent's weapon aside or knock the guard himself down.

Unfortunately, when Rodregas hit this guard his opponent responded, slamming shield against shield. Rodregas had gotten too comfortable with his opponents not being able to match his strength. This guard though must have had a sigil of strength and cleanly blocked him. The Eternal Guard immediately launched himself forward, and Rodregas' own speed worked against him. As Rodregas' short sword hit nothing but air, he felt the sharp agony of the guard's blade piercing his side.

Rodregas used his speed and reflexes to throw himself back. But as he did, he felt another sharp cut hit his upper arm, only a light wound he thought, but the other men were moving in now that he was off balance.

Rodregas twisted sideways and leaped forward as he fell, grabbed one slaver who had come in close, and brought him down with him. With a quick stab into the man's groin, Rodregas took the slaver permanently out of the fight. Rodregas rolled off the squirming body and threw himself up to a standing position. He almost went down again, as he saw, and felt an arrow pierce his thigh.

Rodregas saw the Eternal Guard who had blocked his shield coming to finish him, a stocky man with enormous arms. He was coming in carefully, shield up, sword in position. A warrior of skill and strength. Rodregas made up his mind not to underestimate him a second time.

Rodregas struggled to stay standing and spread his feet wide for balance and locked his legs straight to keep them from buckling under him. He felt cold and knew he was losing blood fast. Rodregas knew that this was probably it. They had gambled and lost, there were just too many of them.

He could hear Doi'van in an equal desperate fight behind him, but he dared not look to see how his friend was doing.

One thing was uncomplicated to him, he did not want to die without taking out this Eternal Guardsmen first. If they killed most of the slavers and the guards, there was an excellent chance that the slaves could escape. If Rodregas and Doi'van died without taking the Eternal Guards out, then they would have died in vain. Rodregas hoped Imeraldä would get away.

His shoulder jerked to the left, and he guessed that an arrow had hit him. Rodregas threw himself toward the Guardsmen. He blocked the sword blow with his borrowed shield but did not have the angle to avoid a direct impact. The blue steel sword sliced through the shield and Rodregas jerked his arm back, fearing that he would lose it.

Rodregas lunged in close and abandoned his useless shield and short sword, in desperation, grabbing his opponent's shield with both hands and pulled him in close. The guard tried to shrug him off. His bearded face looked angry. His eyes, a light blue, stared at Rodregas with revulsion. He was probably wondering how Rodregas could be strong enough to take on an Eternal Guardsman with a sigil.

Rodregas growled at him, letting him feel his anger and rage at taking slaves to be used by the Immortalists. Rodregas had seen what would happen to them. He had suffered for years with a subtle inner rot at letting the evil continue. In all the ways that mattered Rodregas knew he was no better than this man, he had spent most of his life as a glorified slaver. Rodregas had no moral grounds on which to kill these men, but inside of him there was no mercy. He had crossed a line and could no longer live with the evil.

The guardsmen's strength kept Rodregas from

ripping the shield away, and the burly man moved his body to swing his sword in close and finish the fight. Rodregas pulled the guard's shield closer and grabbed the man's other arm in a desperate attempt to stop him from bring his sword to bear, he saw the man grimace in pain from the strength of Rodregas grip.

Rodregas instantly tightened his grip on the man's arm, the chain mail did nothing to protect his opponent from his Celestial strength and the arm turned to pulp. The man tried to pull away but Rodregas now released the shield and grabbed the man's lower face, which was exposed by the half helm, and squeezed.

Rodregas felt the guard's face give way to his rage and Celestial strength. For a moment the guard continued to struggle, but Rodregas pulled him closer with one hand and with the added leverage ripped his opponent's face away.

Rodregas felt a stab in his back as he took either an arrow or a sword. He was groggy with pain, and both weak and filled with rage. The dying guard in his hands was thrashing in unspeakable pain. As the guard collapsed to the ground, Rodregas fell with him. He tried to once more roll to the side, struggling away from a potential final stroke.

Rodregas' face was covered in gore and blood. It was hard for him to see. He struggled back up, but fell. Then Rodregas felt a presence to his right. It was too small to be Doi'van and Rodregas staggered over-reaching for him, determined to take one final slaver with him.

His wounded leg buckled again, and Rodregas tried to reach for the ground to slow his fall, but something was wrong with his arm and it did not move. For a split second, he saw the ground coming up to hit him in the face. And then... darkness.

CHAPTER 10
THE OTHER KIND OF PAIN

Rodregas laid there looking at blue swirls for a long time, wondering where he was. He was not sure if he was awake; his mind seemed heavy with dreams and shifting images. It took him a long time before he remembered the battle. With the memory came concern for Doi'van and Imeraldä, and a surge of adrenaline that gave him the energy to wake up.

Rodregas tried to sit up, but his body, which had been so strong since that day at Raven Keep, now only responded sluggishly. He was sleepy but had the impression that he had been sleeping a very long time.

Rodregas must have moved enough to get some attention because a man, or to be more accurate, an adult male Nymph, moved into his sight. The amount of hair coming out of the ears of an adult Nymph always surprised Rodregas. He was glad that was one trait that Imeraldä did not seem to have. He knew the thought to be a silly one even as it crossed his mind. It was quickly replaced with concern. For a second, he thought they had tied him down, but Rodregas could see enough to determine that his restraints were tightly tucked bed sheets. He must be very weak.

"Easy there, young man," said the old Nymph. The elderly man helped Rodregas sit up and held a bowl to his mouth. "My name is Durien and I am a healer. Please slowly drink this. Rinse your mouth out with it, as your mouth is probably parched after all this time." The drink tasted like tea or maybe a light broth. As soon as Rodregas drank it, he realized he was starving.

"I need more," Rodregas croaked as he finished the bowl.

The man, who unlike any Nymph Rodregas was familiar with, had his hair pulled back in a high ponytail, nodded but said, "Slowly, too much right-away is not good for you."

Rodregas nodded and cleared his throat. His mouth and throat were dry and felt like it had sand in it. While the bed was normal enough, the walls of the room were strange and seemed to be made of woven branches, and some hide or canvas, pulled between tree branches to form an oval shape.

"Doi'van and Imeraldä, do they live?" he got the words out, though it hurt his throat to speak.

"Oh, yes, Imeraldä is fine," the Nymph healer responded. "She was not hurt at all. Doi'van was injured badly, but not as badly as you are. You both should be dead from your wounds several times over. I thought at first you both had a sigil of healing. That would be the only way I know for you two to be alive, but Imeraldä says that you are both 'of the blood.' You are a lucky man, even with your ancestry, to be alive."

"May I speak to them?" Rodregas asked as he looked around the room or tent. It amazed him that they had found a safe place to recover from the battle.

"Of course," the healer responded, "But let's get

something more nourishing in you and maybe we can move you around a bit. Your body has sat still too long. Then you will take a nap. When you awake, I will get you Imeraldä. Doi'van is doing better than you, but I don't think he is up to doing any visiting yet." Rodregas nodded in relief at his words, and soon enough he was once again sleeping.

The next day, sometime around midmorning judging from the light coming in through the opening that seemed to function like a window, Imeraldä entered along with a young, handsome Nymph. He was tall with green hair and with a confident bearing to his presence. He greeted Rodregas with a dazzling smile.

"I see that you are looking much better," said the unknown Nymph.

Imeraldä gave the tall Nymph an enormous hug, one that looked far more intimate than Rodregas was comfortable with. She said, "Rodregas, we are so lucky that I could get Jordane to come. Durien was working so hard trying to heal you, but your body is so hard to work with. He says that the same innate magical ability that makes your body so strong also requires a lot of power to heal. I had to leave and run to Fariste to get Jordane to come." She was smiling like the sun as she spoke. "He was so good to come and just leave at the last moment," she added.

Rodregas thought she would start hugging the Nymph again. But she caught herself and came over to him, and gave him a careful hug, and started fussing with his pillows.

Rodregas wanted to pull her closer and inhale her scent. He had thought he would die, an experience that Rodregas of late knew too often. He wanted to pull Imeraldä down into the bed and celebrate being alive. His body was probably too weak to do more than cuddle, but Imeraldä seemed to act very friendly with the healer.

Rodregas was not sure if something had changed between them while he was healing. The possibility that he had lost what they had just started to explore together made Rodregas' heart heavy.

"So, I have been wanting to ask you a question," said Jordane. "Are the two of you related? You and Doi'van?"

Rodregas was caught off guard at the ridiculous question. "Not to mention the obvious," Rodregas said, "but Doi'van is an Orqui Hellborn from across the Long Sea and I am..." Rodregas paused in confusion. What exactly was he now? He reached for the closest comparison and said, "I have some Celestial blood, but I am human."

"Oh," Jordane said, "well that is strange, you know that you are also part Hellborn, right? Hellborns are very rare in this part of the world, and your bodies feel so similar, that I thought you might be related through a... well, a distant relation."

Rodregas heart stopped at the words and he asked in a rush, "you are saying I am Hellborn? That is impossible!"

"Can we wait one moment?" asked Imeraldä, raising her hand. "I think we need to bring Doi'van in to be part of this conversation." Rodregas just nodded, stunned at the news.

As Imeraldä left the room to get Doi'van, Jordane stepped closer and slowly moved his hand from Rodregas' feet to his head, his eyes half closed. Rodregas wondered what he could sense.

"You are a Nymph of the flesh?" Rodregas asked him. Contrary to his earlier pleasant mood, the Nymph froze at those words.

With an awkward smile the green-haired Nymph

said, "we prefer the term Nymph of Life. Truly, life is as powerful an element as any."

"Sorry," Rodregas said, realizing he had accidentally insulted the healer. "I have never spent much time with Nymphs." Rodregas' tone was quieter. The Nymph seemed young and smart and gifted. Rodregas knew he did not have to like him. But from Imeraldä's introduction, this Nymph was well known and powerful among his people, and he had saved both Rodregas' and Doi'van's lives.

There was an awkward moment until Doi'van appeared at the door. He walked with the help of a tall walking stick and Imeraldä. His arm and side were both covered in bandages. Durien followed him in with a heavy stool, which Doi'van quickly sat down on.

The old healer immediately left the room, and Jordane stood quietly listening. Rodregas was a little hesitant to speak freely in front of the healer, but he trusted Imeraldä's judgement.

"Rodregas, you look much better than last I saw you," said Doi'van. "But what is so important that it takes me away from a very important nap?" Doi'van's body looked worse for the wear, but his eyes showed his natural curiosity and intelligence. Rodregas did not think he minded coming over to visit.

Rodregas smiled, Given the way Doi'van talked about pain when training them with the staff, he must be immune to pain.

Imeraldä repeated Jordane's question. "Jordane asked Rodregas if you two were related as being Hellborn is very rare in the Eastern Kingdoms." Doi'van's surprised expression matched Rodregas response. Imeraldä added, "While I cannot sense the feel and nature of a body like I can a tree, I know the flavor of various magic, and I had thought a few times that I sensed the feel of brimstone and fire not just with Doi'van, but with both of you."

Rodregas could feel his eyes widen as Imeraldä confirmed what Jordane had felt. He had been thinking while Doi'van was being fetched, and he had a question for his friend. "Doi'van, you told us, you were taken quickly after you entered the Eastern Kingdoms. You have a strong physical essence and strong magical power, but both are of Infernal origin. The Immortalists should not be interested in either. Which did they show interest in?" Rodregas asked.

"Both really, I did not understand why they wanted me. I thought if you were Hellborn you were safe from the Immortalists," Doi'van replied. "They would cut me to see how fast I would heal and do tests where they were clearly testing my physical side. But they seemed just as excited about my magical power. This surprised me. It was the first time I was aware that I enough magic to tempt an Immortalist."

Doi'van paused then added, "They seem to think I was of great worth. I think Taiga wanted a lot of money for me. The thing is, Taiga kept me in a distant cell. Though he had me for two years, he only showed me to others for sale a handful of times."

"You suggest that the Guild Dealer, Taiga, and the Immortalist Ravenhurr are breaking 'The First Law?'" asked Jordane. His voice, for the first time, seemed serious and a little nervous.

The three companions shared a confused look at the question. The two men turned to Imeraldä who asked, "Jordane, you know I have had little proper training in magic and these two are warriors. I have heard of 'The First Law', but can you explain?"

Jordane looked surprised, but then nodded. "It is a

law set forth by both the Celestials and the Infernals. Do you know the sources of the magic that we use?" he asked her.

Imeraldä nodded, "Sure, there are three sources of magic: Celestial, Infernal and Elemental. It is one reason I am prized for my potential as I am strong in two. My Ælven ancestry is strong with Celestial magic, but my Nymph side is strong in elemental magic. If an Immortalist takes my power, he or she would become strong in both."

"Correct," Jordane said. "The exact dynamics is a topic of debate among magi. I go along with the theory that the only native source of magic to our world is the elemental. The High Ælves of your father's people who are so rich in magic also have a lot of Celestials blood in their heritage. The Elemental magic of nature is the only native kind of magic to the mortal realm. Only Nymphs through their connection to the One Tree are born strong in Elemental magic. The Orqui are strong with Infernal magic. Magic is the raw energy for spells, no matter what its source." He looked at them to make sure they understood.

Rodregas felt like he was once again a child in the Cathedral of the Heavens learning the basics of magic. All three were extremely interested in the theory that Jordane was sharing. But Rodregas was not sure what any of this had to do with mistaking him for a Hellborn.

He noticed that while Imeraldä's expression was one of simple enjoyment, at refining her knowledge with an expert, Doi'van's seemed almost made of rock. It seemed as if he feared that if he moved, they would challenge his inclusion in the discussion.

Jordane, apparently satisfied with their attention, continued with his explanation, "Mortals, to a greater or lesser extent, have an ability to tap into the magic that has overflowed into our realm from the Celestial and Infernal Realms. I, for one, believe that if our connections to these realms were cut," Jordane made a motion like a knife cutting a loaf of bread, "that in a few years we would have no magic but Elemental."

"Luckily, I can think of no way for such a thing to happen. But a mortal's ability to use magic is very limited by your heritage. The Immortalists have overcome this limitation by steeling other's people's natural, but different, connection.

"So," Jordane continued, "if a mortal can add a High Ælf's potent ability to tap the Celestial power, he gains Celestial power. If the same magic user can also tap into the Elemental powers, he again becomes far more powerful. The end goal of the Immortalists is to become a Celestial God. There are limitations, if a mortal were to incorporate a small bugs connection to the Celestial, he would gain in power. But if he were to incorporate a thousand bugs, he would only gain the same connection as that single bug. So instead he might try a mouse to gain its greater essence."

At this point Jordane paused, and he went from an expression of lecturing to one of nervousness. Rodregas almost expected him to look around for someone listening. When next he spoke, his words were quiet and drawn out. "The Gods and Infernals have been at war from the beginning of time. They are opposites of the balance of creation and destruction. But when mortals began to combine the various kinds of power, the two eternal enemies agreed on one thing. This became 'The First Law.'"

"Mortals can work to become Gods through growing in power. But a mortal must choose only one path: Celestial or Infernal. A mortal cannot steal the other to add to their power. That is The First Law."

"Why?" asked Doi'van, his deep voice sounding both menacing and curious.

"Nobody knows for sure," said Jordane. "The Gods and Infernals do not explain their actions, but most believe that if someone tapped into all three. They would have the potential to break the great balance between the magical realms. This is something that neither want," he added.

Rodregas spoke, "so if Ravenhurr, who was a friend of the Guild Dealer Taiga, was part of a group of Immortalists who have been breaking 'The First Law'. He might have already added Infernal power to his own Celestial. And when I took on Ravenhurr's power, I also added the Infernal power, which is natural for a Hellborn. It could also be a reason that the gods might have answered my prayers and helped me succeed against Ravenhurr."

"The Gods might not be against all Immortalists, but just the ones who are tapping into the Infernal power?" asked Doi'van.

Jordane looked unsure, "I am surprised that the consequences were not far more dire for any Immortalist if the Gods or Daemons knew. Though it sounds like if they helped in the ascension ceremony the result to Ravenhurr was quite serious."

"All Immortalists deserve to die for their crimes," Rodregas answered. His angry response did not surprise the others.

"Agreed," said Doi'van, raising his hand in a calming gesture, "but it might be helpful to understand what actions the gods might continue to help us undertake."

"True," Rodregas added calming down. "Doi'van, do you remember the names of the other Immortalists who were interested in purchasing you for their rituals?"

"I heard no names," Doi'van answered, "but I heard

one of them referred to as 'The Ambassador.' They treated him with great respect. I understood he was a particularly important person."

"I wonder if that is Ambassador Vandret?" asked Jordane. "He is said to be very close to Taiga. Some claim he is one of the few people that Taiga both respects and trusts. He serves as the at large Ambassador for the Immortalist and is the only one that most come across."

"Ambassador Vandret?" Rodregas responded thoughtfully. "He visited Ravenhurr about five years ago. Ravenhurr seemed eager to have him visit, which was unusual for him. Ravenhurr was very solitary."

"What else do you remember about any conversation between Vandret and Ravenhurr?" asked Imeraldä of Rodregas.

"Nothing, I was a guard who did my duty and kept my nose out of things. I was not in their presence enough to overhear a conversation."

The four talked more and then split up. To Rodregas' discomfort, Jordane and Imeraldä left together. Doi'van trailed the others and then stepped back toward Rodregas's room. Rodregas sagged against the bed, the wound of losing Imeraldä hurting more than those of his flesh.

"You said you knew she was a Nymph," stated Doi'van.

Rodregas nodded. He wanted sympathy, but he knew that the straight talking Doi'van was not likely to give him any. "I know. It is just that, well, I was hoping for more time."

"If you can accept her for who she is, then your time is not over," said Doi'van, his voice softer than usual.

"None of us is simple," continued the Hellborn. "The two of us have become friends, even though I am a

Hellborn. In me flows the blood of the Daemons of the Infernal."

He paused and then his voice cracked, showing a trace of a deep emotion for the first time, "You treat me like any man, even a friend. You must do the same for Imeraldä, for you two to be lovers, you must learn to share her with others. She has a lot of love to give. Do not be so selfish as to want it all to yourself." With that he gave a friendly punch to Rodregas' side, causing Rodregas to grunt in pain, and Doi'van followed the other two out the door.

Rodregas laid in the bed, his mind whirling with thoughts. At first, he thought about the implications of what Jordane had shared. But then his mind went back again and again, over his and Imeraldä's time during the last few weeks, and then back to Doi'van's words. He knew his friend spoke the truth, but he was not sure about his ability to do what he needed, to keep his relationship with the beautiful Ælven Nymph.

CHAPTER 11
THE NATURE OF BONDS

The next few days Rodregas and Doi'van recovered quickly under the powerful healing magic of Jordane. Rodregas spent most of his time dreaming that the handsome young Nymph would head back to his own home.

They were staying in a tiny village that seemed to be mostly a forest with compact rooms built into it. Rodregas could not figure out any set pattern to the place or its boundaries. There might have been a dozen or even hundreds of Nymphs living there. Though all the Nymphs were friendly, he was eager to leave.

On the third day after waking, Jordane was doing one of his mystic checks, running his hand a foot above Rodregas' reclining body. Occasionally, his hand seemed to move in the air, very similar to a baker working bread dough. "Well," Rodregas finally said, "I feel fine now. I thank you for your healing, but I think I am ready to leave."

Jordane nodded. His face held his usual expression of good cheer. "Your body heals fast and is fascinating to work with." A cloud went over his smile when he added, "Your body and spirit were not in very good alignment, and your connection was terribly fractured. Truly, it has been more effort to fix your spiritual wounds than your physical ones."

Jordane's smile returned when he added, "While true healing takes a lifetime of both inner and outer work, you are physically healthy enough to be on your way. And while I enjoy the challenge of working on your unique body, your presence too long among us will bring danger down on us."

Rodregas nodded, but asked, "And Doi'van, is he healthy enough to travel and fight if needed?"

"He needs to let go of some of his doubts and learn to focus on his inner self, but his physical wounds are healed."

Rodregas paused. He did not fully understand what Jordane was saying. But he understood that they were healthy enough to go. He then asked that he feared the answer of, "do you know if Imeraldä is coming with us, or if she will stay with you?" He should have asked her that himself during the last few days. But he was afraid to ask the beautiful young woman. He was afraid of what the answer might be.

"Do you truly understand Imeraldä's dual nature?" asked Jordane.

"She is a half Nymph. What does that have to do with her going or staying?" Rodregas asked.

"Nothing, but it does if you love her." Jordane said with a smile. His expression showed nothing but his normal cheer.

Instead of answering the Nymph's question, Rodregas asked him one instead. "Do you love her?"

"I would not travel this distance for anyone else. Imeraldä is an amazing young woman, intelligent, charming and potentially the most powerful magi I have ever encountered. I cherish every moment with her."

Rodregas' heart sank at the news. Life with the

powerful healer would be a far better one than one spent with his lost crusade against the Immortalist.

"Since you would ask me such a personal question, I have one for you." Jordane responded, "You are struggling with what it means that Imeraldä is a half Nymph, but have you thought about what is means that she is a half Ælf? Ælf woman, when they mate with a Ælven man, form a spiritual and magical life-bond. It is a bond that lasts all their lives and connects them on multiple levels as no other race is connected. That is why the Ælves take so long to choose a mate, and almost never choose one outside of their race. They mate for life, not out of choice, but because that is their nature."

Jordane stood silently as Rodregas sat up in bed and thought on the healer's words. "She is not as free with her body as most Nymphs," he said.

"No, she is not. She only lies with men who she truly feels a powerful connection," Jordane answered.

Rodregas had known that fact but had not really thought about it. "Are you saying that Imeraldä forms a life-bond like a Ælf? But while a Ælf has only one, that she has a bond with you and a bond with me?" he asked.

"Yes, I know of few other cases like this. She will always know where you are. And my guess is you will know where she is. But there are deeper implications. The mating bond is one of the dominant sources of power for the Ælven peoples," he said.

Rodregas did not understand fully what Jordane meant, but he added, "If Imeraldä is bonded to me, then we will always be connected?" He asked, but he thought he already knew the answer.

Jordane nodded. "She will love and bond with others, but it bonds you to her for all time."

Rodregas sat quietly, stunned by the news. No more words passed between the two until Jordane was about to leave.

"Do you know where the weapons are from the Eternal Guards? We are going to need them if we will do better during our next raid." Rodregas was getting his mind back to business. The news that he would never truly be separated from Imeraldä revived his spirit.

"Oh, we claimed the weapons as salvage. It has helped to pay for your healing, and equipping the people you rescued. As their rescuers, you were responsible for getting them properly outfitted and on their way back to their homes."

Rodregas sat shocked for a moment and then he just exploded. "WHAT! You cannot do that. Do you have any idea how much we need that gear? We bled for it! We put our lives at risk to rescue your people, and all we ask for in return is the weapons!" Rodregas breathed deep, trying to calm himself, but it was no use.

"DOI'VAN!" Rodregas yelled. He stepped out of his room which, unlike a normal room in a human house, opened directly outside. He ducked under a branch and bolted through the two trees and through a bush and to the door to Doi'van's room. Doi'van was standing up, his walking stick now unneeded held ready to fight at Rodregas' bellow.

"What alarms you?" he asked. He seemed to be listening for attack.

"These bastards are trying to take our armor and swords! We nearly died because it was the right thing to do to rescue the Nymphs, especially with the children being part of the caravan."

Doi'van agreed in a growl, "there are probably Dire

Steeds from the Eternal Guards."

"By the Celestial Winds," said Rodregas, "I might be as strong as a Celestial Lion, but we will get chopped to insignificant pieces until we have decent armor and weapons."

"But why would they keep the armor?" growled Doi'van. "These people do not seem to be warriors. What good would it do them?" Doi'van tossed his wild black mane of hair and his eyes lit with rage that more than matched Rodregas's.

Rodregas suddenly realized that he better not feed the Hellborn's rage. He knew those with Infernal blood's legendary reputation for berserker rages. They seldom survived the rampages but were nearly unstoppable when they fell into one.

Rodregas breathed deeply, trying to lower his own anger and frustration. Jordane stepped outside the room Rodregas had been staying in and into the small clearing that was the center of the Nymph Dwello, the tent like structure that they used for houses.

"Gentleman, please," said Jordane. "You must have understood that this village took a monumental risk in taking you in. The only way Imeraldä could get the support of the dwello's elders was to offer the bounty of the Eternal Guard's equipment."

As if called from Jordane's words, Imeraldä landed in the clearing, leaping from one of the nearby trees. She looked a bit out of breath, like she had sprinted at a run to the Dwello.

She took a quick look at Doi'van and Rodregas and paled. Doi'van's eyes were literally glowing red, and he was tossing his horned head with his wild black hair flying. Imeraldä had not seen him in such a mood before, not even during the battle with the slave caravan.

Imeraldä thought Rodregas was only marginally better. The muscles of his neck and shoulders were hunched up and she could feel his anger through her bond with him. But he was also breathing deeply, and through the bond she knew he was trying to control himself. Imeraldä saw that Rodregas was also watching Doi'van. She thought he also recognized the danger of a Hellborn rage.

Imeraldä reached out to Rodregas first to get him to calm down and help manage Doi'van. Imeraldä focused on their bond and looked him in the eyes and said, "Rodregas getting angry will not change things, let us sit down and talk to the village elders. They are thankful for what we have done. They need payment for their risk, but they understand we have needs."

Rodregas nodded and seemed to be calming down until Jordane spoke, "No, you made your agreement. Imeraldä, you have said that the equipment of the Eternal Guard was ours. While our warriors are not as renown as some other races, we have several worthy of such armor and good gear is critical for our own survival."

Imeraldä could see both men's renewed rage at Jordane's words. She knew she should calm them down, but her first thought was how stupid men could be, men of all races. Sure, it would have been great for them to get their better-quality armor, but they were only alive because of her.

She was the one who had to come back and shot the last guards with the Black Yew bow. She was no warrior but had gone back with only a few arrows and rescued them. She had patched them up, rounded up the rescued slaves and sought a refuge.

"Are you insane?" she asked them in a voice that was as cold as her anger.

Imeraldä, her voice dripping scorn, added, "It was only because one of the slaves had family at the local village that we could find this refuge. Then, no matter how valiant the efforts of healer Durien, he barely kept you two from death's door."

"So, what did I do?" she asked the two men. "I nearly ran myself to exhaustion fetching Jordane to heal you. I was using my relationship to rescue you. Who I have known less than a season. And now that I have gone through all this effort you are going to get mad. Mad at the only reason you two are alive to complain at all? Well, to the Infernal River with you." With that, Imeraldä turned and jumped back into the trees.

The half Nymph's anger, though not meant to cool the warriors, had that effect as both men stood in shock at Imeraldä's normally calm demeanor. Doi'van wilted like a flower without water in the sun of the Burning Lands. The great Hellborn literally sat down on the ground. Rodregas sagged as the truth behind the half Ælf's words sank in.

Jordane stood watching the scene, without his normal expression of cheer. Finally, Rodregas turned to Jordane and said, "Imeraldä is right and I apologize for our anger. We misplaced it. My life and the life of my friend are well worth the price. We are in your debt."

At Rodregas' words Jordane nodded and then stepped into the trees, disappearing as the Nymphs had a habit of doing when in nature.

"I had better go apologize to Imeraldä," said Rodregas.

"You should wait awhile and let her rage cool first," suggested Doi'van slowly. He spoke as one who was awfully familiar with rage.

Rodregas realized that Doi'van was probably right, so he sat back and tried to think of the right words to speak when the timing was better.

Unfortunately, when Rodregas did speak to Imeraldä, his explanations and apology were not well received. She listened but seemed to have little sympathy. He decided that the only thing left to do was for him and Doi'van to get what gear they could, and head back out.

CHAPTER 12
TO WALK AN OLD PATH

It surprised Rodregas to find a pile of equipment outside his door the next morning, and Imeraldä sorting through the pile. It appeared to be mostly their equipment plus miscellaneous pieces of slaver gear.

Doi'van stood watching nearby, clearly not sure what to make of it any more than Rodregas.

When Rodregas tried to apologize again, Imeraldä ignored him and instead said, "We traded the Eternal Guard equipment for safe harbor here at the village for healing. But there were also regular slavers. I claimed their equipment, and any money that was in their personal money pouches."

"Your armor got pretty chopped up," she continued, "and Doi'van did not have any armor to start with. I have been trading excess gear and coins to have your leather armor repaired, and to refit some other armor to fit Doi'van. We still have our three horses, but none of them were too great to begin with. The two grays were good for pulling carriages, the other was too old."

"True," Rodregas said, nodding his agreement.

"Jordane knows horses," she went on, "and we could trade our three horses for one of the Eternal Guards' horses. I will be honest; he is a big ugly brute and his Dire blood is marginal. But Jordane thinks he can handle Doi'van's weight. The Nymphs were not that interested in keeping him because he is too big for them."

Doi'van said, "A steed that can handle me? That would make an agreeable change."

Imeraldä continued, "he along with the two best of the slavers' horses that I claimed. That means we now have three decent riding horses. Not the warhorses I know you want, but an upgrade on what we had. The local armorer was also able to piece together some chain mail that was decent quality and a good leather weapon harness for Doi'van. The chain mail should fit over both of your leather armors."

Imeraldä added, "I could recover only about a score of the arrows we used, but I have been working with some wood nymphs and the fletcher and we now have an excellent quality of arrows."

Doi'van, at her motion towards his armor, picked up the pile of chain mail and tried it over his head. The opening on top fit over his huge horned head. Doi'van guessed that it had been the chain of the large overweight slaver that he had killed. While the equipment was of average quality, Rodregas was smiling because there were three sets of everything plus a pack horse for equipment.

Imeraldä was planning on joining them. While that was what his heart hoped for, he was not sure if it was the smartest move.

When they were working on putting the tack on the horses, he asked her. "Imeraldä, I want to make sure you want to continue with us. I mean I love being with you, but while Doi'van and I are warriors, when you joined us it was only as a travel companion. If you want to stay with the village, or stay with Jordane, I will understand." He paused for a moment before adding, "you know they will hunt us, if not because of Ravenhurr's death, then because of the missing Eternal Guards."

"You know that I killed more slavers with the Black Yew bow than either you or Doi'van?" asked Imeraldä with a snort.

"Your abilities are not the question," Rodregas responded. "As a Forest Nymph and an archer, you have shown yourself deadly. As you gain control over your magical powers, you will only become more dangerous. The question is whether you want to fight?"

Imeraldä nodded, and she hesitated. "I will be honest," she said. "I am a little torn, I have never been as afraid as during and after the battle. I have truly come to care for both of you. I have met few men of such character as to fight to save children, especially against the Guild of the Celestial Path and all their power." She continued, "I want to be with you. I want to share this journey, but the two of you were so close to dying on me, and next time I might not save you and you might die...," she paused. "I could handle dying, but I am not sure I could handle having you die in my arms."

"Imeraldä," said Doi'van, "we must all walk our own paths. Rodregas and I have made a choice, we will fight.

Whether the Gods are on our side, we will fight. You need to find your own path. You are talented and young and have the world at your feet. We cherish the time that you joined us."

Rodregas nodded, Doi'van's words had captured his own thoughts. He was no boy to put his own needs over another. "I agree, I cherish the time we have had together, but you must walk your own path. The Grimoires and mithril chain and bow are yours to keep. My gifts to you. Your gifts to me were far greater."

"So where do you go now?" asked Imeraldä. "You can't look for slavers or patrols on the road; they will be reinforced after the caravan went missing."

Rodregas nodded. His thoughts had traveled in a similar direction. "I have been thinking about what you said, about it making sense for me to get a greater sigil. I have more magic than I need. There is only one other group besides the Guild that are allowed to give sigils, the Knights of the Soaring Stars."

Imeraldä and Doi'van were intrigued by what Rodregas was hinting at. He continued, "I was a squire in the Knighthood who was never raised. As you probably know they do not raise most squires to knighthood. Only those of the most noble blood and those of greatest talent in both magic and the arts of a warrior. I was neither. I had thought I would make a career in the army of the Ramig Empire," he paused after admitting that. His time as a squire was like a dream to him, and his time in the army had been a living nightmare.

"Once a year, directly after they raise this year's fresh group of knights, they hold a great competition. This is a five-day tournament which comes to a head in a grand melee battle of the finalist. Any squire is eligible to compete who has enough magic to take at least a lessor sigil. They raise the winner of this competition to knighthood," Rodregas added.

"You mean to enter the tournament for the right to knighthood and a greater sigil?" asked Doi'van.

"I have been thinking about it since Imeraldä suggested a sigil would really help me. They hold the tournament twenty days after mid-summer at the Great Cathedral of Heaven. I believe that to be in about ten days and it is about a seven-day ride from this village," said Rodregas.

"You would challenge for knighthood," said Imeraldä quietly. "That is not a terrible idea, while the Guild will hunt for you, they would not expect you to be in such an event. At the Cathedral other warriors will surround you. They would have no room to suspect you."

"There are a few problems. I would need to show proof that I was a squire, which I have," said Rodregas. As he spoke, he reached into his pouch and pulled out his old squire patch. He showed them the old beaten cloth, the one memento that he had taken with him from his old life. The only problem would be if someone asked too many questions about when and where he had trained.

"It might not work," said Rodregas. "but I think it worth the effort to try."

Doi'van nodded but said, "it is a worthy goal. But what of me? The knighthood will not welcome a Hellborn at the Cathedral as they assume we follow the Infernal Daemons."

Rodregas nodded but said, "If you are ok with calling yourself and acting as my sworn man, you could enter the Cathedral and stay with me. They won't be happy about it, but they cannot challenge who I bring with me."

"I would love to figure out a way to smuggle you into the Sigil Chamber, but that is not likely... but we can try to figure out a way," Rodregas added.

"And what about Nymphs?" asked Imeraldä.

"What do you mean?" asked Rodregas.

"If I was your sworn 'man' could you also bring me into the Cathedral?" she asked.

Rodregas nodded, "yes, Orqui and Ælves have joined the knighthood in the past. Nymphs have never shown an interest in joining the knighthood."

"I am still hesitant to say that your cause is mine. But I wish to keep traveling with you two. I have always heard stories of the knights and would enjoy visiting the Cathedral of the Heavens. It is supposed to be a place of great magic and the location of many myths and stories."

Rodregas nodded, he could not help smiling. He enjoyed the company of the two of them. It would be good to continue to travel together.

The next day Imeraldä arranged to send a group of fellow Forest Nymphs back to The Farm to put a roof on the old farmhouse. It was probably not worth the cost of some of their excess equipment and limited coins, but the three of them all had wonderful memories of the farm and liked the idea of putting a roof back on the structure. The Nymphs with their connection with nature were the only humanoids unlikely to be attacked by the Dire Cats.

The next morning Rodregas had his stuff all spread out in the room he had been using, organizing what would go where. They had left the trunk in the barn back at the farm, but much of its contents was now in his saddlebag.

When Jordane walked in, Rodregas signaled the tall Nymph to wait a moment, as he rolled his gear up. He was wrapping some of the Grimoires they were not reading, and the small mechanical toy frog that he had picked up in Ravenhurr's laboratory, when Jordane made a funny sound and stepped forward.

Jordane seemed to be staring at the contents of the blanket, and Rodregas wondered if he had recognized a grimoire. Jordane pointed at the newly wrapped blanket and said, "excuse me, but can I see that?"

Rodregas nodded and curiously handled the half-wrapped package over to the Nymph, wondering what had captured his attention. The Nymph slowly laid the package on the bed and unwrapped it. His hand passed over the contents in a motion similar to what he had done while working on Rodregas. To Rodregas' surprise, he stopped at the small toy frog. Jordane glanced over to him as if asking for permission and Rodregas nodded his ok.

Jordane reached down and carefully picked up the small frog and cupped it in his hands. His eyes were closed in concentration. He looked up at Rodregas with a confused expression and asked, "do you know what this is?"

"Not really, I found it in Raven Keep. It felt of magic, so I took it. I thought it might be worth something."

Jordane smiled and laughed as he said, "worth something indeed. This is a lessor Sigil of Healing."

It was Rodregas who gasped this time and said, "Infernals Rivers! We had a Sigil of Healing all this time? If we had inscribed this sigil back at The Farm, we would never have needed your help."

Jordane smiled and said, "not sure about that, but it would have made the healing a lot easier."

The two of them quickly gathered the others. Doi'van laughed at the irony of recognizing what they had had all this time, only after Jordane had worked so hard. Imeraldä seemed a little embarrassed that she had not recognized its purpose.

All agreed that no matter what might happen with the greater sigils that the three should inscribe the minor Sigil of Healing. They well knew its benefits to warriors and mages alike. Jordane agreed to do the inscribing and show the others the technique. In return Imeraldä would inscribe Jordane, who was also eager for the sigil. Though it was fully possible for someone with magic to apply it to themselves.

Jordane had his hand out with the palm facing up, with the frog sitting in the middle. At Jordane's direction, Rodregas put his own hand, palm down, on top of it. Jordane then said, "This will hurt a bit, it will feel like someone is drawing a pattern under your skin. If you pull away before it is done, you will mess up the pattern and it will use up your magic without adding the benefits of the sigil."

As Jordane finished speaking he looked in Rodregas' eyes until he nodded his understanding. He knew what was coming. He could feel Jordane's magic pouring across his hands and into the frog. A sensation emanating from the frog filled his senses. Without Rodregas' conscious will, his own magic raised from the core of his being. The two magic forces seemed to mix and then enter the frog. They seemed to pour from the frog back into his own body. That power felt like a thousand tiny knives digging into his flesh.

His body tightened and he could feel Jordane's hands hold him firm. Rodregas struggled to keep his arm from spasming in pain. He knew that Jordane could not really keep his arm from moving if he fought too hard. He kept thinking the ordeal would be over soon. When it continued, he worried about his ability to keep from jerking away from the small frog figurine. Just when he was sure that he could not keep his arm still the pain reduced and finally stopped.

As Jordane relaxed his grip and released him, Rodregas shook his arm and then his body, trying to feel the difference. It felt almost like someone had drawn all over him from the inside, but there was no visible difference. There was no sign that a bit of his own magic had been used up in creating a permanent effect.

Rodregas sat and watched as Doi'van and then Imeraldä undertook the inscription of the minor sigil. From Rodregas' perspective, the next two seemed to withstand the pain a lot better than then he had.

After all three were completed, Imeraldä used her magic to inscribe the enhancement on Jordane. The healing sigil was the only sigil commonly used by magic users. A few magi used sigils that improved memory or allowed one to store excess magic. But the enhanced healing and longer life that was achieved made it the one minor sigil that was worth the cost.

After the sensation faded Rodregas felt no different from before. Rodregas had the feeling that Jordane would have liked to keep the little frog. It was a powerful tool in the hands of an Elemental Healer like Jordane, but Rodregas was not willing to give it up, and Jordane never asked.

The next morning, they headed out for the Cathedral of the Heavens, the center of the Order of the Soaring Stars, and one of the most important spiritual locations for everyone who worshiped the Celestial Gods.

CHAPTER 13
A CHALLENGING PAST

They arrived at the town that served the Cathedral of Heaven eight days later. It was late in the afternoon, and they were all tired from travel. They had to hustle through the town of Oravue to reach the fortress in time to register for the upcoming tournament.

Oravue was a good-sized town, with paved roads of brick winding up and down the sides of the hill. Though separated by a fair distance because of the magic of the ley lines, the Cathedral visually dominated the town. Rodregas thought the town was one of the most beautiful that he knew. It disappointed him to have to hurry through it without pausing to get to the Cathedral before dark.

While the Cathedral was one of the most impressive fortresses in the known world. The town, in contrast was without walls or visible defenses of any kind, unless you counted all the winding stairs and streets. That quickly got the three companions lost several times on their way to the Cathedral.

They had built the Cathedral of the Heavens into and around the top of a small granite hilltop with short cliffs and a river making for a natural fortification on three sides. The walls were almost a hundred feet high in most places and seemed constructed of the very sides of the hill.

Because they built directly in the very bedrock of the earth, knocking down the fortress walls was not an option for an opposing army.

They had tapped the powerful ley lines to provide magical protections as great as the physical. The Cathedral's defenses gave it the reputation as one of the most impenetrable fortress in the Eastern Kingdoms. Rodregas feared that what could not be taken by force, could be easily taken by politics and fear.

Once through the enormous gates, Rodregas, Doi'van and Imeraldä came into full view of the Great Cathedral of the Heavens. The Cathedral served as both fortress and a temple to the Celestial Gods, and its thick walls were a balance of the practical and the artistic. Its towering white walls were adorned with statues and engravings. With the highest floor adorned with slim stained-glass windows and arches and on the heights were a series of small towers and domes.

Rodregas had forgotten how striking the building was, and all three stood to admire it for a long moment before moving forward into the large open courtyard in front of the central building.

In front of the Cathedral's central keep was a grandly engraved table of gleaming oak. Which looked to be more suitable for the dining hall of a noble than the practical service it was providing in the great courtyard. The three men behind the table were Lord Knights of the Order, behind them stood young squires eager to be of service at the word of the Lord Knights. In front of the table was a line of men who were warriors waiting to talk to the knights.

The knighthood was split into two grand divisions; those with minor sigils who were Knights of the Order, and the rare Lord Knights who had gained the greater sigils. From their ranks was chosen the Grand Marshal of the Order, the physical and spiritual leader of the Order of the Soaring Stars.

Rodregas' eyes fell on a man who sat in a beautifully carved chair, a match for the table that sat just behind the knights. He was tall and graceful with striking dark eyes and features. His long dark hair was pulled back. He wore not the clothing of the knights but the robes of an Immortalist Sorcerer. Across his chest was a sash. Rodregas guessed him to be either a special ambassador to the Knights or possibly Vandret, the Immortalist Ambassador at large.

Rodregas' blood froze at the sight, though he did his best to remain casual. He knew that the Guild would have a representative at the Cathedral but had not expected him to be so closely watching the registration table.

Rodregas fell into old habits of survival. He kept his eyes to himself and embraced the feeling of the fatigue from travel on the open road.

When it became his turn to approach the table, Rodregas stood there silently. The knight, an older man with a short gray beard, who was missing his left hand, waved him forward. The Lord Knight slowly looked up at the tall figure before him and after a quick examination went to the oddly mismatched pair that stood at each shoulder.

"You are a squire who wishes to register for the tournament?" asked the Lord Knight. While the Knight had probably asked this to many people that day, his tone suggested genuine curiosity at the odd group.

Rodregas grunted acknowledgment and dropped his hand with the Patch of his Knightly Chapter in it. The

Knight Captain picked it up and studied the detailed patterns woven into the fabric.

"Chapter and heredity?" the Knight asked.

"Sir Saurrien was my mentor, Quirren was his mentor, and Bitress was his, Chapter of the Silver Mace," Rodregas answered.

The Knight nodded. The answer matched the pattern on the patch. "I thought Sir Saurrien was long dead? What is your name?" he asked.

"I was his last student, my name is Rodregas," he said. The knight waited, expecting more, but that was all he said. The knight waited a moment, then shrugged, and wrote his name on the scroll in front of him.

Rodregas' heart froze as the sorcerer stood up and strode over to the table. He reached out and casually touched the shoulder of the Lord Knight to get his attention.

"Sir Intreg, do you mind asking a few questions to confirm his status?" The Knight seemed uncomfortable under the hand of the sorcerer but nodded and said to Rodregas, "What is the eighth law of Chivalry?"

"Thou shalt never offer combat to someone who is not equal in strength, unless in defense of the honor of the Order, for Justice for the oppressed or in defense of the weak," he answered.

Sir Intreg nodded and then asked, "a question of law: two messenger couriers stop at a keep with priority messages and switch out his horses. The local lord, who owns the fresh horses, finds that both of the messenger's horses are lame, and are no longer any good. One messenger is from a neighboring lord and one from the Guild of the Celestial Path. What rights does the lord have in this situation?" Rodregas noticed the sorcerer seemed to stiffen at the question.

Rodregas' mind swirled. The first questions had been easy, but it had been a very long time since he had studied law. The sorcerer's body language directed his memory to the answer.

Rodregas said, "the local lord is responsible for replacing the messenger's lame old horse with one of equal value to what they gave. There is nothing to be done for the Immortalist messenger's horse. It is the responsibility of the local lords to provide mounts for the Guild at the local lord's expense." He made sure his voice remained rough with no emotion coloring his response, just a simple squire giving a by-the-book answer.

The Lord Knight nodded and said, "welcome to the tournament squire Rodregas." He then turned to look up at the sorcerer and asked him, "any other questions, Ambassador Vandret?"

The sorcerer addressed his question directly to Rodregas, "I noticed you have a Hellborn with you. Bringing one of his kind to the Cathedral of the Heavens, shows that you would insult the very faith of the Knights?"

Rodregas knew this question would come up and had the natural answer, "They are my sworn followers, and are sworn to the All-Father Grímnr." Such an oath could not honorably be challenged.

"Truly?" the sorcerer said. "the Oath of Fealty by one of Infernal birth? I would see that." He turned to Doi'van who loomed over all of them. Doi'van had watched the show with a cold interest.

The sorcerer spoke with a command that dripped venom, "on your knees Hellborn and swear the oath of fealty, in the name of the All-Father to this squire, where we can all see."

Doi'van paused for a heartbeat, and then pulled his sword out in a smooth gesture. For a moment Rodregas thought a battle was to be had, but then Doi'van dropped to his knees in front of Rodregas. He took the sword onto his arms, as if in morning sword meditation, and spoke the words of the Oath.

"I swear my life and fealty to the Squire Rodregas in the name of the All-Father Grímnr and the Celestial Gods."

Rodregas nodded and responded as was required, "As the All-Father Grímnir protects and guards his people. I swear to honor your oath in the name of the All-Father." Rodregas reached down and picked up the sword across Doi'van's arms and lifted it up. "As I lift up your sword, so do I lift up your honor and make it mine."

As he finished the oath, he handed the sword back to Doi'van, who responded with the final, "My arm shall be your arm, my sword your sword, my honor your honor, for my whole life from this moment."

Rodregas had expected to have to claim his followers as bound by a life oath of fealty. A knight would never have demanded to see the oath sworn. He felt guilt seize his stomach at what had happened. Doi'van had been forced to swear the oath, due to not wanting to blow their cover.

Rodregas swore to himself that he would lift the oath as soon as they could. That Doi'van had trusted him enough to say such an oath, which could put his very soul in jeopardy if broken, was a powerful statement to their growing friendship and humbled Rodregas.

Rodregas looked back at the sorcerer who seemed surprised at watching the oath sworn, "satisfied, sir?"

The sorcerer waved his hand, dismissing them, and without a word went back to his chair, sitting down as if a king in his throne. The Lord Knight called for a squire who he commanded to find them a room. Rodregas sensed that the Lord Knight was not happy with what had happened, but he said no words of apology.

As a young squire led away the three, Rodregas asked the boy about the sorcerer at the table.

"That is the Immortalist Vandret, the High Ambassador from the Guild. He is powerful. We are told to do whatever he commands, but also told to stay as far away from him as possible," said the young boy who could not have been much over twelve years old.

Rodregas nodded and said, "sounds like excellent advice."

Rodregas looked over at Doi'van and Imeraldä as the three entered the room. Doi'van looked grim but brushed off Rodregas's apologies. After a brief rest and finding food, the other two headed out to see what they could learn about what he would face in the tournament.

Doi'van looked no happier when the two returned late that evening. Rodregas almost had to smile. "Is it that bad?" he asked.

Doi'van missed his amused tone, or he was simply not in the mood to hear it. "The news is not good," Doi'van agreed.

Doi'van grabbed the far too small stool beside the bed, which was the only other piece of furniture in the little dorm room that they had been assigned. Rodregas knew it was only because of his visitor status and having 'servants' that he had his own room. Most squires would share housing during the tournament.

Rodregas watched the stool curiously as Doi'van sat, to see if it would hold the massive weight of the Hellborn. His guess was that the weight would crush it. To his surprise it held, though the stool gave a groan at the weight.

"We counted over a hundred here for the tournament, all are trained warriors. Most should not be any problem, but at least a handful are of the blood," Doi'van said.

"I think a few are minor sigil warriors," said Imeraldä.

"If they already have sigils, why are they competing?" asked Doi'van.

"She is probably right," Rodregas said. "If someone who was a squire managed to get a sigil, it would tempt him to come back and earn the title and the prestige of knighthood."

"It does not matter if they are of the blood or minor sigil warriors," said Doi'van. "There are a few who will be a challenge physically, but that is not the problem. Either way, you should be physically more powerful. It is the nature of the competitions that I am worried about." Doi'van paused as he ordered the coming conversation in his mind.

Rodregas knew him well enough to wait until he was ready. It had surprised Rodregas when Doi'van had refused to take back his oath when they had had some privacy. Doi'van said he took his oaths too seriously to play such games. So Rodregas had sworn the same oath to Doi'van, which Doi'van had accepted. Rodregas felt good at this shared oath.

Doi'van though was more focused on the task than the oath. He stated, "each competition is worth points. The top five winners of each round of competition earns five points; those that place six through ten earn four points, eleven through fifteen earn three points and so on. There are five unique events if you include the final melee."

Rodregas nodded. He had not remembered the point system, but he knew well that a knight is unique for his mastering of five distinct fighting styles.

Doi'van continued, "the first they call 'open fist'. Which does not really make any sense, it is barehanded without armor. I think you are likely to do very well with that contest. In fact, I think you would be wise to finish as one of the winners. The next is the bow...," Doi'van glancing at Imeraldä.

Rodregas could not help but smile, "I know you guys think of my skill with the bow, in terms of my inability to use the Black Yew bows. But really, I can shoot a bow fine."

Doi'van and Imeraldä looked at him doubtfully. "The challenge," said Doi'van, "is not to be good but to out-shoot over one hundred other highly skilled warriors, and the targets are multiple and difficult including a moving target. Unfortunately, all the targets are within normal range for a human. Your strength will not help. The pleasant news is this is a competition of skill and they provide the bows. The unwelcome news is that it is up to each competing squire to have his own equipment for the other three competitions."

"they limit the sword and the shield competition to light armor. You will be at a disadvantage against some with better armor, but you should still finish high. The genuine problem will be the fourth and fifth rounds. The completions with the lance and the melee with the mace. Both have no limit to the armor that can be worn, and the lance is a mounted competition."

"You should see some of the horses!" said Imeraldä. "They are beautiful." She smiled, but Doi'van did not see beautiful animals but a problem.

"She is correct, most have trained warhorses and more than a few are Dire Steeds. I will be honest with you,

Rodregas, I am not sure that this will work. These warriors are trained in the lance's use and their warhorses will negate your personal advantage in physical might."

Doi'van paused and said, "the biggest problem is that you don't have decent armor and your chief competition will. They're not allowed full plate, that is reserved for greater sigil warriors, but the best are close to it. I am not sure how you can survive such a fight. If you succeed the ultimate competition is an open melee of the top ten finalist wearing full armor and fighting with mace or warhammer. Your body is far stronger than theirs, but not as strong as night bronze or mithril." Doi'van shook his head. "I don't know how you can compete with simple steel chain mail against all the top finishers at once!"

"Rodregas," Doi'van said, "I think you should give up on this task. The Cathedral is busy and none will know or care if we leave."

Imeraldä nodded, but something about the way she stood told Rodregas that she knew he would not do this.

"Have you done the math?" Rodregas asked. "What if I get five points on the hand-to-hand and five with the sword and shield and maybe two with the bow? Would twelve points get me to the final melee?"

"Unlikely," answered Doi'van. "I have asked around and fifteen seems to be the magic number. It varies year to year, but that is what we need to get to the last round."

"Did you know that three times during the history of the Order warriors have finished with perfect twenty-five points? The last time was over forty years ago by 'the traitor.'" Imeraldä explained, "I was talking to one of the older knights."

"Who is this traitor?" asked Doi'van.

"I don't know," answered Imeraldä.

"It is Lord General Sigoria of the Eternal Guard," Rodregas said. "He was once the Grand Marshal of the Order before he turned traitor and joined the Immortalists. He is hated by the knighthood, but he was a magnificent warrior, the kind that we have to face if we fight the Eternal Guard." Rodregas responded.

"We can't be afraid of the competition. I may die, but if I win, I can earn a greater sigil, maybe even bring Doi'van into the chamber as my servant. If both Doi'van and I had a greater sigil, we would be much more likely to survive the upcoming battles," Rodregas said.

"We would still get spitted like a pig in the roasting pit without decent armor," said Doi'van, "but as the Gods have yet to provide the armor, we will show these human squires the armor of our faith and the armor of our courage. I just don't enjoy having to watch you fight such battles, and not be able to fight myself," growled Doi'van in his deep voice.

"Yeah, what he said," Imeraldä stated, "I wish I could do the bow competition for you. I could get you five points there even with a regular bow, otherwise I am happy to watch you big boys show how tough and strong you are."

Rodregas smiled at Doi'van's and Imeraldä's courage, even though their personalities were opposites. Imeraldä was as light-hearted as Doi'van was thoughtful.

"One question," Rodregas asked, "do we have a hammer or a mace?"

Two days later the dawn found Rodregas facing his first opponent. This first foe looked very young. The warrior nodded to him like Rodregas should know him. Rodregas wondered if this man had been a friend of the previous occupant of his new body? He looked like he might speak, but Rodregas shook his head.

They marked the great outer courtyard off with chalk into ten squares. The contestants stood around the squares waiting their turn to enter. The watching knights would push anyone who fell out during the fight back into the square. The knights and non-competing squires and pages were not allowed within a long pace of the squares. Rodregas knew Imeraldä and Doi'van were atop the wall, the closest spot allowed for spectators who were not of the knighthood.

They had already fought two rounds before Rodregas had his first turn. The rules were simple. Two went in, and one came out. The contestants were bare of hand and foot. There were no fancy speeches to start the match. A bell sounded and the next round began.

Rodregas kept his weight low and his hands up. Doi'van and he had discussed the best approach. Both agreed the best strategy would be to use his full strength and speed to be quick and as brutal as he could without killing. Doi'van suggested body blows were best, as a full-strength punch into the face would likely kill a normal human.

The boy who faced him was fair-haired and smiling, seeming to relish the match. His stance was like Rodregas's own footwork. Rodregas went slowly but steadily, keeping his guard up. The boy kept his hands up. When Rodregas went in low, the boyish man took the blows to his body and went for Rodregas' face. Against another opponent, it was the right move.

Unfortunately for the boy, his blow seemed to come at Rodregas slowly. Rodregas easily dodged as he landed a forceful blow to his opponent's chest. Rodregas was used to sparring with Doi'van, and was surprised, when his opponent went flying into the line of watchers and did not get back up.

Rodregas waited a moment and then looked at the knight who stood outside the match. The knight did not look as surprised at the quickness of the match as Rodregas. He nodded toward Rodregas. He left the square, and the knight sent the next two in.

By mid-morning Rodregas had cleared out all comers into his square without major effort. He noticed that all the other squares were still going on. His matches had ended faster than the others. His body's balance of strength and speed were at a full advantage in hand-to-hand fighting. He fought three others at the end of the afternoon; all three had won their group of matches. Rodregas thought they might have been tough opponents if they had not been so beaten up. Between the natural durability of his body and the minor Sigil of Healing, he was feeling fine.

The knights were clearly trying to find the best five among the competitors. They were not trying to find out who was the best among the five. Rodregas watched several fighters that clearly were of the blood or had minor sigils, but he did not fight any that could have offered him a genuine challenge.

At the end, after he defeated his last opponents, they tied a bright yellow ribbon to his upper arm and wrote down his name as a top five finishers. The top five got bright yellow armbands, the sixth to tenth finishers white bands, the eleventh through fifteenth red bands, sixteenth through twentieth blue bands and twenty-first to twenty-fifth received a green band.

Rodregas felt more nervous the next day with the

archery competition. While the knights provided the bows for all contestants, they did not have them available for practice. The only bows that the three had were the Black Yews, which Rodregas continued to struggle to use for even the simplest of shots.

While Rodregas had learned to shoot the bow when he was trained as a squire, and was proficient in it, he had not shot one in a long time. He trailed behind the others and watched them shoot. There were five shots that you had to make: a man shaped target at twenty paces, a crouching man shape at thirty, a standard round target on a hay bale at forty, and another round target at fifty paces. Finally, there was a round target dragged in hops and jumps across the field with a rope pulled by squires in armor.

As the first round of contestants lined up behind the rope to shoot, Rodregas watched the technique of the better archers and mentally went through his old training. He knew the best archers focused on their breathing and keeping your eyes where you wanted the arrow to go. Releasing the string at two-thirds of the way through your exhale was the best way to hit your target.

Rodregas became nervous as he waited. The quality of the archery impressed him. Everyone knew what they were about. He ended up being behind a slim youthful man. Rodregas almost thought the squire might have some Ælf blood. It also looked like he might have a broken nose from the previous day's competition.

The youthful man did very well, hitting all five targets. His shot on the moving target only nicked the edge, but that was still impressive.

Rodregas stepped forward and picked up the bow. It felt light and a little awkward. Rodregas focused on his breathing. He had five targets and five arrows. He shot at the nearest target shaped like a man. The arrow sailed over its right shoulder. Rodregas tensed up, but knew that would kill any chances of hitting his next targets.

He released the second arrow at the crouching man and the arrow hit low to the left, but he hit the target. He nailed the next standard target almost in the middle but missed the last two completely.

Rodregas was among those who were first out of this round of the tournament and spent the rest of the day watching the archery competition. The only relief he felt was that only one of the other winners with the yellow ribbons on their arm also gained a second one. He found out his name was Geriodon. Rodregas also saw that two others who had the white second place ribbons from the day before also earned white ribbons in the day's contest. That meant that Geriodon was winning so far with ten points. The other two, named Karun and Nordien, both had eight points.

On the third morning, Rodregas stood ready to enter his square. The format was the same as the first day. He thought his chances were better today. He was used to the sword and shield.

Rodregas stood with his chain mail over his repaired studded leather armor; a long sword and a shield, both from the dead slavers were in his hands. The rules were not to fight to the death. A knight stood in the middle of the square and would declare the winner of the match.

Rodregas' first opponent looked like a grizzled army veteran; he had a red ribbon and a blue ribbon, so he was a man of some skill. Rodregas knew he had to do well today, or he had no chance. He stepped into the square. The sands of the ground shifted slightly under his weight as he circled his opponent.

The veteran was taking him seriously, going in slowly with his knees bent and his feet keeping active. Rodregas would have no skill advantage here. Rodregas was hesitant to bash his sword too much, as it was of average quality. While the sword should be fine for his first match, he hoped to be fighting all day today.

He went forward, leading with his round shield. He pushed his opponent back with some hard swings. Rodregas swung his shield aggressively, he hit the man's sword with his shield and then banged the other man's shield hard. Rodregas' goal was to see if he could out muscle the man while staying protected by the shield. It worked! His opponent, though set for a heavy blow, was not expecting the strength of Rodregas' bash.

Still, his opponent was too good to fall, even when surprised. As he half fell backwards, he used the momentum to slide down, and try to land a blow under the shield. Rodregas had both quickness and strength on his side. He blocked the blow with his sword and then bashed down quick and hard multiple times with his shield. He thought he heard a bone break.

Rodregas paused, and the knight signaled him as victor with a finger to the Heavens. Rodregas followed this pattern throughout the day. He kept using his sword more to block than to attack and kept using his shield offensively. This allowed him to take advantage of his unnatural strength to overwhelm his foes.

According to the contest rules, he could replace his sword or shield after every fourth match if need be. By the last match, he was on his third and final shield. Most of the rest of the matches were with squires with no ribbons. But as the afternoon wrapped up his last match was against Karun who had two second place white ribbons on her arm.

Rodregas was sure this match would decide who got the yellow first place ribbon and who would get the white. If Rodregas won, it would give him ten total points after three competitions. It would give Karun twelve points if she once more came in second. If he lost, it would be much harder. Karun would have thirteen, and he would have nine points. He was not sure how Geriodon, or Nordien, or the other leading contestants were doing.

At the bell, the two circled. Karun was a sizeable woman. She was tall and unusually muscular. She moved with an easy cat-like grace and was attractive, in an about to kick your ass, athletic way. She was probably of the blood and strong. She had her brown hair woven into a tight braid and wore a well-fitting chain and leather armor. Her sword and shield seemed to be of excellent quality.

Rodregas tried to get a good hold on his shield. It was battered and not looking good. The top of its handle was loose. His sword was possibly worse with chips and a crack starting high up. As the two circled each other, Rodregas' realized that his first impression, that she was of the blood, was clearly true. She was both quicker and stronger than a normal human. She was also highly skilled, and while not as physically gifted as Rodregas, she was powerful.

She was also intelligent. She must have been watching Rodregas in earlier matches, as she refused to let him get in close with her shield to his shield and let him out muscle her. She moved quickly and fluidly, keeping her distance.

Her sword wove in and out, back and forth. Rodregas blocked one blow only to find two others coming at him. He quickly found himself on the defensive and suffered both a cut on his upper hand and cheek. He worried that the knight would end the match and give Karun the victory.

He tried to use his speed to advantage and trap her sword. But he nearly lost his sword instead. He realized that he was outclassed. Her skills were better than his own and Rodregas' physical abilities were not so much greater than hers, as to counter her superior equipment.

For the first time in the tournament, Rodregas lost control of the flow of the match as suddenly she moved in, swinging hard. She went in close with her shield, wedging it to his, a move he had been trying to do, but he was not expecting her to initiate it. His shield was pushed to his left for just a second. She swung hard at his open side; he had time to block her stroke, but his sword shattered when the two swords collided. Her sword was at his throat before he could do anything and the officiating knight yelled a stop to the match, handing the yellow band to the smiling Karun and the white second place finish to Rodregas.

Doi'van and Imeraldä met him at the entrance to the cafeteria. Rodregas stalked in without looking at them and stood quietly in line to get a bowl of stew and a chunk of bread. They sat down away from where most of the other squires were eating. The other two sat quietly until all three had finished the repast.

"So how did Geriodon and Nordien finish?" asked Rodregas.

Doi'van spoke, "Geriodon finished first place which puts him in the total lead with a perfect fifteen points. Nordien only got a third-place red ribbon, so he has only eleven, Karun is now second with thirteen points."

Rodregas nodded. With only nine points he was

unlikely to compete in the final championship melee round. "Imeraldä, can you do me a favor?" Rodregas asked.

"Sure, but I am not sure how I can help," she said.

Rodregas nodded, but said, "Can you go around to the other top finishers and talk to them, and to the other squires and try to get a feel for them. See if you can find out who people want to win and why?"

The odd request confused Imeraldä, but she nodded, and after a few minutes slipped away to the food line and within moments was in an animated discussion with a few squires at another table. Who were happy to talk to the beautiful visitor.

Rodregas thought Doi'van might ask, but he showed no interest and instead said, "While most of the knights are too high and mighty to talk to a Hellborn, the staff is not so closed mouthed. Many of them have never seen a Hellborn and were curious to talk to one. I have learned a few interesting things. They say the greater sigils are guarded twenty-four hours a day in a magnificent chamber in the very heart of the Cathedral."

"And did you ask if they allowed in sworn men with a new knight?" asked Rodregas with a smile. He had known where the sigil chamber was located but was impressed that the Hellborn had found out intelligence, in a place where you would think none would be happy by his very presence.

"The topic did come up," said Doi'van with a chuckle like rocks in a landslide. "While guards are usually not allowed in, it is not unusual for close friends or advisors to go in with some of those of the blood. To share their wisdom on the best sigils to take on."

"I will assume," said Rodregas, "that they had never heard of a Nymph entering the chamber, much less one of the Hellborn?"

"Ælves are not uncommon and actually more Orqui than I expected. One servant thought Nymphs used to go in during his father's father's time, but not anytime recently. No one could even imagine a Hellborn going into the Chamber," agreed Doi'van.

"Well, as far behind as we are, we might not even get the chance to bully our way in," Rodregas said. Doi'van nodded in grim agreement, and that comment seemed to end the conversation.

As Rodregas headed out to the sands of the Cathedral arena for the jousting match, it relieved him to see Imeraldä waiting at the entrance to talk to him. She had been out all night on her mission.

"Well, I have to say, I am exhausted of talking, so I will make this quick," she said with her normal sunny smile. Rodregas had to admit she looked tired.

"First, Geriodon is much disliked. He is gruff, unfriendly and too serious to like. The squires and knights universally dislike him. This is his third attempt to achieve knighthood, and he has gotten closer each time. While he is the odds-on favorite to achieve it this year, no one wants him to win," she said.

"I chatted with him," she continued, "and he is rather unpleasant and needs to take a bath. But he is also straightforward. When I asked him why he wanted to be a knight..." she paused, then added, "he said that some damned knights have to stand up and fight."

"You think he is an honorable man?" Rodregas guessed.

"I think Geriodon is a 'holier than thou' stick in the mud, who needs to learn to bathe and not mumble when he speaks. And yes, he is probably one of the few men here that deserves knighthood."

Rodregas nodded and said, "What about Nordien?"

"Nordien is the opposite to Geriodon; smooth and friendly... and tried to have sex with me within our first conversation, which was also the only decent thing he said. He seems to really dislike Geriodon and Karun. He comes from a powerful blood line and rich family and feels he should already be a knight and not be forced to be in the tournament."

"So, why is Nordien in the tournament and not knighted the usual way?" Rodregas asked.

"From what I can gather, Nordien is friendly with the Immortalists, including Ambassador Vandret. Most people believe that he only wants to be knighted so he can then leave the knighthood and join the Eternal Guard as an officer."

Rodregas nodded. That was not too surprising. They usually make ex-knights officers. The training of squires was much prized and unmatched. But the officers of the Eternal Guard lived in much nicer style and luxury than the knighthood.

"The Grand Marshal might not be willing to stand up to the Immortalists, but he would be more than willing to skip giving knighthood to someone, who was planning to leave anyhow," said Rodregas.

They had made it to the stables and Doi'van put the saddle and tack onto Doom Hoof, the horse that Doi'van had been riding. The horse had some dire blood, but while big and strong the beast was slow, but he was the best horse they had for this kind of combat.

"So finally, Karun," said Imeraldä, "Not too much is known about her; she was an orphan and of the blood and strong. She is said to be very skilled, and she is liked well enough, but no one seems to be an actual friend. This is her first contest and trained by a knight errant. There is a rumor that she might be an actual Blood Princess, a child of a God. No one knew for sure or who that God might be."

"Really? That is rare if true. What is your gut instinct about her?" Rodregas asked.

"Well, I am not sure, but while she barely talked to me, I kind of liked her."

Rodregas nodded, he had a similar positive impression from his brief meeting.

"Thank you for looking into their backgrounds, Imeraldä. You should go get some sleep; the joust will go on for hours."

She nodded as he got in the saddle. But before he could ride out, she asked, "I don't suppose you want to explain why you wanted to know more about them?"

"I am not sure, just thinking about options," he answered. Then he pulled Doom Hoof through a wide turn and tried to get him moving and warmed up. If the beast felt any excitement or nervousness, he was not showing it. Which Rodregas admitted was better than the opposite reaction. But the horse felt sluggish compared to his own mount. Hopefully, the horse's positive qualities would shine in the tournament.

As Rodregas circled around the courtyard warming up his horse, he noticed fewer horses than he expected. After Doom Hoof seemed awake, he headed over to where Doi'van stood. For this competition they allowed each squire a servant to provide support, mostly help with equipment, especially fresh lances.

"Where is everyone?" he asked Doi'van.

Doi'van did not look up from the ground where he

was trying to straighten out a shield without doing more damage to it, and responded, "I wondered that myself. Apparently, most squires drop out by this point. A lot have been injured, especially during yesterday's sword and shield competition, and many others quit for not having any points. If you are going into the most dangerous part of the competition, where you may be seriously injured or killed, and you have only one or two points, why bother?"

Doi'van added, "to be honest, I am surprised how many are left. There are still quite a few naive fools out there."

"So how many are left now?" Rodregas asked.

"Fifty-four, on my last count," Doi'van said.

Rodregas was a little worried about his shield and wondered if he should jump in and rescue it from the powerful grip of the Hellborn, but he held his tongue and let Doi'van handle the equipment.

"I see you are employing the forces of the Infernal Realm to aid you in the joust," said a voice behind Rodregas.

Rodregas unfortunately recognized the voice as that of Ambassador Vandret, even before he turned and saw him standing there. Two nervous looking squires were standing behind him, one holding a glass and a bottle of wine. The tall graceful Immortalist wore dark robes of deepest black with swirling gold patterns embroidered on it. His hair was pulled back and to the side in an unusual looking style.

"My Lord," Rodregas responded. "Is there something that I can help you with?"

"I understand that your other servant, the Nymph girl, was out making inquiries last night," said Vandret.

Rodregas paused at that, unsure of how to respond.

Finally, he said, "it is always good to know who your enemies are, and who might be your friends."

"I don't think you have many friends here," said Vandret.

"I have those I need," responded Rodregas, "I hear that you are exceedingly popular. They say that Nordien carries your colors and is your champion."

Rodregas thought he saw the Ambassador's eyebrow rise slowly, but there was no hesitation to his response. "As an Ambassador to the knighthood, I have no favorites. Though as one who works to join the Celestials Gods in the Heavens, I have an abiding dislike for anything that stinks of the Infernal." His voice was smooth, very reasonable, and intolerably smug.

Rodregas spoke before he could help himself, "Really? I heard that you and the Guild Dealer Taiga, rather liked the smell of the Infernal. In fact, I heard that it smells very familiar to you."

Rodregas immediately felt ice in his belly at his words. He knew his hint at such knowledge was enough to turn Vandret fully against him. The Immortalist's eyes blazed with fury and Rodregas had no problem thinking the Infernal Realms were reflected in those cold eyes.

Strangely, it was the one who looked the part of an Infernal Daemon that broke the tense moment. Doi'van casually stood up to his impressive height and said, "this is the best I can do with this shield, and here is your lance." The Hellborn promptly handed Rodregas the items. As Rodregas sat on his horse juggling the gear Doi'van finished with saying, "now stop teasing the nice Ambassador and go win a pretty ribbon." His voice was light and teasing even though it was deep enough to vibrate rock.

Rodregas realized his best move was to go quickly, before the angry-looking sorcerer could act, and he moved Doom Hoof around and into line.

The judges seemed to pair up the contestants depending on the quality of the armor. Either that or Rodregas got lucky. His first opponent's armor was not much better than his own. As Doom Hoof plodded forward Rodregas landed a solid strike on his opponent's shield. It was probably no less than the strike he received in return. But Rodregas could hold on to his big steed and absorb the blow. His opponent landed on the ground with a crash. When you were knocked off your mount, you had the choice to get back on again and face the same opponent. The winner of two out of three rounds won the match.

Rodregas' opponent did not get up. He circled around and checked on the man. Rodregas could not tell if the man was alive or dead, so he dismounted and took off the man's helm. The man was covered in sweat and was surprisingly old. He was alive, if unconscious. A few young squire ran out and helped to drag the man to get medical care.

Rodregas' next opponent followed in like manner, though he got up and gave Rodregas a second round. Rodregas circled around to Doi'van who held his spare shields, and the provided lances. "This next one is wearing full plate armor, but it is just regular steel. If you can take him down, you should be in the top ten or fifteen," Doi'van said.

Rodregas flexed his shoulders. He might have the physical power of a Celestial Lion but blows from mounted lancers still hurt. "I think I need to change shields," he said.

Doi'van glanced at what remained of Rodregas' shield and nodded and handed him one of their other shields. It was not in great shape, but it was whole.

Rodregas watched a few of the other matches before it was his turn again. Except for him, everyone remaining wore half plate armor. Rodregas' next opponent was shining in the sun in his steel, which was better than him having to face night bronze, but still not very reassuring.

The flag fell and Rodregas dug his heals into Doom Hoof's side and the mount plodded forward. His opponent's horse looked almost as powerful, but much faster. The collision happened before Rodregas was fully expecting it, but he caught it with his shield. But he felt himself lift out of the saddle and hit the ground hard.

"Great," Rodregas muttered to himself, "he has a Dire Steed and better armor."

Rodregas rolled over and pushed himself up, Doom Hoof stood nosing the sand looking for food. "The damned beast should pull plows, not be in a tournament for knighthood." Rodregas thought. Rodregas' opponent was turning around, probably to ask for his surrender. Rodregas painfully climbed back up on Doom Hoof and circled the horse back to Doi'van for a new lance and shield.

Doi'van handed over the equipment and said, "How did you break a shield on a single joust?"

Rodregas grunted a non-committal response and tried to find a comfortable position to hold his lance.

"This is our last shield so when it is gone, we are done," Doi'van said.

Rodregas nodded in response. He had to get right back to the tilt, as it was still his turn to fight.

Rodregas' opponent was waiting for his return, and was at full speed, as soon as the flag fell. Doom Hoof was barely into a trot before the new opponent came into range. Rodregas knew he could not exchange blows straight up against the more heavily armored and mounted opponent and win. He dropped away in the saddle, away from his charging opponent, and with a speed that his opponent could not match, stood up in his stirrups and swung his lance into the man. That move was similar to one move Doi'van had taught him with the quarterstaff. A normal lancer did not have the strength to swing the heavy lance in such a way.

His blow landed higher than the shield and Rodregas drove his lance into the side of the man's shoulder. Shattered pieces of wood filled the air. His opponent flew out of the saddle, an ungainly sight, and landed hard on the arena floor. He did not get back up. After a few minutes, the official signaled Rodregas' victory.

Rodregas headed back to Doi'van. The Hellborn said, "I don't think that technique is what the knights had in mind." His voice showed his pleasure, knowing that a move he had taught Rodregas had led to his victory.

Rodregas nodded and said, "Decided that my advantage of strength was being matched by armor and steel, so it was time to use agility. I was not sure it would work."

"It will be harder the next time. Good luck," Doi'van said.

Rodregas' next opponent for the joust was riding a powerful war steed and was in the dark less reflective brown of night bronze armor. Rodregas recognized the simple gray banner of Geriodon. His arm was decorated with the ribbons of his accomplishments in the tournament to date.

As the flag fell, it seemed like Geriodon was half-way to Rodregas before Doom Hoof started to move. Rodregas knew that the only way he could dodge the lance was if his timing was perfect. He raised himself up as the lance lowered down and dodged to the right. But the lance followed him this time, and he felt his body being ripped off the saddle.

CHAPTER 14
THE ORDER

Rodregas blinked at the sunlight and raised his hand to create some shade. Pain shot through his body at the movement. He felt his body, now without armor, for any serious wounds.

"The good news is that while the tip of the lance sliced into your chest a bit, it did not pierce your ribs, and should heal quickly thanks to what Jordane did," said Doi'van standing above him.

Rodregas realized he was lying on the ground over by where Doi'van had been keeping the lances and equipment. The spare lances were gone. He had lost. Doi'van was referring to the healing sigil. He wisely did not say it out loud as every squire there would have been asking about where they had gotten one.

Rodregas got up, but quickly decided it was smarter to stay lying down for now. "Where did we finish?" he asked.

"We did pretty good. There were more than a few that cannot go on, even if they finish higher. You finished eighth overall in the tournament, with a second-place white ribbon for the joust. Several of those who would now be higher are too injured to continue. So you are now in sixth place overall. Geriodon and Nordien were the top two finishers," said Doi'van.

Rodregas nodded. The pain was easier to manage knowing that he was still in the running for the tournament championship.

Imeraldä stepped into his sight shaking her head, "you men are crazy sometimes, you actually look pleased! If your armor had not held you would be dead now. And it is not like you are fighting someone who deserves to die. Most of these men are honorable warriors."

Rodregas nodded. "True, hopefully another day of this though, and we will be back to fighting those we should be fighting. It will be far harder to stop us if I achieve a greater sigil."

Imeraldä crouched down. She had a profoundly serious expression on her face, and Rodregas had a sense that he would not like what she said next. "Rodregas," she said slowly, "we are not doing this for vanity right?"

Rodregas nodded, he sensed she knew the answer to the question, but was going somewhere with the query. She looked around to make sure others in the arena could not overhear. "We attacked a slave caravan because there were children and innocents that needed rescuing though the odds were against us." She said. Rodregas nodded in response.

"On the way here to check on you I passed the healers tent," she continued. "The healers have cleaned the wounds and cast their healing chants and spells, but I think some of them won't make it. I think we should use the minor Sigil of Healing on them. At least the most critical of them." She paused at Rodregas' surprised look and then quickly added, "I know it is illegal for anyone, but the Immortalists or the Order of the Soaring Stars to use sigils, but that is a law made by the Immortalists!"

"But Imeraldä," said Doi'van, "the final competition of the tournament is tomorrow, and he is very close to earning knighthood and a greater sigil." Though he spoke in opposition, his tone was flat as if he simply weighed facts.

Rodregas froze for a moment, and then simply nodded. He had made this decision the moment he took on a body that was not his. He was either a monster now, or he was a warrior fighting for justice. He struggled up to his feet and said, "go get the figurine out of my trunk, keep it hidden. Doi'van and I will meet you outside of the infirmary."

It pleased Rodregas that neither Doi'van nor Imeraldä looked surprised. He was not the only one who had decided that someone had to do the right thing, and that they were those people.

As Rodregas and Doi'van met Imeraldä outside the infirmary doors, he could hear people in pain coming through the tent flaps. The sight inside was not pretty. It was not the warm and open space of the Nymph's healing room, but full of crowded cots and kneeling chatting figures in the yellow robes of the clerics of Paeon, God of Healing.

Rodregas was sore himself. Even walking shot pain up his shoulders, and into his neck. But the men and women in the room looked like they had come off a battlefield. The majority were covered in bandages stained red with blood. Splints holding together broken bones were also in obvious evidence. At least the enchantment against flying insects seemed to be holding, otherwise it would have been even worse.

Imeraldä led the two men over to a corner where a youthful man lay; he was unconscious and looked near death. From his wounds, Rodregas guessed he had been injured during the sword and shield competition.

To Rodregas' relief, no one was paying them any attention, not even to Doi'van. Rodregas and Doi'van did their best to block the view of others. Imeraldä gathered the limp, pale hand that should have belonged to an old man, not a young one, and slipped the small frog figurine into it. Quickly, she channeled the power. Rodregas could feel the instinctive rise of the man's own power. Then the squire squirmed weakly in pain.

Both Doi'van and Rodregas reached out and steadied the young man until it was over. Imeraldä straightened the sheets for the young squire. She then led Rodregas and Doi'van to the figure of a woman. She was short and muscular and older than average for the tournament. Her bed was more exposed and Rodregas could feel the attention of one healer. He seemed to be afraid to come over even when the body started to shake in pain.

After they stepped away from the female squire, the healer came over to the other side of the bed from Rodregas and Doi'van and touched the woman's neck. He looked reassured at her healthy vital signs and asked, "what did you do?" He looked nervous, though Rodregas was not sure why.

Imeraldä spoke up, "I hope it does not offend you, but I am part Nymph and our healing powers work differently than yours. She should heal faster for the next few days." Rodregas hid his relieved smile. It was an excellent cover story.

"Thank you," said the healer. "Do you have the strength to heal a few others? I think we will lose several more otherwise." Rodregas could not tell if the healer believed Imeraldä's story, or recognized what was going on, and was going along with it to save his patients.

"I would be happy to help them, but I have to do it as privately as possible," said Imeraldä. The healer did not seem to take the odd request as being unusual, and stepped away, after leading them to two more patients.

The healer thanked Imeraldä for her healing work and the three were heading out the door when a frail voice called out, "Rodregas, may I speak to you?"

Rodregas turned around and noticed for the first time, the tall shapely form of Karun, who had defeated him with sword and shield. She had propped herself up now on the bed and waved them over. Her arm was broken, and they had heavily bandaged her side. She was seriously injured, but her complexion looked good, and he did not think her life was in danger. His heart froze though at her quiet whisper.

"You share a minor sigil freely for being in the great Cathedral itself," her voice was but a whisper, her eyes more curious than challenging.

"They would likely die without our aid," said Imeraldä. Doi'van nodded next to her. Rodregas thought Doi'van was strangely silent. He guessed that the Hellborn was afraid to speak, even in a whisper. His voice was like granite breaking and traveled.

"You risk your life to save strangers?" the female squire asked. Her voice still sounded curious, and she glanced at Doi'van, whose giant horned shape could not help but loom over everyone.

Rodregas said, "yes, we do. You seem like an

honorable squire, would you also like a minor Sigil of Healing?"

He thought she would laugh at his question at first, but then she whispered, "that simple?"

"Almost." Rodregas said. "Promise to say nothing about this and also promise that you will use your sigil wisely."

"You are creating your own little Shadow Order?" she asked. She was referring to stories of secret orders of knighthood that lived in the 'shadows.'

Rodregas started to say no, but then thought the idea had some advantages, "Welcome to the Order of...," he paused. He almost said, "the Celestial Lions." But while he might be filled with the essence of a Celestial Lion, his closest companions were of elemental and Infernal power. So instead he went with the simpler, "the Lion." It was the only real symbol that he could think of quickly.

"What of the others?" she asked.

Her question confused Rodregas, and he asked, "what others?"

Karun answered, "There are a lot of exceptionally good squires here, honorable men and women who could benefit from the sigil. But lack the royal blood or coin, to gain knighthood from the Order of the Soaring Stars, and only one can earn it through the tournament." Rodregas' head was spinning at the idea. They were being hunted by the Immortalists and gaining some allies was not a terrible idea. But their luck would only hold so far.

Doi'van spoke now, trying hard to be quiet, "only warriors you would swear have a powerful sense of honor, and no one who would serve the Immortalists."

Karun glanced around the room nervously at Doi'van's voice. It was just not made for covert conversations and his words were dangerous. She nodded thoughtfully and the four quickly agreed that they would share the sigil with anyone who was skilled, honorable and had no love for the Immortalist Guild of the Celestial Path.

They returned to their rooms that night tired. The four of them had tracked down twelve more squires. All had at least two ribbons; and all swore secrecy at the source of their sigil. The biggest surprise was probably Geriodon, who had beaten Rodregas earlier that day. Rodregas could not argue against sharing the minor sigil as he clearly fit the description of a worthy candidate.

Geriodon was more than happy to swear that he had no love for the Guild, and that Justice should be dealt to all equally. But before accepting the sigil he wanted to be sure that any Shadow Order he joined, was mostly about secrecy to protect themselves, and that he could still compete for knighthood in the Order of the Soaring Stars.

It still surprised Rodregas when the gruff squire took on the minor sigil, it was one of the most common and favored lessor sigils. But it would also consume some of a squires natural magic and making the chances of taking a greater sigil harder. He guessed the squire lacked the power necessary to take a greater sigil. Such power was very rare. There were less than a dozen Lord Knights in the entire Order. Though that was partly because some who gained the greater sigil later joined the Eternal Guard.

Rodregas dropped into his cot, tired and exhausted. Even with his healing sigil he needed a full night's rest, but duty did not wait for what a man needed.

Imeraldä woke him slightly after dawn, and Rodregas could tell that both she and Doi'van had spent the few hours left of the night, working on what was left of their equipment. They sewed the tear in both his leather shirt and chain up, the first with thread, the second with steel wire. For a mace, Doi'van had bought a piece of round solid steel from the smithy. It was a crude thing, but of the proper size to qualify for the tournament.

Rodregas dressed and ate quickly and walked out to the sands of the arena. The arena smelled fresh. Sometime during the early morning, it must have rained, and young squires had raked the sands.

The ultimate competition of the tournament was a true melee. Only the top ten finishers qualified. There was no taking turns. The ten were spread out in a circle. In the center of the arena was a shield painted with the seal of the knighthood, a winged sword in the clouds. The squire who claimed that shield and made it to the Cathedral's Grand Hall with it, would be knighted on the spot by the Grand Marshal of the Order.

This day would decide Rodregas' fate. It was likely to end in defeat. He stood flexing his sore shoulders, waiting for the flag to drop. Across from him was Geriodon, who was standing tall and ready in his mithril and night bronze armor. He looked to have gotten much more sleep than Rodregas, and now the warrior also had a minor Sigil of Healing. What minor advantage Rodregas might have had was no longer.

Directly to Rodregas' left stood the tall graceful figure of Nordien, he was as tall as Rodregas if not as muscular and his armor was spectacular. Geriodon's armor of mithril and night bronze armor was probably a family heirloom and looked of solid craftsmanship. Nordien's armor was a work of art. The shining armor was just short of full plate, his great helm had a purple feather sticking out the top, and he had a short, matching cape coming out the back.

Rodregas was the only one of the ten to be in leather with steel chain mail. Not to mention that his chain and leather were held together by wire and thread. Instead of a warhammer or mace with flanges and carefully wrapped handles, he held what was basically a metal pipe for a weapon. He could not help but feel a little foolish.

Rodregas decided that he would go after Nordien first. He would make sure the favorite of Ambassador Vandret would not win if nothing else. If Geriodon became a knight, at least an honorable man had won the day. Several of the squires were being seen to by attendants, making sure everything was secure and waiting for the start of the match.

Rodregas thought he was alone until he heard Imeraldä speak from behind him, "Did you see who is watching from the Great Hall's door?" she asked. Rodregas glanced over. It was Vandret. He stood tall and handsome, young squires surrounding him ready to serve. Rodregas thought the Immortalist was in turn watching him.

Rodregas would have to leave quickly after the tournament, as the sorcerer was growing suspicious of them. Rodregas would have loved to kill him, but Vandret was a powerful sorcerer capable of magic that made him nearly impossible to kill.

"Do you remember The Lion?" asked Imeraldä.

"What?" Rodregas asked. His answer sounded as confused as he felt.

"The Celestial Lion. Do you remember him? The way he walked; the way he moved," she said.

"Of course," he said. No one could forget seeing any Celestial animal, much less the Great Lion.

"The noble beasts of the Celestial Realm are not just magical animals. They are far more. They are the embodiment of magic, totems for ideas that represent the Celestials, The White Stag, The Moon Wolf, The Great Lion, The Six-legged Stallion." The half Nymph paused for a moment until Rodregas nodded. She added, "Dire beasts are animals with magic who are more powerful, smarter, and stronger because of their magic. Celestial Beasts are far more. You saw that for yourself, didn't you?" she asked softly. Rodregas nodded again. It was interesting what she said, but he was not sure why she was bringing it up now.

"Only the most powerful Immortalist have ever taken on the essence of a Celestial. It is their ultimate evolution before they become Gods," Imeraldä continued. Her eyes wandering around the arena, waiting. Her voice had a casual quality, but Rodregas sensed she thought what she said was particularly important.

"When Doi'van sees you, he thinks of you as one of the blood, a noble. Most of the men and women in this circle are that; faster, stronger because they descend from a Celestial God. But you are not that." She finished that last as an emphatic statement.

"The Celestial animals all represent something." She paused, looking at him directly in the eyes for the first time. "What does The Great Lion represent?" she asked.

Rodregas was silent for a moment and then answered, "the Great Lion is the Celestial guardian, the Protector of the Pride. The sound of his roar signals defiance against all odds." He spoke words he knew he had learned as a child at the temple.

Imeraldä nodded, a smile starting to appear on her face, "and what would happen if this group of squires tried to take on a Celestial Lion?" she asked.

Rodregas laughed at the idea and then stopped cold. He nodded thoughtfully, he understood her point now. The two sat quietly for the remaining minutes. The dread in his heart was gone. It had no place in the heart of a lion.

While no speeches had started the other matches, for the first time Rodregas saw the Grand Marshal himself step forward. His name was Faurrenida. The Grand Marshal was an older man and not a pretty one. His face had more scars than anything else. He spoke with a rough voice like he was permanently hoarse from barking commands.

"Today," he yelled out, "we have a match of men and women ready to become knights, to be the very Champions of the Gods on this world. They are all worthy, but there will be only one new knight this day." Faurrenida looked around slowly, catching each of them by the eye. Rodregas was caught up in the commanding presence of the man.

"To the Order and to the Celestial Gods!" his voice was half command and half prayer.

Everyone including combatants and those watching from walls and window responded, so that the words swirled around the arena. "To the Order and to the Celestial Gods!"

This time the Grand Marshal seemed to look around at all the spectators until finally he nodded, satisfied. Without another word, he strode out of the circle. Imeraldä followed him as did all the squire's attendants. It was time for the final match.

Rodregas left his shield and mace relaxed at his side and strode over to Nordien, who stood with shield and mace at the ready. Instead of attacking he asked the tall man, "are people right, do you plan to serve the Immortalists if you gain a sigil?" The squire looked around, a little confused. He held himself ready to fight as others had already started around them.

He was not expecting a conversation, but no one was

near enough to hear. "The Immortalists are the genuine power of the Kingdom. To tie one's self to the greatest power in the land is only smart," Nordien responded before adding, "but, I plan not to add just a sigil, but a Greater Sigil, this day people will call me Lord."

"So, you do not deny it," said Rodregas.

"It is not to a squire I am going to either admit or deny such claims. Now fight me." His voice was smooth, but the end was more a command than anything.

Rodregas laughed and let Nordien see his smile. "Well," Rodregas said, "let us see how well you will do in battle against an Immortalist." With that, Rodregas charged. He dropped his poor mace and slammed into Nordien with all his speed and strength.

Rodregas hit shield first, then instantly dropped his own shield, grabbed on to Nordien's shield and ripped it out of the other man's hands. Nordien's mace was made of night bronze. It was enchanted since the end glowed with a sickly yellow color. It almost nailed Rodregas in the head. He dodged down and then got in close, and with his hands free grabbed the opposing squire from the top and bottom edges of his breastplate. Rodregas then heaved the armored man in the air, something even he could only do for a moment, and then slammed him down onto the smooth sands of the arena.

Nordien hit with such force that his arms and legs flew like a small doll's. Rodregas fell on top of the armored form, grabbed the bottom of the helmet, and yanked it off. Unfortunately, it was firmly secured. When Rodregas ripped it off, he took a good section of jaw with the helm. Rodregas then threw the helm aside and punched the man in the face, full strength, several times. His first hit smashed into the front of Nordien's face. The second blow shattered it. The third blow smashed the head to a pulp. This man would not serve the Immoralist as a Lord Captain.

Rodregas should pick up Nordien's mace and shield, but he knew that without plate armor, he could not afford a long drawn out series of pounding matches. Rodregas would fight like a lion instead. He charged the next closest squire, who was approaching another squire. His new opponent never knew he was coming. He was heavily covered in armor with little visibility. He never saw Rodregas jumping on him from behind. This opponent was smaller and crashed to the ground at the unexpected weight of the attack. Rodregas was more careful in ripping off this squire's helm and punched him in the face but once. It was enough.

He took out four other squires before anyone seemed to realize that he had changed the rules. Not to his surprise, it was Geriodon who was the first to face him and fend him off. Rodregas almost ran face into the squire's mace, barely throwing himself down in time to miss the blow.

Rodregas knew that for this to work, he had to keep up the momentum. He spun around and ran around his opponent, circling him at a breakneck speed. Geriodon responded perfectly. He kept one foot planted and spun tight to help counter Rodregas' speed. It should have worked.

And it worked for several long moments. Rodregas kept running in a circle around Geriodon just outside the range of his mace. He dug into the sand with his feet as he ran and kept running. Minutes went by before Geriodon's own spin move went a little too fast as he tired. Then Rodregas threw himself into the man and wrestled him to the ground.

Even as Rodregas carefully ripped Geriodon's helmet

off, the squire kept fighting. This man was a true fighter and Rodregas wished that he could also become a knight, but there could be only one winner today. Rodregas' fist stopped the squire's struggles.

He looked around, and to his alarm, he saw the last remaining squire running toward the hall with the shield. It was understood that you did not claim the shield until the last opponent was down. But the winner was the first to take the shield to the Grand Hall.

Rodregas jumped up and ran, his arms pumping. He was almost as surprised as the armored squire, with how fast he caught him, and knocked him to the ground. This squire thrust the shield at him and dropped to the ground, surrendering the fight. Rodregas looked around the arena to make sure no one was left to fight, and then headed into the grand hall, carrying the shield of the tournament champion.

As he walked down the hallway into the main ceremonial chamber that was in the center of the main floor, knights stood along the hallway walls. As Rodregas passed, they all said the same words to him, "Welcome to the Order, my brother." Several reached out and shook his hand or showed other signs of welcome. Others looked at him strangely put off by the way he had won the melee. He felt a little unsteady, not sure what to make of both the welcome and the uncomfortable looks.

As he passed through the doors in the main central chamber, the Grand Marshal stood at the far end waiting. In the chamber were both knights and squires. Many smiled, but Rodregas thought a few looked like the ones in the hall, not sure what to think of this new knight.

Rodregas was not surprised that when he knelt in front of the Grand Marshal, Vandret stepped forward and demanded. "Grand Marshal, you are not thinking of knighting this fiend, are you? He killed a fellow squire out there. And he consorts with Hellborns, not proper citizens of the Eastern Kingdom. You do the Order of the Soaring Stars a disservice to make him a knight." Vandret's voice was slow and reasonable sounding, and he spoke not so much to the Grand Marshal as to the audience of knights in the Grand Hall.

"I follow the rules and traditions of the Order as they have stood for centuries, Ambassador. While there are many considerations that go into raising a squire to knighthood, the tournament is the exception. The rules are simple; win, and you win knighthood. While undue bloodshed can disqualify you, a single death during the melee is not unusual." While the Grand Marshal spoke, he did not look at the audience. He looked at Vandret, and he did not look happy at the interruption.

"But clearly he already has a greater sigil. No man can fight like that who does not have one. He is an impostor. He steals this knighthood from more deserving squires," Vandret said. At this last point, Rodregas saw many people nodding, but he remained silent. It was not his turn to answer any question other than from the Grand Marshal.

Grand Marshal Faurrenida's voice made his displeasure of arguing with a non-knight clear, as he said, "While a knight may enter both the Lesser and Greater Sigil Chambers, and take any sigil as his level of magic might allow, it is not a sigil he earns today. It is a knighthood. Now, the discussion is over." Growled Marshal Faurrenida.

To forestall any further argument, the Grand Marshal stepped forward quickly and drew his sword. The sword gleamed with the highest quality blue steel and it all but shimmered as if there was something wet running its length. Marshal Faurrenida laid the sword on Rodregas' right shoulder and said, "A Squire, you come to us this day. Think well and be sure on your decision to swear these oaths."

Faurrenida paused for a second, and then slowly added. "Will you swear to uphold the Rules of Chivalry, to serve the Order of the Soaring Stars with honor, and to serve faithfully in the name of the Celestial Gods?"

"My Lord Grand Marshal, I so swear in the name of the Celestial Gods." Strangely, instead of being excited, he felt tired. In some ways, he was adding another burden, and it was heavy.

"Arise, Sir Rodregas, Knight of the Soaring Stars and be made welcome in the Cathedral of the Heavens."

Applause filled the room, though it was muted. Rodregas looked for Doi'van and Imeraldä and he was sad to see that they had not been there to share his moment. Vandret at least had left. The next few hours went by quickly. They introduced him to many of his fellow knights.

Many were curious to see if he would try to take a greater sigil in the Sigil Chamber that lay below. Few knights had enough power to take a greater sigil, but it always added to the drama to see if a new knight had sufficient power. Though many clearly thought he already had a greater sigil, and everyone knew that taking two greater sigils was all but unknown.

It was late as the other knights went to find sleep when both Doi'van and Imeraldä suddenly both appeared. He could see from their body language that they were ready to do more than congratulate him.

CHAPTER 15
DARK SHADOWS

Doi'van led the three deeper into the magnificent fortress and said, "Sir Rodregas, congratulations on becoming a Knight of the Soaring Stars, but I fear Ambassador Vandret is getting suspicious. Since you now may enter the Chamber that holds the greater sigils. I think you need to go there now."

Rodregas nodded, "can I bring you two into the Chamber as my advisors?"

"That seems to be allowed," said Imeraldä, "Traditionally that is more about fathers with sons, not half-bloods and Hellborns, but I think we might have a bigger problem." She stopped speaking mid-sentence, and Rodregas curiously looked back at her, but she was staring ahead. A figure stood there, tall and graceful. He had appeared in the long hallway out of nowhere, as if by magic. It was the Immortalist Vandret.

"The three of you are all together, and far away from the others, how convenient for me." Vandret casually reached out toward the side wall, and they could vaguely hear him mumble a few words. A second later, the sound of doors slamming and bolts and locks sliding closed echoed in the hallway from every direction. "I hope you don't mind, but I don't want to be interrupted."

Rodregas reached for his sword, but remembered that he did not have one. He froze for a second, unsure of what to do. Then Vandret spit on the ground and spoke a guttural sound. Suddenly Rodregas' and the others' feet were stuck to the ground, and no matter how hard they pulled their feet would not move.

"You know there is a reason that the Immortalist Sorcerers rule this land." The sorcerer said in a very pleased voice, "I have a few questions for you though before I leave your dried-up husks behind for the rats."

Rodregas growled to himself and pulled the only weapon he had, a small dagger, and threw it hard straight at Vandret. A second dagger flew almost in the same heartbeat from Doi'van. The sorcerer waved in the air and both daggers flew to the side and clattered off the wall.

The sorcerer smiled. Standing tall, he was clearly enjoying being able to use his power out of sight of the knights. Rodregas had to admit the Immortalist seemed very relaxed and in control. His expensive black and gold robes were perfectly cut, his black hair was slicked back with scented oils. He might wear the body of a twenty-year-old, but he showed all the self-confidence of a man who counted his age in decades if not centuries.

Vandret's voice reflected the articulation and grace of a man who had all the time in the world to enjoy the finer things. "Let us dispense with the silly games and lies. I want to be clear about something. You killed Nordien, who was a friend of mine. You all die this day. There is no need for you to use deceptions or exaggerations. You will die today. So speak the truth and it will be a less interesting death."

Rodregas was furious at himself, having just achieved the knighthood he had always dreamed of, to then to be caught this close to the Sigil Chamber. That was life. There were no simple victories. "What do you want to know?" Rodregas asked.

"An Immortalist sorcerer disappeared this past spring, and then this summer, someone ambushed a caravan with fresh stock for the Menagerie. I believe these two events are connected, and I even think you might be the connection," Vandret said. His words gaining an edge of anger at the end.

Rodregas glanced at the other two. Doi'van met his inquiring look but did not respond. The Hellborn was waiting for Rodregas to take the lead.

Imeraldä was huddled behind Doi'van's great bulk. For a moment Rodregas thought she was hiding from fear of the great sorcerer. Then he saw she was reading a grimoire that she must have had with her. Her fingers were making patterns in the air. She was too busy to look up at Rodregas, but the new knight almost smiled.

He did not understand what she was trying to do, but at least they had something to try. He needed to keep Vandret busy, to give Imeraldä time to cast whatever spell she was working on. Rodregas turned to Vandret and said, "well, since you are killing us today, how about we make things interesting for both sides? I will answer any question of yours with the truth, every time that you answer a question of mine."

Vandret's expression darkened, and he almost hissed his outrage, "you would bargain with me, with your life held by a string?"

For a reason that Rodregas was sure reflected a deep character flaw, he felt his face break out in a large bright smile, as he said, "I have what to lose?"

Vandret stared at him for several long moments

before he shrugged and said, "very well, ask me your question, but then you will answer mine or you die."

Rodregas nodded. He had no lack of questions but was not sure which to ask first. He decided going small first would cause a less violent reaction. Rodregas said, "how did you find us down here?"

Vandret's expression at the question was like he had asked why the sky is blue. He nearly sneered the answer, "magic, a simple tracking spell." Vandret did not go small with his first question, "are you three responsible for the disappearance of the Immortalist Sorcerer Ravenhurr?"

"Yes and no," responded Rodregas. He almost left it at that, but continued with a proper answer. He wanted the sorcerer to follow his example of how to answer, "I killed Ravenhurr during the Ceremony of Ascension. I threw him into his own consuming flames. The other two I did not meet until afterwards."

At Rodregas' response, Vandret stared at him. "You killed an Immortalist Sorcerer by yourself in his tower? You truly claim that?"

Rodregas almost laughed. He chuckled a bit as he said, "first, you want me to admit that I killed an Immortalist Sorcerer, and when I do, you don't believe me. An old soldier like me just can't win."

Vandret was too smart not to pick up his hint, "An old soldier?" he asked quietly.

"My turn to ask a question," said Rodregas. "How did you connect the three of us to these crimes?"

Vandret shrugged and smiled, and said, "to be honest, I did not really think you were the ones. I did not like you, and the way you hung out with non-Celestials. It is unnatural. Now, it is my turn to ask a question."

"Actually," interrupted Rodregas, "you already

asked me about being an old soldier. I will answer that first. I was a sergeant in Ravenhurr's guard. I have become what I learned to hate more than anything, an Immortalist."

Rodregas paused and took a deep breath. What he said next was hard even for himself to say, "In truth, I am an old man who had his time on this world and did not do much with it. But now I have stolen the body of a very promising young man. I will die feeling guilty for what I have done. I plan to take a few of you with me before I die. Now, it is my turn for a question," he said.

Rodregas hoped that Imeraldä would do whatever she was planning, soon. The conversation was escalating, and he did not think they had much time before things got deadly. Rodregas asked, "Why did the Immortalist Guild Dealer Taiga capture my friend Doi'van, and keep him in his Menagerie of Sky, for two years before selling him to Ravenhurr? He is a Hellborn and should have been of no interest to those trying to become Celestial Gods."

Vandret became still at this question. For a long moment he neither moved nor spoke. Rodregas wondered briefly if he even breathed, or if the powerful sorcerer had moved beyond such mortal needs. Finally, Vandret said, "I cannot say what was in the minds of others."

Vandret raised his hand to cast a spell. Rodregas spoke quickly, trying to keep the sorcerer engaged in conversation and not killing them. "Are you saying there are not Immortalists, led by Master Taiga who are breaking 'The First Law' set by both the Gods and the Daemon Lords, to keep the balance between the Realms?"

Vandret went pale at Rodregas words and stood up very tall. For the first time genuine anger was in his words, "you do not know what you are asking of. You are barely a lowly knight, and yet you would ask questions of those so much greater than you?"

The Immortalist went from anger to laughter, but his laughter did not last long. His laughter was like all things Immortalist, beautiful but cold. When it ended, he said, "time for the three of you to die."

What Rodregas did next he knew was meaningless, but he hoped it would give Imeraldä a few more moments. He reached inside where he used to find his little 'itch,' except his former magical power was now a raging volcano of energy. He had learned from Imeraldä a spell to make light. It was a simple and fast spell.

He waved his hands, mumbled the incantation, and cast the spell with every bit of power he had. The magic headed straight at Vandret in a stream of energy that felt like a river of lava flowing from his hands. The spell failed, with not so much as a flicker of light. Rodregas lacked the discipline to channel the spell so quickly.

Vandret's senses were acute on all things arcane, and he felt the coming flood of power, as if it was a real physical thing. Vandret spread his hands and made a frantic move that sent a corona of power around him. It was a magical shield of some kind.

No focused magic came near the Immortalist, simply a surge of unfocused power. Vandret kept his hands up, clearly expecting another magical attack, but what next flew toward the sorcerer startled both of them. Imeraldä was flying down the hallway, and she had her dagger drawn. The sorcerer was not prepared for an attack from the beautiful half-blood. He could not stop her from landing right in front of him. She did not land smoothly, falling and stumbling into Vandret's lower body, making the surprised sorcerer step back.

She attacked even as she landed and thrust her

dagger into Vandret's stomach. The dagger did not sink far; a few inches. Rodregas expected Vandret to get his hands up and fend her off, but the sorcerer seemed in shock.

Imeraldä pulled the dagger out, and then viciously stuck it back in the sorcerer's stomach. Her body moved with the stroke, using every ounce of strength she had. Still, the blade only penetrated a few inches into the powerful Immortalist. But Vandret screamed and fell to the floor and dragged himself away from his attacker.

As soon as they heard the high pitch of Vandret scream, both Doi'van's and Rodregas' feet were free. Rodregas stumbled for a moment, but was running, even as he caught himself.

Imeraldä was stepping forward with the dagger to finish Vandret, but Rodregas caught her arm and said, "Stop. He will be as strong as I am. Let me and Doi'van get in close." She hesitated but nodded and handed her dagger to him.

Doi'van pounded past the two and grabbed Vandret and picked him off the ground, by the front of his robes, and gave the sorcerer a vicious backhanded slap across the face. It was with enough power to have snapped a normal man's neck, but Vandret looked more startled than hurt.

"Gag him and don't let him move his fingers," said Imeraldä. Even as Doi'van nodded, he slapped his open palm against Vandret's mouth and used his other hand to grab one of the sorcerer's free hands. Rodregas knelt down and grabbed the other.

"Put him on the ground and kneel on him," Rodregas said to Doi'van. The Hellborn nodded and pushed the sorcerer down on the icy stone floor. He straddled the man with his knees, pinning his shoulders down.

"I want to ask him a few more questions. If either of

you think he will cast a spell, kill him." The other two nodded at Rodregas. Rodregas reached down and slid the blade under the sorcerer's chin and said, "one spell and you die." He then nodded to Doi'van, and the Hellborn lifted his hand a few inches from Vandret's mouth.

Vandret pleaded, "please, I am bleeding. I need to see a healer." Rodregas stared at the sorcerer in disbelief. He suffered a few minor injuries, and he expected they would just go get him a healer? The man killed people to steal their bodies and power. How could he think they would respond to such a request? "I need a healer now," Vandret demanded. His voice tone changing to one of command.

"We will get you a healer as soon as you finish answering our questions," said Doi'van, his voice more growl than speech. "First tell us who among the Immortalists are trying to break 'The First Law' and why,"

"I can't," Vandret whimpered. "I mean that I know nothing about Immortalists breaking The First Law." He suddenly groaned and would have doubled up if Doi'van had not been sitting on his chest. Imeraldä smiled at his reaction. She was poking her fingers into his two wounds.

Strangely, when he spoke next the tone of his voice strengthened with the pain. Rodregas thought that it had been a long time since Vandret had faced any uncomfortable physical injury, a very, very long time. But his chin came up and his body tried to straighten as he said, "I am an Ambassador for the Immortalist Guild of the Celestial Path. A friend to the Guild Dealer Taiga himself. How dare you?" Then he said a single word and from his mouth poured a huge wind, Doi'van flayed around trying to hold on to Vandret, but he lost his grip and hit the ceiling hard.

Rodregas crunched the fingers he was holding and

heard them snap, even as he was being pushed away. With the snapping of the fingers, the wind stopped. Rodregas then dropped the hand, grabbed Vandret's head and twisted.

He remembered that day in Raven Tower when he had easily snapped the adept Korin's neck. His arms bunched up, his muscles rippling with the strain. Vandret was an Immortalist. His neck did not snap easily, but it snapped. Rodregas did not stop snapping it until he had the man's face looking into the rock below.

The three sat there for a minute and then stepped away, to rest against the far wall, to get some distance from Vandret's body. After a few minutes Doi'van said, "Well, one more Immortalist down, that's good." The other two nodded.

Rodregas said, "we did not learn much though. We still don't understand why they are interested in Infernal power now, and willing to break The First Law."

"You mean if that is what they are doing. We really don't know for sure, other than by Ravenhurr," said Imeraldä.

Doi'van, sounding like granite as he said, "I know Taiga is involved."

The other two nodded but did not pursue that thought. Rodregas said, "we are just starting to figure out that there is something big going on. I can't believe even the Immortalists would be crazy enough to go up against both the Celestial Gods and the Daemon Lords of the Infernal."

Imeraldä nodded and said, "what reward is so great as to be even better than Godhood?" The three sat silent for a few minutes, soaking in that question.

Rodregas looked at Imeraldä and asked, "well, we can't answer that today. But I do want to know how you broke Vandret's spell?"

Imeraldä nodded and with a smile said, "I always hoped that if I had to take on a sorcerer, it would be in the forest where I would have an edge, but no, it had to be in a hallway! I had to work around the spell. The spell was one to hold you from walking or running. I tried to dance or hop," she said with a smile. "But he was too good, he had those covered. But I have been practicing a spell to float in the air, and that worked. The spell was not designed to stop someone from floating in place. And then I told Doi'van to throw me at Vandret."

"That was a crazy chance, as an Immortalist he could have split you in two with his bare hands," said Rodregas.

"I know," she said, her voice a little shaken. "But we were out of options and it was the only thing I could think of." Then she added with more confidence, "Plus, while everyone knows a knight might learn a bit of magic, a sorcerer never learns to fight. They have servants for that."

The three shared a smile at that. Rodregas was very glad that he had insisted that she learn the fundamentals of blade work. "So, what now?" he asked.

"Now we go see if we can get some greater sigils," said Doi'van.

"We?" Rodregas asked. "Will you take a greater sigil even it if cost you most of your magic?"

Doi'van nodded and said, "I like to learn magic, but we are on a mission, one that is very important. The Immortalists, especially the Guild Dealer Taiga, must be stopped. I will be of most use as a warrior. We already have a powerful Magi," he said with a smile. Imeraldä smiled back at the compliment.

"Taking a greater sigil has certain political ramifications, if I ever return to my home. But, I have been having human knights tell me how inappropriate and terrible it would be for a Hellborn to have a greater sigil. It has really made me want to take one." Doi'van added with a mischievous smile and a shake of his horns, that Rodregas had learned meant defiance.

After stashing the body, in what appeared to be an unused bedroom, the three started back the way they had been going, continuing their walk to the Chamber of Sigils.

CHAPTER 16
TO RAISE A SWORD

Rodregas was careful to walk with the confidence due of a new knight eager for his award. Doi'van and Imeraldä followed two steps behind, both playing the role of faithful servants to the hilt. He saw the engraved doors ahead of them, a pair of knights on each side of the door. The doors were large enough that the three of them could have entered abreast through the threshold. The doors were solid, looking as if they were made of entire trees. Bound in night bronze, they looked like they could handle a battering ram better than even the front gates.

The two knights stood tall next to the doors, but their heads tracked Rodregas and his two companions. Rodregas vaguely remembered one as Gorin, an older man who under more prosperous times for the knighthood would now be enjoying his retirement.

"Gorin!" Rodregas yelled boastfully, "Open the doors, the Grand Marshal says that I may review my choices." Rodregas walked over and slapped the knight on the arm, laying it on heavily. Luckily, his success on the field had him in an excellent mood. Rodregas waved at the heavy doors as if wiggling his fingers could open them.

"Sir Rodregas, you look good for having just completed the tournament this day," said Gorin. "I would not expect you to be moving around much."

Rodregas nodded. He could not explain that he already had a minor sigil of healing. He smiled and said, "I am too excited to lie down and groan in pain! My mind races with the possibilities. Now that I am officially a knight, I want to bring my sworn men into the chamber and figure out what sigil I should choose." At his words, the men's faces tightened, and they looked at his supposed advisors.

Rodregas nodded his understanding. He also knew from his own 'illustrious' career as a guard that the others would follow the rules. They were not officers to be making judgments. "I know you don't like my servants being a Hellborn and a Nymph," he said keeping his voice light. "They are my sworn men and I trust them. It is my call and my right. Now open the doors." At the last part he let a sergeant's voice ring out and it was more order than request. And like all dutiful soldiers, they immediately carried out his order.

The door had a strange mechanism such as Rodregas had never seen before. Gorin lifted a large handle and solid squares of night bronze slid out of the floor and the ceiling. When both the top and the bottom fully released the guard pushed the doors wide.

The three immediately pushed through and Rodregas

said, "You can close the doors. I will pound on them when we are ready to leave." With a nervous nod, the doors slid closed behind them.

As the door closed Gorin hastily added, "remember not to touch anything until the Grand Marshal is present."

Doi'van nodded at the now closed doors and raised his torch. The three gazed around the room in wonderment. In response to the torch the room seemed to respond with a light of its own, which came from all directions. The chamber was enormous with a tall vaulted ceiling like some temple, but no rows of seats or prayer mats did this temple hold. Instead, it was filled with giant animals in frozen poses.

The twelve mythical animals of the Celestial Realm. The sight of the majestic totem animals, each symbolizing unique attributes, made all three stands still, staring. The glorious beasts were full size. But, for their lack of movement, Rodregas would have thought they must have traveled to the Celestial Realm itself.

"Oh, my Gods, they look real. I thought they would be made of stone like the frog," said Imeraldä.

Rodregas nodded. The Celestial animals looked to be made of flesh and bone, except they all stood perfectly still on short stone pedestals. Strangely, the room did not smell of damp stone like the rest of the Cathedral, but the air smelled of the outdoors in spring.

Rodregas' eyes were drawn to the enormous lion that reared up not far into the gathered animals, and just to the right of the center. He walked over to it. It looked like it could have been the twin for the beast the Creation Fire on top of Raven Keep had devoured. He stepped up close, looking up at the beast. The magnificent creature was massive! The beast's mouth was open, not as if he would roar, but in a relaxed pose. He looked like they had caught him stalking forward while on the hunt. Rodregas stepped up and just stared at him. He was beautiful.

"Don't touch," barked Doi'van.

Rodregas nodded, he knew not to touch, but then realized that his hand was raised and had been reaching out to stroke the lion's mane. He knew that this was the greater sigil that he wanted to gain. It was a perfect circle. He had taken in the essence of the Celestial Lion back at Raven Keep, and now Rodregas would consume his own magical power with the greater sigil of a Celestial Lion and become a perfect vessel for its power.

Rodregas forced himself to step back. This was their chance for Doi'van, and he would not get a second chance if needed. He looked over at the other two. Once Rodregas had turned around from the Great Lion, Doi'van walked between the pedestals joining Imeraldä as she looked around. He stood in front of the great six-legged stallion, the steed the Gods themselves ride, and then walked over to the Great White Stag of the forest and then to the giant War Eagle that guarded the Celestial sky.

It was a sight to take the breath from any mortal, a score of beasts that appeared to have been taken right from the heavens. "How were the greater sigils created?" Rodregas wondered out loud. While the leaser sigils appeared to be simple sculpture empowered by magic, these truly appeared real. Yet what magic could capture such powerful beasts for the use of creating sigils? Had the greater sigils been gifts to mortals from the Gods themselves?

Rodregas yearned to reach out and touch, to see if they felt like flesh or stone. But to do so would set his path for the rest of his life. If he was strong enough for two as

Imeraldä thought, then he could be a lion and what else?

"Well, Doi'van, what do you think?" Rodregas asked. "I will choose the Great Lion, but it would be great to have a pride, or maybe the Moon Wolf or the Mountain Bear."

Doi'van nodded and walked over to the Mountain Bear. It was a kind of bear that Rodregas had not heard of, even larger than 'his' lion. The bear had a thick tail and its teeth seemed far larger than any bear he had heard of.

Doi'van stood there looking up at the magnificent beast for a long moment. Then he cocked his head; his nose went up as if he smelled something. He stepped around the great bear and headed toward the back wall. The Twelve figures, while separated, were clustered in the middle of the grand chamber. The four walls of the room seemed to be set back with the ceiling gently coming down in the form of grand arches.

In one of the grand arches was the door they had entered. The stone around the door was the gray of the local granite. The three others were made of a black featureless stone that Rodregas did not recognize. As he followed Doi'van into the shadows of the distant arch, Rodregas smelled what had attracted Doi'van, the odor of brimstone and hellfire.

Rodregas stepped back in shock; what was the smell of the Infernal Realm doing here in the Cathedral of the Heavens?

Doi'van however, did not step back but stepped forward, reaching out to the stone. When he touched it, suddenly there was another doorway. It was the twin of the primary entrance, except here there were no guards. Doi'van reached for the long handle, but Rodregas quickly said, "stop!"

Doi'van looked back at him, and Rodregas could see

that he was under no magical geis controlling his will, just curiosity of what the source of the Infernal smell was down here. But what Doi'van said to him was, "where is Imeraldä?"

At these words Rodregas whirled around and looked throughout the grand chamber. Both of their eyes were drawn to where they heard a third door being opened. As they had found a door smelling of the fires of hell, so apparently had Imeraldä found a door. She was opening hers. They both ran to catch up with her before she got in. They dared not run full out as they dodged around the greater sigils, knowing any touch would be permanent.

They were not in time to stop Imeraldä from entering through the other hidden door. Rodregas could feel Imeraldä in front of him, but she and the door disappeared. She had been there and then she was gone. But he knew that a doorway was there. His eyes were of no use, so he closed them and walked toward where he knew she was. He always knew where she was now. He felt Doi'van grab onto his shoulder and follow him.

When he opened his eyes, he saw that they had entered another magnificent chamber. At first, he thought it was the same size as the first chamber, until his eyes saw the vast tree in the middle and followed it up and then up. The tree soared above them so high that Rodregas thought it must be far higher than the Cathedral itself. The size of the tree was impossible.

As Rodregas stopped beside Imeraldä, he tried to see the shape of the leaf to identify the type of tree, but the leaves were so high up he could only see a very general shape. The shape of the trunk reminded him of a white oak, but the color was a darker gray with touches of striped brown.

The trunk of the tree was huge, thicker than the towers of the keep. But that made no sense to Rodregas. The chamber seemed to be the same size as the one they had entered, if the Cathedral had had a tower in the middle of the central keep he would have seen the structure. Yet, the tree trunk was not that close to them from the door and was not near any of the walls. So it was either smaller around, which was impossible because of the height, or the chamber must be far smaller and much larger. Rodregas shook his head in confusion.

"What is that?" whispered Doi'van as confused as Rodregas.

Imeraldä smiled a soft smile, one that for a brief moment brought memories of the two of them back at The Farm. "I," she started and then paused as if caught up in her own words, "I think that is the One Tree." At their look of confusion, she said, "The legendary source of all Elemental Power. While most Nymphs serve the Gods or Daemons like all mortals, the One Tree is our source. The ultimate expression of Mother Gaea's love for the world. It is to us like water is for a fish. I don't know how to even explain it to one not of our people. But I did not think it was real. When Nymphs talked about it, I thought it a concept of what we are as a people. How can it be here?"

Imeraldä started forward. Rodregas caught her arm, holding her back. He was not sure what to say, but Doi'van was. "Before you examine it, can you come look at what we found? And I want to see what might be behind the last wall."

At that comment Rodregas felt his head turn around as if to look through the Chamber walls to study the fourth wall. As they stepped out of the door the three of them rushed to the fourth wall. However, they could find nothing but the black stone of the wall; no door appeared under any fingertips.

"Well... nothing here," said Imeraldä. "What did you find earlier?" she asked.

"It is behind that door, we have not opened it yet, but it smells of the Infernal Realm," Doi'van said nodding over to the other exposed door.

"What door? I see nothing but black stone." she said.

"What?" Rodregas exclaimed. "You don't see that door?" Doi'van and he shared a look of confusion. The three walked back to the door that Doi'van had found and could see. Rodregas waited as Doi'van touched the handle but stopped him before he opened it.

"Do you see anything?" he asked her. Imeraldä eyes opened wide when Doi'van fully opened the doors and revealed the room. It was in a style identical to the first room of the Celestials, except instead of great animals on pedestals, it held crouching daemons in pits. The previous vague smell of brimstone and hellfire wafted fully into the room.

Doi'van and Rodregas stepped into the room but paused when Imeraldä did not follow. He looked back, and she looked confused, squinting as if the room was not fully illuminated by the glowing daemons in their pits.

"Can you not see into the room?" Rodregas asked.

"No, I can't see anything, you must have gone somewhere, but you seemed to walk right into the wall to me? I think I smell something like rotten eggs? I don't know why, but I really don't want to go in."

Doi'van and Rodregas shared another look and then, nodding, stepped out of the chamber. The three of them stood silent for a minute.

Finally, Doi'van spoke, "Maybe you need a

connection to see the doors and the room? All of us worship the Celestials and we were all drawn to their sigils, especially Rodregas. I was drawn to the door here, which makes sense. This room, like the Celestial Chamber, seems to have similar beasts of the Infernal realm. It also drew Rodregas to a lesser extent, which might show that we were right about Ravenhurr, experimenting with taking Infernal power. Imeraldä has no connection to the Infernal Realm and therefore is blind to it."

The three nodded slowly, caught up in the mystery of the hidden chambers. Imeraldä said, "The need for a connection to sense the rooms would be true for the knights. We know that they don't normally allow Hellborn nor Nymphs in. In that case there might be another room behind the fourth wall, that we don't have a connection to, and therefore cannot sense."

The others nodded. Rodregas thought they were heading along the right path in their thinking.

Imeraldä asked, "does the presence of daemon figures in this Infernal room mean these are greater sigils as well? Ones that require Infernal sourced magic to work? That kind of makes sense if you can have greater sigils that are the shapes of the Celestial animals. Why not daemons of the Infernal Realm as well? But what is the One Tree? It is not a beast of a realm, it is the symbol of the Nymph people. It can't be a sigil, can it?" she asked.

Doi'van nodded, "yes. Greater sigils in the Burning Lands take the form of daemons. But the tree I know nothing of."

The three of them stood there, each caught up in their own thoughts. Finally, Doi'van spoke, "I will see what lies in this Chamber. Will you be all right?" he asked Imeraldä. She nodded and seemed relieved to be free to head back to the doorway of the One Tree.

Rodregas feared for her. He was not sure what the consequences would be if she touched the One Tree. He wanted to follow her, but he followed Doi'van into the Infernal chamber instead. "Was his own Infernal power drawing him to follow?" He wondered.

Rodregas and Doi'van circled the chamber. Rodregas was not as familiar with the daemons of the Infernal Realms as he was with the majestic beasts of the Celestial Realm. He looked at a wolf with the tail of a serpent but with large beautiful white wings. Then he slowly walked next to a magnificent bull with bat wings, and a head that appeared to be very human.

While he had been drawn to the Infernal Chamber both figures repulsed him. They mocked the natural order. It was not just that they seemed to combine multiple unconnected animals, but the size and shapes were wrong.

Rodregas looked up from his examination of the strange bull daemon and looked for Doi'van. He must have been more familiar with the powers of the various creatures. Doi'van had walked past many of the figures until he stood at one toward the back. The shape was a powerfully built dragon with wings partially spread as if getting ready to fly. But unlike a proper dragon, this one had three heads at the end of long serpentine necks; one was that of a wolf, one was of an eagle and one was of a lion. "What is it?" he asked Doi'van.

"A Bunei. They are powerful fighters, but also lead packs of daemons in combat and have powerful magical abilities. Most of these others are powerful and dangerous, but a Bunei is more than a simple fighter. They are known as the Pack Leader, the stories of them were my favorites as a boy.

I think I might see what happens when I touch it," Doi'van said.

"Is that wise?" Rodregas asked. He was worried for his friend.

Doi'van was asking himself the same thing. He looked over at Rodregas and shrugged. "We both have the power of the Infernal Realm in us. Is it easier for us to follow the path of righteousness, to let the power burn free or to take on the form of a greater sigil, and bind it? I think we must choose carefully." Doi'van said, then added, "For me the Bunei feels right."

Doi'van paused in that thoughtful way he had, considering all sides before taking action. "If it consumes my Infernal power, I will gain its strengths. If I am lucky, what magic ability I have left will be mortal or Celestial in nature. The Bunei are creatures of magic, they are both exceptional warriors and magicians. They are known to help others find their destiny. I cannot pass this chance up."

Rodregas nodded; they both knew they would not get this chance twice. Doi'van saw in the Bunei what Rodregas had felt in the Great Lion in the Celestial Chamber.

"See any good Infernal sigils for me?" Rodregas asked. "I should bind my Infernal magic. I will never be a great Magi." Rodregas had not expected an answer, but Doi'van surprised him by nodding his great horned head, and pointing to a corner, that strangely was the only one in shadow.

"I think the Ni'Barrbari, the daemon known as the Night Panther, would add a bit of subtly to your Celestial Lion. While hunters, they are also healers and not as vicious as most of the others. It might also be easier if you can gain both Infernal and Celestial greater sigils that share some similarities."

Rodregas nodded and walked toward where Doi'van had pointed, having to circle around what appeared to be a bear with the front feet of a stork and the overlarge head of an owl. Rodregas felt his skin crawl, and he almost left the chamber, but then the cat shape behind the daemon became clear.

The Daemonic shape seemed to be missing the odd combinations of the others. It looked like the large Panthers he had heard of that were found in the southern jungles. It had no mane like the lions he knew and its fur was black. It was the darkest black he had ever seen. This was why, at first, he had not seen the shape in the dark. It seemed to soak in and blend in with the shadows.

Unlike the Celestial Lion that seemed to have been caught in the middle of stalking forward. The Night Panther was sitting and seemed to be watching the world. The daemon's eyes were golden cat eyes, like glowing embers in a campfire, not the burning red of most of the other creatures.

The only daemonic aspect to the creature was a pair of horns coming out the sides of his head, not that dissimilar to Doi'van's curving up and back protecting the skull. Only the tips were different; while Doi'van's curved up, these curled down at the end.

While Doi'van had seen a lion's head on another man-like shape in the distance, and Doi'van's dragon had a lion's head, he felt drawn to this shape. While he was not as attracted as he had felt with the Celestial Lion, he guessed that this was as good a match as he would find among the Infernal Daemons.

Rodregas looked back toward Doi'van but could no longer see him. He knew he should check on him and

Imeraldä, but he also knew that they had all chosen to walk this path. It had been a more interesting path than expected, but they all wanted to see where it led. He reached up and petted the black horned head of the creature. Its ears had the only hint of non-black on the beast, a slight touch of silver. The fur was not as soft as it looked and was rough to the touch.

Rodregas realized his hand was sinking into the skin. He tried to pull back but felt himself being drawn into the panther. He pulled away, but then he stopped and let himself sink into the shape of the magnificent daemon.

Panic set in as his mouth sank into the creature's head. He tried to hold his breath, but he was too late for such an action. Rodregas tried to move, but his arms refused to reach out and push the Daemon away. His arms felt wrong, like he had no arms to push.

Then, genuine panic set in and he tried to fight his way free. Something was wrong. The greater sigil was not becoming part of him, he was being made part of the sigil. Maybe these were not like the Celestial sigils at all, but some kind of trap. He choked, as instead of breathing air he felt liquid enter his mouth and pour into his lungs. He was drowning in the creature! He had to get out, or he would die. He could not move and was unable to breathe and trying to do anything to get free. His panic faded into anger. If he was to die, he would die fighting.

Rodregas roared his defiance to the Infernal Realm. He reared up and swiped his claws at any that would try to take on a powerful Ni'Barrbari! Let any who would fight him know they took on the night itself and the night had claws! He gathered his powerful hind quarters and pounced free with a roar and felt his body soar out of its confinement!

As he landed on the ground from his leap, he realized that he could feel his arms and legs again. He was human. But he knew he had been a cat, a Night Panther, for a moment. He stood in shock. Was this what it felt like to take on a greater sigil?

Rodregas stood up. He felt strength and other things he was not sure how to describe. He looked around the room and the dim light now seemed far brighter. He started walking over toward where he had left Doi'van, and this time he got to see the result of taking on a greater sigil as the dragon reared up. All three heads howled, and the wings beat, and the dragon seemed to fly. For just a moment there were two daemon dragons. Then one of them fell toward the ground only to sink into the shape of Doi'van.

Doi'van staggered, and Rodregas reached out and caught him to keep him from falling. Apparently, being a three headed daemon dragon did not include a cat-like ability to land from a fall. Rodregas steadied his friend and then Doi'van shook himself and looked around, confused.

"Are you all right?" Rodregas asked.

Doi'van said, "Let's get out of this chamber." Rodregas nodded, as he wanted to check on Imeraldä. Doi'van seemed to have his balance back. Rodregas wondered if Doi'van had lost his balance, because he had been trying to fly, instead of walk.

As they approached where Imeraldä had shown them the door, he was dismayed to see only black stone again. "Damn," he whispered. He closed his eyes, and once again tried to feel where Imeraldä was. It was no doubt part of the life-bond. He went to the middle where the door had been, and with his eyes closed, simply walked to where he sensed her. Doi'van trusted in Rodregas to find her with his clawed hand resting on his shoulder.

When he felt he had gone farther than he should have been able to, he opened his eyes to see, that he had indeed stepped through the open doorway. Rodregas glanced around this other grand chamber for Imeraldä. But she was nowhere to be seen. He ran to the base of the One Tree, finding that it took longer to run from the door to the tree than he had expected. It was huge. He felt like he was approaching a mountain, not a tree.

Doi'van seemed unsteady and Rodregas wondered if his own experiences had prepared him more naturally for this. Rodregas had changed bodies before.

"Doi'van, why don't you sit down and rest for a second? I will check on Imeraldä." Doi'van nodded his thanks and sank down on the floor. Doi'van seemed to need to think more than rest, but either way Rodregas went to check on Imeraldä. He hoped she had not touched the One Tree.

"Imeraldä!" he yelled. "Where are you?" Rodregas circled the tree, something that he quickly realized might take a while to accomplish. Then he saw her. Rodregas had been trying to look into the tree, thinking of his experience of being pulled into the Night Panther. But then he heard a noise and looked up and saw that she was on a branch high above, looking tiny. She seemed to be trying to reach something.

"Imeraldä!" he yelled at her. She was caught up in whatever she was doing or could not hear him. How had she gotten up there? The branches were way beyond reach. She was a Forest Nymph, and he had seen her move in trees like a squirrel. Still, she seemed very vulnerable high up there. He had to get to her.

Rodregas took off his harness and boots and grabbed

the ridges of the bark. He had climbed walls where you stuck your toes in the crack left by old mortar worn away. The bark of the tree, like the rest of the tree, was on an epic scale and provided good leverage for climbing. He did not look at how high he had to go but simply climbed. The climb took far longer than he hoped, and he could not see Imeraldä as he climbed. He was finally getting close to the first of the branches of the tree when he heard Doi'van yell.

"Rodregas, what in the name of the Celestial Winds are you doing?" He paused in his climb, his toes caught in the bark. Rodregas could feel the wetness of blood on his toes, and he felt like he would slip at any moment.

He breathed deep and yelled, "I am climbing the damn 'One Tree,' what does it look like? Now, shut up before I fall." He continued his climb, finally reaching a branch. The branch was on such a scale that he had to climb the branch coming up its side. The bark of the branch was smoother and offered less of a grip. Finally, he got to the top, which was broad and rather cup-like against the main trunk. Though he worried about Imeraldä, he let himself rest for a moment to recover.

After a few minutes, Rodregas got up and looked around for Imeraldä. He saw that she was far out on another impossibly thin branch. By the Celestial Winds! He swore to himself. She was a Forest Nymph. He should just leave her there. She could do this far easier than he.

Rodregas had an urge to leap from his branch to the other like a cat. Maybe he could have made it, but if he missed it was at least a hundred feet down. So, he climbed the bark over to the other branch and then walked on the top, which slowly swayed as he carefully walked on the massive branch. He followed Imeraldä out on the branch until it started getting thin and began swaying more. Then he sat on the branch.

He did not know what to do next. His body relaxed when he heard Imeraldä's voice. "Are you trying to kill me swaying the branch with your great weight?" she asked, "Or are you trying to rescue a Forest Nymph from a tree?" The laughter that followed was pure and open and even he had to laugh with it.

"So," he asked, "what are you doing?"

"This is the One Tree. And well, I am at least half Nymph. So I reached out and touched the tree, and nothing happened. As a forest Nymph trees sort of speak to me. Speaking to the One Tree was wonderful! The One Tree is here and everywhere. Somehow it can be reached from here is the best way to describe it. There is no sigil to be had like the other chambers. The tree 'spoke' to me as trees do, and it explained about The Blessing of the One Tree, that is probably why it can be reached here like the greater sigils." Imeraldä spoke in a conversational tone, but also like her own story amazed her.

She continued, "I think for a Nymph The Blessing of the One Tree opens you to the natural world and connects you to Elemental Magic, but not by binding it into a shape. It heals your spirit and makes you more..., well, more of a Nymph," she said. Her voice was a tone of sunlight and happiness. For reasons Rodregas did not understand, he felt happy for her.

"So, why do you have to climb up a hundred feet to the end of a branch to get a blessing from a tree?"

Imeraldä laughed and then yelled down to Doi'van who was watching them from the chamber floor, "Take your boots off, and your harness and your weapons, and climb up on the top of one of the big roots. That should work, you have to be on the One Tree and then I will show you The Blessing."

Doi'van looked like he wanted to argue, but with Rodregas' nod of encouragement he followed her odd request, and Imeraldä stepped closer and she held three golden fruits. The fruits looked like giant acorns, but rounder and softer. She handed Rodregas one and then waited for Doi'van to follow her instructions. Then, warning him to be ready, she dropped one fruit which the Hellborn caught with his normal dexterity.

"Stay on the root," she warned him. "You cannot take one The Blessings off the tree; it will wither and die if you try." She winked at Rodregas as she said this.

Imeraldä then ate the acorn-shaped fruit; it took some work. It seemed to be harder than any ripe fruit Rodregas knew of, but he followed her example and found that while it was tart, it was amazing. It tasted of... Rodregas did not know what to call the flavor. The words that came to mind were sunlight and rain and the smell of a forest at night. When Rodregas finished the fruit completely he was sad that it was gone.

Imeraldä seemed in great humor. "Come on," she said. She dropped to her hands on the edge of the branch, and then with one hand touching the side of the tree, slid down the trunk with ease as if she was only feet from the ground. Rodregas saw her standing on the ground. She smiled and waved at him to follow her.

Rodregas followed her example. He was nervous at the great height, but between his Celestial essence and now the Night Panther's sigil, he probably would not die. Sure enough, he was on the ground like he had slid down a normal size tree and not the hundred feet that he had climbed.

Doi'van looked at them; he seemed amused and with

a deep laugh of his own made a big show of jumping off the root he was standing on. The few feet of his jump seemed to lack any magical qualities.

"So, other than making the most memorable snack of my life, you say this was the equivalent of a greater sigil? So, am I stronger, faster or what?" Doi'van asked.

Imeraldä shrugged and said, "No. None of that. You are more, well, I think the only way to describe it is more nymph like. There are tales of eating The Blessings of the One Tree, most of the greatest Nymphs of our history claim to have eaten The Blessing fruit. Nymphs gain a little of all kinds of elemental power. I do not understand what effect it will have with you two, as you did not have any elemental magic, or you did not before," she said.

With a shrug she added, "I do not think it will help much on the battlefield."

Rodregas nodded. It might have little practical effect, but he knew that while a greater sigil might make him an exceptional fighter, it had no real inherent value. It made one better at fighting. Somehow, he knew The Blessing Fruit was inherently a positive thing. He remembered on hot sunny days as a kid the wonderful pleasure of lying under a tree, when the town would be hot in the summer, but in the tree's shade it was simply perfect. It was a random thought, but a pleasant one.

Doi'van interrupted his memory by sharing his own self-reflection. "I embraced my Infernal side by taking on the sigil of the Bunei daemon, only to immediately become a part Nymph. I seem destined to always be the oddest of Hellborn."

He shook his head, Rodregas thought not in his usual defiance, but in amusement in all that had happened. So very much like Doi'van to always be thinking, Rodregas thought with a smile.

Rodregas said to Imeraldä, "I think we both feel the importance of The Blessing fruit and I thank you for sharing it."

She nodded and said, "I am so happy that I went with you to sneak in the Sigil Chamber, otherwise I would never have been able to receive The Blessing of the One Tree. No matter how successful we are now against the Immortalists, it has blessed me as few of my people have."

Imeraldä looked like she wanted to talk and Rodregas hated to break the mood, but they needed to get back to business. "We should return to the main chamber. The Grand Marshal will come soon for the official moment for me to take on a greater sigil, and I don't think we want them to find these chambers."

As Rodregas walked from the chamber of the One Tree, he felt more regret than when he had left the Infernal chamber. Though in all likelihood the sigil from the Night Panther would prove to be of more use on his quest.

The three walked as one to the Celestial Lion. They looked first at the majestic animal and then at Rodregas. "Are you sure I have the magical strength to take on two greater sigils?" he asked Imeraldä.

"Few have had such strength. I have heard that taking a second greater sigil consumes more power than the first. It is not just twice as much, but far more. Only the most powerful have such magic, but you have the magic of a powerful Immortalist sorcerer. I can't promise it, but you should have such magical strength."

Doi'van and Imeraldä watched silently as he reached out to touch the Celestial Lion, his hand again drawn to its mane. This time no voice spoke up to warn him away. The fur of the mane was rough to the touch, not unlike the texture of the Night Panther. Strangely, Rodregas smelled grass.

EPILOGUE
BEGINNINGS

His large frame stalked through the grass, eager for the hunt to begin. The Great Lion twitched his ears to the right. He had expected his nemesis, the White Stag, but instead walked a woman. Her short legs somehow kept pace with him. Her hair, as golden as his own fur, rained down her back. She appeared in the form of a beautiful young Ælf, wearing a glowing short white dress adorned with many pouches.

"Why do you hunt with me, Goddess?" the Lion growled.

The Goddess Blodeuwald answered, "I am proud of you. I shared my favor with you as a matter of convenience. You were where I needed someone. I hoped you might succeed. It was a gamble, but with my divine blessing you have gathered the hunters that will be needed."

The great Lion shook his head. The ways of the winds and the speech of gods were the same, fickle, and not to be understood. Yet, he sensed that somehow the words sounded fair and right that he could not really explain.

Blodeuwald smiled at him, a smile that answered nothing but claimed to answer everything. The two continued to walk through the tall grass. After a few minutes she spoke, "The Gods and Daemon Lords can choose one champion in the mortal world. But we are only allowed to speak to them in dreams. I have tried to reach out to you, but until now you did not think the dreams real."

They continued to walk through the sweet-smelling grass as she continued, "For this moment you are enough in the Celestial Realm for me to talk with you. I have to ask you a question: I don't understand why you have chosen that."

As the golden Ælf spoke she raised her slim perfect hand and pointed at his shadow. He lowered his majestic head and studied the dark shape. The Great Lion had to admit the shadow was odd, slimmer than his great bulk, strangely dark in the day, and the shadow's eyes seem to glow the bright yellow color of burning embers.

He shook his majestic head and mane as if to free it from the strange shadow, and growled, "You are a Goddess. You tell me."

Blodeuwald nodded, she forgot to walk for a moment, as if in deep thought, but still she kept up with the Great Lion stalking through the grassland. "I can see all that is seen by one of my followers. I cannot see into the Infernal or Elemental Realms, and I think you have entered both. I do not know what this means."

The two continued through the grass for a few moments in silence. The Great Lion did not understand the Goddess' questions. But he understood his own power, which in its way was as great as any god's. He growled, "do you wish me to fight? Is our pride in danger?"

Blodeuwald nodded, "Yes and yes. In their grand quest for power, The Immortalist Taiga, and his followers, such as that vermin Vandret, must all be stopped. They do not understand that if they upset the balance that the ultimate battle between Infernal and Celestial could destroy all."

She paused and then added in a voice that he almost thought he sensed fear in, "I think we must find the sword Caledfwlch. The other gods will not like it. They might even oppose finding it, but it might be our only hope."

The majestic head of the lion nodded, and the Goddess stepped away and was gone, but they could hear the roar that followed across the grasslands and into the forest and to the peaks of the mountains beyond. For a moment, the Heavenly Realm was silent. All the creatures knew the roar. The great Celestial Lion was on the hunt, and when he found his prey, there would be a battle to shake the realms.

As the roar faded in the heavens, a new Lord Knight, and the chosen Paladin of a Goddess, stood in the Cathedral of the Heavens. Rodregas heard the roar because it was his. The other hunters in his pride were at his side and ready. It was time to start the hunt.

###

Thank you for reading The Celestial Paladin! Please consider writing a review from where you purchased it. Reviews are extremely helpful! I invite you to read The Hellborn Prince, the second book of the Order of the Lion. To find out more about my stories and receive a free short story join my mailing list: **www.gilhough.com/free-stuff/** Follow me on twitter **@Gilhough**

Resources

Celestial - Led by the All-Father Grímnr and a pantheon of gods, most of who are his children, but also includes those who have ascended to the Celestial Realm. The realm is also the habitat of the Celestial beasts who symbolize varies aspects of the gods.

Infernal - Led by the High Prince Sathariel and his court of Daemon Lords in a realm of fire and chaos and constant struggle. The realm is full of minor daemons that symbolize various aspects of the Daemon Lords.

Elemental - The One Tree connects the power of the natural realm and exists both within the mortal realm and beside it. One aspect of the Elemental realm is One Tree, and another is Gaea the Great Mother, and the four elemental dragons: EArth, FIre, WAter and AIr.

The Guild of the Celestial Path - The organization of hundreds of Sorcerers who rule an extensive section of the Eastern Kingdoms. Each Immortalist Sorcerer rules their own town. The Guild protects their mutual interest. It unites the Immortalist Sorcerers in their desire to strengthen themselves over time until they achieve godhood.

The Eternal Guards - The standing army of the Guild of the Celestial Path. They enforce the will of the Guild. Besides their martial prowess and training, all members are sigil warriors and use enchanted armor and weapons to increase their effectiveness.

The Order of the Soaring Stars - An ancient order of knights who live by a strict code of conduct. Besides their martial prowess and training, they are sigil warriors and use enchanted armor to increase their effectiveness. The Celestial Gods traditionally pick their Paladins from their membership.

Sigil Warriors - Those who are born with magical talent but do not wish to be sorcerers or magi can inscribe a sigil on their magic that uses up a portion of their magical ability. Lesser sigils are simple, such as health, strength, quickness. Greater Sigils are more complex and mimic the powers of Celestial Beasts or Infernal Daemons.

Dire Beasts - The offspring of a natural animal and either a Celestial animal or an Infernal daemon during the annual Wild Hunt when they enter the mortal world. Dire Beasts who are 'of the Blood' are direct descendants, while most dire beast will be several generations removed, but still show signs of their ancestry.

Night bronze - Heavy armor usually only worn by warriors who are part Celestial or Infernal or have a sigil of strength, because of the armor's heavyweight. The metal is highly magical and can hold powerful enchantments. Though extraordinarily strong, it does not hold an edge well and is seldom used to produce sharp bladed weapon.

Mithril - Silvery metal light in weight. It can be beaten like copper and polished like glass, light and yet harder than tempered steel. The metal is magical and can hold enchantments, but not as strong as night bronze. It makes excellent armor for those not strong enough to use night bronze.

Blue steel - Steel that is enchanted by Nymphs and holds an enhanced strength and edge. The most powerful of these weapons are known as being 'kissed by fire'.

About the Author

Gil Hough was born in Detroit, Michigan and raised on the waters of lake St. Clair, spending his youth reading and boating. After graduating from Grand Valley State University, where he mainly studied his love of the sport of rowing, he left for various adventures which included several years of non-violent reconciliation work in Northern Ireland through the Brethren Volunteer Service, working with refuges from Central America seeking political asylum, and teaching English as a second language in Torreon, Mexico.

Gil settled in Knoxville, Tennessee, where he lives today. After spending four years organizing Appalachian communities, he worked as the Tennessee Director of Renewable Programs at the Southern Alliance for Clean Energy, until he moved on to developing renewable projects with RSI Entech LLC. He is a founding member of TenneSEIA (Tennessee Solar Energy Industries Association) where he serves as Executive Director, advocating for the orderly and sustained development of solar energy.

Made in the USA
Monee, IL
04 August 2021